"How dare you come back here with your child, expecting me to open my heart to her? Yes, I'll be kind to her. Yes, I'll treat her with the care I give all children. But have you forgotten that when you left me all those years ago, you didn't even care enough to ask if the sex we'd shared might possibly have resulted in a child of our own?"

Hoarsely, Linc whispered her name. His eyes burning, he put out a hand to touch her.

"Camille, are you saying—"

"I'm saying I'll be good to your little girl while you're here in Blossom, Linc. But don't expect miracles."

Turning from him, she rushed through the fence rails and, blinded by a sudden gush of hot tears, fumbled with the horse's reins. She didn't want to know about Linc's life away from Blossom, about his daughter's mother…she didn't want to know anything that might draw her back into something that would surely destroy her.…

Dear Reader,

The plantation setting in this story is not a figment of my imagination. My daughter, Sally, actually lived on a "cotton farm," as they are now called, in the Mississippi Delta. From my first glimpse of the huge house set in the middle of hot, flat delta land white with cotton as far as the eye could see, my writer's heart beat a little faster. I knew I was looking at the setting for my next book. Sometimes on our frequent visits, as I stand on the top floor of that house and look out, I have the feeling that the clock has somehow stopped here. I knew I must try to convey to my readers a sense of the unique Southern culture that has remarkably survived in America. And if my grandson, Josh, should decide one day to farm cotton like his daddy, he will be the fifth generation in his family to do so.

Welcome to Twin Willows!

Karen Young

KAREN YOUNG
Beyond Summer

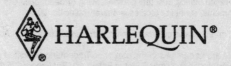

HARLEQUIN®

TORONTO • NEW YORK • LONDON
AMSTERDAM • PARIS • SYDNEY • HAMBURG
STOCKHOLM • ATHENS • TOKYO • MILAN • MADRID
PRAGUE • WARSAW • BUDAPEST • AUCKLAND

ISBN-13: 978-0-373-36112-0
ISBN-10:   0-373-36112-2

BEYOND SUMMER

www.eHarlequin.com

Printed in U.S.A.

KAREN YOUNG

RITA® Award and *Romantic Times BOOKreviews* award winner Karen Young is one of the most innovative writers of romance fiction today. She is the author of numerous novels published by MIRA Books, Harlequin Books and Silhouette Books and is highly touted as a spellbinding storyteller. Karen currently lives in Texas.

To my grandson, Josh

PROLOGUE

"AND SO, the time has come to say goodbye...."

Goodbye, Pearce.

Camille Wyatt stared at the huge spray of blood-red roses that adorned the top of the casket where her husband lay in peace at last. It had taken him more than fifteen years, but he had finally managed it. As surely as if he'd put a gun to his head and pulled the trigger, Pearce had finally killed himself.

"It is often difficult to accept the passing of so young a man as Pearce...."

Thirty-eight last week. She'd planned a quiet dinner at home with a few close friends. But Pearce had begun celebrating early at the country club. An hour and a half past the dinner hour, they'd eaten without him. At midnight, Camille had received a call from the club manager to come and get him.

Happy birthday, Pearce.

"But we are left with precious legacies—love and laughter and caring...."

Guilt and shame and failure. She had never been able to give him what he needed. Friendship and loyalty hadn't been enough for Pearce. He'd wanted her heart. But her heart wasn't hers to give. It had been lost long ago.

Forgive me, Pearce.

"Ashes to ashes..."

If only their last moments hadn't been spent in anger. If only she hadn't let him slam out of the house like that. A word from her and he would have melted in her arms, weeping, promising. She'd done that a hundred times before. Why not just one more time?

I'm sorry, Pearce.

"...dust to dust. We commend this soul to Thee."

So sorry.

Someone touched her hand. She glanced up, her vision still haunted by ghosts. The minister stood before her, extending one long-stemmed rose. He said something in a soft, sympathetic tone. She nodded, accepting the rose. He reached for her arm and she got to her feet. She became aware of the low voices of other mourners as they rose from the chairs neatly spaced under the green funeral awning. Those who were standing began to move away from the flowers mounding the casket.

Bright June sunshine poured down on the scene. From its perch in an ancient magnolia tree came the pure, mellifluous song of a mockingbird. The smell of honeysuckle growing along the lacy iron fence that enclosed the cemetery was sweet and evocative. Death on a summer afternoon seemed an intrusion.

Camille blinked when someone took her hand and squeezed it. "Such a tragedy. I'm so sorry."

"Thank you," she murmured.

Someone hugged her. "If you need anything..."

"...so kind of you."

"We'll really miss him...."

"Yes."

"So sad..."

Jessica Perkins, her best friend, hugged her fiercely. "I'll call you."

Camille nodded and swallowed against the constriction in her throat.

"Go home. Get some rest. You look done in."

Camille's attempt to smile failed.

Jessica squeezed her hand. "Don't worry about Sunny Day. I'll handle everything until you get back."

"Thanks, Jess."

Pete, Jessica's husband, swept her up in a mute rough-gentle embrace that required no words.

She felt bereft when they moved on. Thank God the line of mourners was growing shorter. She was near the end of her endurance. Christine, her brother's wife, gave her a brief hug, brushing her cheek against Camille's and kissing the air. "A bad break, Camille. Pearce was a sweet guy."

"Yes, he was," Camille murmured, her throat thick with unshed tears.

She felt an arm go around her shoulders. She looked up into the pale blue eyes of her brother. "Jack—" She opened her mouth to ask him to help her get away. All she wanted was to be back at Willow Wind, closed up in her bedroom. She needed to put the nightmare of the past three days behind her.

"Thank you, one and all, for your kindness," Jack said, blind to the appeal in her expression. He turned on a practiced smile, his voice lifted just enough to reach the little groups that had formed as people gravitated to friends and acquaintances not frequently met. "This is a sad occasion. Pearce Wyatt was as close to me as a brother, and I know a day won't go by the rest of my life that I won't miss him."

Oh, please. Not another speech. Not here. Not now. Camille made a soft, distressed sound. She could not stand another minute of this.

Jack squeezed her shoulder a little too hard. "Naturally there'll be food and refreshments at Willow Wood for the rest of the day. I hope you'll all come by. There's plenty, believe me. Camille here—" he looked down at her with an expression of brotherly sympathy "—is grateful for your support. Right, honey?" Without waiting for her reply, he flashed another perfect smile. "Come on back to Willow Wood and allow her to tell you so personally."

She stared at him, beyond speech. Even Jack, as insensitive as he could be, couldn't demand this from her today of all days. Willow Wood, an antebellum plantation, was a showplace. Many of the people attending Pearce's funeral had never been inside and would seize any excuse to get a look at it. But *today...*

Looking around, she could see Jack's constituents smiling with pleasurable anticipation. If Jack was throwing open the doors of Willow Wood, she knew they'd expect to walk the two hundred yards of landscaped lawn that separated the two plantations and take a look at its twin, Pearce's home—*her home!*—Willow Wind.

One of Jack's cronies sidled up, and Camille seized the opportunity to escape. She'd traveled to the cemetery with Jack and Christine in their Mercedes. Focusing on it blindly, she started across the thick grass carpet. She made it to the car and was reaching to open the door when she became aware that someone was standing there. A masculine hand grasped the handle and opened the door for her.

She looked up, her lips trembling too much to support a polite smile. And then politeness and gratitude were forgotten. Her hand froze on the door frame. Shock drained the color from her face as she met the eyes of the one man she'd expected never to see again.

"Linc!"

"Camille, I—" He swallowed, his gaze moving toward the flower-deck mound that covered Pearce's remains, then returned to look deeply into her eyes. "I'm sorry about Pearce."

"Thank you."

"He was always special to me."

She barely heard him, her heart was slamming so against her ribs. Lincoln Cantrell here. Back in Blossom. She felt dizzy, disoriented. Putting out her other hand, she braced herself against the Mercedes.

"Camille, are you all right?" His deep, husky tone took on a sharper note. He stepped closer, his topaz eyes dark with concern.

"Y-yes, I'm all right."

"Are you sure? You look pale." He started to touch her. "Come on, get inside and—"

"No!" She flinched, avoiding his hand. Small particles of light danced across her field of vision. She blinked to banish them. He was saying something, she knew, but his voice seemed to come to her through a long, dark tunnel. Suddenly, she welcomed the darkness, welcomed the oblivion that beckoned. Giving in to it, she simply relaxed her grip on the door and let the blackness take her.

Linc made a grab for her. Swearing softly, he swept her up and deposited her gently on the seat of the Mercedes as inconspicuously as possible, knowing she wouldn't want to draw the attention of a curious crowd. Quickly, he closed the door, relieved that the windows of the Mercedes were tinted. He didn't think the crowd realized she had fainted. He searched the interior of the car looking for something to revive her and then cursed the plush emptiness.

Camille.

He stole a look at her face. She was even more beautiful than he remembered. He cradled her protectively for a moment longer than he should have while a thousand memories rushed forward like thunderous waters released from a dam. Then, carefully, he maneuvered her so that he could take off her jacket. That done, he studied her anxiously. She was so pale and lifeless.

But beautiful. Still so beautiful.

Again, guiltily, he pushed that thought away. She needed oxygen. Placing her flat on the plush seat, he reached for the bow on her blouse. In his hands it felt too delicate, too fragile. It was the sheerest white silk, light and crisp, yet…insubstantial. Working clumsily, he finally had it loose. Next he unbuttoned the first two buttons to be sure nothing could restrict her breathing, closing his eyes to a glimpse of the soft swell of her breasts covered in wispy white lace.

"Camille," he said softly, rubbing her wrists urgently. There was no response. He frowned, becoming genuinely alarmed. Gently he tapped her cheek. "Camille, please wake up."

His gaze roamed hungrily over the shape of her face. The maturity she'd gained over the past seventeen years had simply enhanced her delicate features. Even while she was unconscious, her beauty took his breath away. Her skin was flawless and creamy. Her hair, in a sleek, smooth chignon, was still that rich blue-black. Did she ever wear it loose and free? Was it still as soft and silky as a kitten's? He shied away from that kind of thinking and framed her face with his hands.

"Please say something, Camille."

She stirred and made a small sound. Her eyes fluttered open, smoky with confusion, and then, as recollection dawned, clearing to vivid morning-glory blue. Reluctantly, he removed his hands.

"Let me up." She refused his help, giving him no option but to back away, making room for her to sit.

"I didn't mean to upset you," he began apologetically. "It must—"

She waved away his words, leaning back against the seat and resting her head as though caving in to exhaustion. Strands of dark hair had escaped to tickle her cheek, giving her a vulnerable look. The pulse at the base of her throat raced. She wasn't yet aware of her unfastened blouse or that he'd removed her jacket.

"Why are you here?" she asked, her tone distant.

"For Pearce. For our friendship."

She turned her head then and looked at him. "I never knew friendship to weigh so heavily on you before."

Words trembled on his tongue, but he'd let the opportunity for explanations slip away seventeen years ago. He turned his gaze to the thinning crowd around Pearce's grave. Nothing he said now would change anything.

Suddenly aware of her disheveled state, Camille began hastily rebuttoning her blouse. "Was this necessary?" she demanded tightly.

"I'm sorry. I was concerned when you were out so long." He shrugged, feeling helpless and awkward. "I didn't know what else to do."

"How did you know about Pearce?" she asked, her hands, retying the silk bow, only slightly unsteady.

"We kept in touch."

Linc didn't miss the tiny frown that pinched her brows. He smothered a curse. Pearce hadn't told her anything, damn it. He wondered how she would react when she knew. Maybe she was stronger than she appeared.

Ten minutes before, she had been in a dead faint, but she'd pulled herself together remarkably fast. Good. She was in for a rude surprise, and that kind of grit would come in handy. He wished things were different. He wished he could spare her. He wished—

Their eyes met again and he could see the questions forming. This was not a good time. She would probably be furious, and who could blame her? Pearce's lawyer would have to be the one to tell her, he decided suddenly.

"You look tired," he said, his tone gentle. "Go home and get some rest."

She laughed shortly, without humor. "Didn't you hear Jack? His constituents won't hesitate to take him up on an invitation to Willow Wood."

"You don't live at Willow Wood anymore, Camille. Willow Wind is your home." His mouth thinned. "And the hell with Jack. He's running for governor, not you. If he has no more consideration than to use Pearce's funeral to stage a political rally, then let him do it without you. Go home and let Abigail pamper you with a little tea and a lot of sympathy and forget Jack."

She looked at him. "How did you know Abby lived with me at Willow Wind?"

He looked away. "Pearce must have mentioned it."

Suspicion made her eyes grow darker, but before she could frame a question, his hand went to the door of the Mercedes. "If you're sure you're okay I'll be shoving off."

Her eyes were cool meeting his. "I'm fine. Thanks for…everything."

He was out of the car as Jack Keating walked up. When he recognized Linc, his ready smile disappeared.

"Well, well, look who's back in town."

Linc straightened slowly but didn't speak. Neither man made a move to shake hands.

"Hell, what's it been…ten or fifteen years, I guess."

"Seventeen."

"Yeah, well, time flies, as they say. So, how's the world treating you, Cantrell?"

"I've managed," Linc replied evenly.

Jack's gaze slid over him swiftly, taking in the cut of his suit and the slim gold wristwatch. "You don't look like a farmer anymore."

"No."

Beyond Linc's shoulder, Jack spotted another influential constituent and, smiling broadly, lifted his hand in a friendly salute. "What line did you say you were in?"

"I didn't."

The smile disappeared as Jack studied him silently for a moment, his eyes cold. "Just passing through, right?" he said deliberately.

"This time." For a second, all the hatred in Linc's soul was reflected in his eyes. Then, ignoring Jack, he bent slightly to look inside the Mercedes at Camille. In that moment, as their eyes locked, the veil of the past was torn away. Her hand lay in her lap, white and oddly touching. Reaching for it, he allowed himself one last brief contact.

"It was a pleasure seeing you again, Camille."

He straightened abruptly and closed the door of the Mercedes. Then, without looking right or left, he turned, pushed his sunglasses over his eyes and walked away.

CHAPTER ONE

"ARE WE ALMOST THERE, Daddy?"

"Almost, punkin." Linc took a right off U.S. 61, turning due west, and then lifted a hand to flip the visor down, blocking the glare reflected off the hood of his four-by-four. His gaze swept across the vast expanse of a cotton field stretching from the road to a distant line of trees that defined the meandering path of Red Creek. Heat shimmered before his eyes. Was there any place hotter than Mississippi in July? Or grittier? A fine coating of red delta dust lay over everything—vehicles, highway signs, the parched grass along the roadside. If he'd been anywhere except in the air-conditioned interior of his vehicle, he knew, grit would be in his eyes and nose, on his jeans, stuck to his shirt. Linc's tawny eyes burned, just remembering.

"Try to be patient a few more miles, baby," he said to the little girl beside him, a dark-haired, blue-eyed miniature angel with a snub nose. At the moment, Nikki's tiny nose was pressed against the window as she gravely studied the monotonous landscape. For the past sixty miles, it had been nothing but cotton fields, row after row, acre after acre. They'd seen a few soybeans and some milo, a grain used mainly for livestock feed, but most of the rich soil of the Mississippi Delta was planted with the traditional crop—cotton.

Finally, a sign erected by the local chamber of commerce—dusty and riddled with holes from target-practicing sharpshooters—announced the town of Blossom.

"Daddy, this is it! This is Blossom, isn't it?"

"This is Blossom, baby."

Nikki's dark curls bounced wildly as she turned her head this way and that, trying to take in the sights on both sides of the street at once. Fascination shaped her small mouth into a small O as they cruised through the sleepy little town.

"Look, there's the square! It's just like you said, Daddy." She pointed to the grassy, fenced-in area about the size of a football field. Robert E. Lee, mounted on a magnificent horse and outfitted in full Confederate regalia, occupied pride of place in the center. Oblivious to the heat, Nikki eagerly rolled down the window on her side.

Along with the heat and humidity, Linc was instantly assaulted with scents that evoked memories of scenes of his youth. The air was sweet with the heady fragrance of gardenias in the sun. Summer insects hummed in chorus, offsetting the strident cry of a blue jay taunting a red squirrel. At the edge of the sidewalk were wooden benches with ornate wrought-iron arms, worn smooth from cradling the backsides of Blossom's idle for more than forty years.

Driving slowly, Linc felt as though he'd traveled back in time. If he blanked out the late-model pickups and the acid-washed jeans, he could easily imagine himself in the fifties. Hell, in eighteen hundred and something. How had these people managed to preserve this aura of timelessness? He felt a wave of nostalgia looking at the old stores. Peabody Mercantile, McMahan Feed and Seed, Sam Byrd's Barbershop... Had nothing changed?

Nikki turned and caught his eye. Her face eager, she pointed to two modest houses of similar design with short, thick columns and deep, shaded front porches, both set close to the street.

"Is that the Twin Willows, Daddy? Is that where we're going?" She craned her small neck trying to see behind the houses. "Where's Kate's Cottage?"

"No, baby, that's not the Twin Willows." He smiled at her downcast look. "Willow Wood and Willow Wind are much, much bigger, and they're a few miles out of town. They're older, too. And painted snow-white. They both have long, curved roads lined with pecan trees leading right up to them."

"Oh." Nikki studied the two houses as though imagining them differently and nodded. "I forgot."

He reached over and tweaked one of her dark, silky curls. How could a four-year-old ever come close to picturing the grandeur of the two antebellum mansions? Still, like a hungry little bird, she had gobbled up every tidbit of information he gave her about the two plantations that had played such a vital role in his childhood. Had he made a mistake plying her imagination with tales of the Twin Willows? Had it been some deep-seated, selfish need that drove him to acquaint his child with his bittersweet past? He prayed that wasn't it. After they lost Joanna, he'd searched for common interests in a need to draw them closer as father and daughter. Then Pearce had died. It seemed like fate, all things considered. Taking Nikki to Blossom had seemed so right. He settled back in his seat. Right or wrong, it was too late to turn back now.

Nikki scooted over next to him and leaned her small head against his arm. Feeling fiercely protective, he slipped his arm around her and brushed a wispy curl from her soft cheek. She was still just a baby, but she had seen too much. For the hundredth time, he cursed the fate that had put his wife and child in that particular shopping center at that moment in time. In the Christmas rush, Joanna had not even seen the drunk driver who slammed into her just as she stepped off the curb. No one was sure how Nikki had escaped. He studied her small, unsmiling face. She'd escaped physical injury, but witnessing everything—the blood, Joanna's broken body, the crowd's hysteria—had taken a bitter toll. In spite of the best counseling his money could buy, she had withdrawn to some safe, secret place inside herself. Since that day, she had not spoken a word to anybody except him.

"Tired, honey?"

She shook her head in solemn denial, and he hid a smile. She had to be pooped. They'd been on the road for more than ten hours. He'd been warned that traveling with a four-year-old would test the patience of a saint, but Nikki blew that theory away. They had made the trip from St. Louis without a hitch. Nikki had been obedient, sweet-natured and quiet. Too quiet.

Her small tummy growled and she clapped both hands over it.

He chuckled. "Somebody's getting hungry, huh, punkin?"

She turned wide blue eyes up at him and nodded.

"Well, we'll grab something fast if we can find a place, and then we've got to go to the grocery store. We can't very well start our new life at Kate's Cottage without groceries, can we?"

"Kate's my grandmother," Nikki said solemnly.

"That's right."

"She died a long time ago."

Linc drew in a breath. Nikki's casual reference to death made him uncomfortable, especially since she had witnessed the accident that took away her own mother. Was all death the same to a child? Swamped by a feeling of inadequacy that was too familiar since he'd become a round-the-clock father, he raked a hand across neck muscles stiff from hours at the wheel.

"Yes, baby, she died a long time ago."

"But we're going to live in her house."

"Uh-huh."

"Kate's Cottage."

"That's right."

"I can have a night-light as long as I want it."

"You bet."

WITHIN AN HOUR word was out in Blossom, Mississippi, that Lincoln Cantrell was back in town. Of course, news traveled fast in a town with a population of 1,361. And Linc Cantrell was news. He'd been a favorite topic of conversation at Sam Byrd's Barbershop from the time he was big enough to spit straight—he'd been a basketball star, an honor student and a good kid, too. Even after seventeen years, folks were still speculating as to why he'd just up and left Blossom. Dropped right out of college and disappeared just about the time his mother and Judge Joe Keating had that car wreck.

Abigail Keating, the judge's sister, was in the hospital in Jackson, and they'd been on their way home after visiting with her. Killed Kate outright, but the judge had lingered a couple of months in a deep coma. Yes, indeed, it had been strange, Linc leaving like that, especially since everybody knew the judge had been paying for his education over at Mississippi State. It was a known fact that he was grooming Linc to manage the plantation while making plans for his own boy, Jack, to go into politics. But Linc wasn't even blood kin. Never would be.

"Well…" Sam was clipping what little hair there was left on Wiley Dawson's head. "Jack is a state senator now and running for governor. I guess if the judge was still around, he'd be proud."

"Certainly he'd be proud," Wiley said as Sam removed the cape from his shoulders with a snap, sending up a cloud of cut hair. "But the Twin Willows need full-time management, which they ain't gettin', what with Jack at the state capital and Pearce Wyatt dead of liver disease."

"Hmmm." Out of respect, Sam didn't dispute that, since Wiley was related to the Wyatts, but the truth was, Pearce Wyatt had simply drunk himself to death. "You're right, though. Here it is smack in the middle of growin' season, and nobody but the hired hands to take charge at Pearce's place. What's Camille going to do, Wiley?"

Wiley scratched his nearly bald pate. "Could be nothin' will change much, Sam. With Pearce ailin' the past four or five years, Jack's manager has been tending to Pearce's land anyway, more or less calling the shots at both places. Now, whether that situation can go on now that the place has come to Camille remains to be seen, I expect."

Sam lifted a skeptical brow. "I can't see Camille buckin' anything her brother wants to do."

"Me neither," said Wiley. "No disrespect meant, but Camille can't run a plantation."

"Something'll have to be done, and fast," Sam pointed out practically. "Cotton pickin' time is right around the corner, mid-September, October. You know

Jack. He likes to keep a strong hand in, especially with anything pertainin' to those two plantations. But with the pressure of his campaign, he sure can't do the job himself. So if Camille doesn't approve of things as they've been goin' the past few years, she'll have to find somebody to manage Willow Wind for her. But then she'd have her hands full, goin' up against Jack.''

Sam rang up a sale on the ancient cash register. ''I heard Linc Cantrell has somebody over at Kate's Cottage openin' it up and gettin' it ready to occupy.''

Wiley's eyes narrowed. ''You don't say.''

Sam nodded slowly. ''I sure heard it.'' He picked up the cape and began folding it. ''I caught a glimpse of him at Pearce's funeral, but he didn't stick around to talk. Wonder how he's made out for himself all these years?''

''I don't know, but I bet he did good,'' Wiley said. ''He was always smart and industrious. Not a lazy bone in that boy.''

''Yep.'' Sam placed the folded cloth on a shelf. ''Big difference between him and Jack, don't you know? Even though they were raised close as brothers, Linc had to work a lot harder than the judge's heir.''

Wiley harrumphed and reached for his cap. ''Well, they weren't brothers when you get right down to it. The judge was plenty generous with Linc, but Jack was his own flesh and blood.''

''Sure enough.'' Sam took off his glasses. ''Still, I always thought Jack seemed more than a little jealous of Linc, them being the same age and all. No doubt about it, Linc outdid him in sports and academics.''

''I guess the judge knew what he was doing sending them off to different schools,'' Wiley mused. ''Jack to Ole Miss and Linc to State. One groomed for politics, the other for farming." He made a clicking sound. "Jack's fulfilling the judge's dreams in a big way all right. And I'll just bet you this, Sam. I bet Linc's done all right for himself, too."

Sam nodded. "I wouldn't argue with that, Wiley." He stared contemplatively through the front plate-glass window. "Hard to know what to make of him comin' back now, ain't it? Makes you wonder what he's got in mind."

"Yep."

With a little smile on his face, Sam began polishing his glasses. "You know what, Wiley? I'd like to be a fly on the wall when Jack Keating hears Linc's gonna be in that cottage right in Jack's own backyard."

"Well, he's got to have a place to stay," Wiley retorted. "We ain't exactly got a four-star hotel around here."

"That's for sure. Nor has Linc got a single, solitary relative."

"You don't suppose he's coming back to Blossom to manage Willow Wind for Camille?" Wiley speculated.

There was a moment of silence while the two men considered the possibility. Then Sam shook his head. "Nah, I wouldn't think so."

Wiley picked up his cap and, looking in the mirror, set it carefully on his head, pulling the bill forward so the words *John Deere* could be seen. "But if that is what he's up to, Jack Keating ain't gonna like it a bit."

"THIS CAN'T BE, Tom."

The lawyer shook his head grimly. "I wish I could tell you otherwise, Camille. Unfortunately, it's all right here in black and white." He straightened the stack of papers and then laid them down again. He was obviously uncomfortable with the situation, as though he were personally responsible. "The plantation itself is mortgaged to the hilt, I'm afraid. The good news is, Pearce managed to hold the house free and clear. So, it's not as if you're going to be homeless, my dear."

Tom Pettigrew had been Pearce's attorney for as long as she could remember. Consequently, he was privy to information about Camille's assets as well. There was no point in dissembling for the sake of her pride.

She smiled bleakly. "You know I won't have enough income to maintain a house like Willow Wind," she told him flatly.

He looked at her sympathetically. "You don't think your little business will generate adequate income?"

Camille smothered a weary sigh, beyond taking offense. No, she didn't think her "little business" would generate enough money to maintain a twelve-room antebellum mansion. Sunny Day Kindergarten had an enrollment of thirty four- and five-year-olds. She had one full-time staff member—Jessica Perkins—and two part-time aides. Her "little business" was nothing near the size it would have to be to carry Willow Wind.

"Well…" Pettigrew sat up a little straighter and tried to look positive. "What about your brother? Under the circumstances, Jack will surely want to come to your assistance."

"I'm not sure he can," she murmured, frowning. She wasn't certain, but she suspected that, financially, Jack was stretched to the maximum right now. A lot of his assets were tied up in the financing of his gubernatorial campaign. Of course he had constituents who'd made substantial contributions, but those funds weren't his to use personally, and certainly not his to turn over to his sister, even if it meant losing Willow Wind. No, she couldn't depend on Jack.

She sighed, staring at her hands. She'd spent the best part of the month since Pearce's funeral trying to sort out his tangled affairs. Coming here today, she'd believed herself prepared to hear the worst, but the reality was turning out to be even more dismal than she had expected.

"Now, don't look so downcast, my dear. Even if Jack is unable to come to your rescue, you're still a long way from ruin. The mortgagee now..." He picked up the papers. "Where did I put that...?" he muttered, moistening a finger so that he could leaf through the stack.

Gloomily, Camille watched him. "Which bank holds the mortgages?" she asked, almost beyond caring.

The lawyer blinked. "Bank? It's not a bank, my dear. No, indeed. Didn't I mention that?" Once more, he began shuffling the papers. He held one up and studied it through his bifocals before handing it over to her. "It's a corporation, as you can see there. Delta Star Enterprises."

She frowned. The name meant nothing to her. "Is it just a big faceless financial monster, Tom, or is Delta Star controlled by someone I can talk to?"

Pettigrew shot her a look of surprise mixed with chagrin. "That Pearce," he said, shaking his head. "I'm just beginning to realize the lengths he went to to protect you, my dear. However, it's a bit awkward, I must say. Under the circumstances, as it were. Particularly now that it's come to—"

A tiny tremor of premonition sent her hand to her throat. She gave Pettigrew a quick, wary look. "Tom, who is Delta Star?"

"Well, fortunately, my dear, it's your old friend Lincoln Cantrell."

CAMILLE STEPPED numbly out of Tom Pettigrew's office into bright July sunshine. Since that brief encounter a month before, she had not allowed herself to think about Linc. She had managed it by concentrating fiercely on sorting out Pearce's affairs. She'd breathed a cautious sigh of relief when, a few days later, it appeared Linc had left Blossom, going back to wherever it was he had come from. His only reason for coming at all had been just what he told her. Pearce was his old friend. Fine. His duty was done. He could stay away for another seventeen years and it wouldn't be long enough for her. She needed no reminder of the naive fool she'd been that long-ago summer when Lincoln Cantrell had been the sun in her sky, the very air she breathed.

She would have to tell Jack. Taking a deep breath, she headed down the sidewalk past the Sears Catalog Store and the barbershop, nodding vaguely to Sam Byrd and Wiley Dawson through the big plate-glass window. Jack's office was in the next block, barely a two-minute walk from Tom Pettigrew's, but she found herself lagging. For the past two years, Pearce had allowed Jack to lease Willow Wind acreage. Pearce had never claimed to be much of a farmer, and as his disease worsened, he'd been glad to turn over the everyday grind of farming cotton to Jack, or rather to Jack's hired hands. The truth was, neither Jack nor Pearce loved farming. Both had other, more compelling interests. Gentlemen planters, Camille thought with a wry twist of her mouth. Neither had ever felt the fierce love for the land that Linc had.

Too late she realized she should have asked Tom

whether Linc meant to involve himself personally in Willow Wind's operation. She tried not to think about it now. Just the thought of him was enough to make her feel as though she were splintering into a thousand pieces.

Surely he wouldn't, she assured herself. Apparently he'd been dealing behind the scenes with Pearce for who knew how long. Maybe he'd be content to stay out of sight.

And out of mind? a wicked little voice taunted. Dear God, she didn't know if she could manage that, too.

Too soon she was at Jack's office. He was going to be unhappy. She didn't know what had happened between him and Linc all those years ago, but something had. Never again had Jack mentioned Linc's name without following it with a scathing, profane opinion as to exactly where Lincoln Cantrell belonged. Sighing, she pushed open the door, dreading what must be done. It was bad enough that the land was mortgaged. Maybe she would put off mentioning exactly who held the mortgages.

"WHAT THE HELL!" Jack stalked across the floor of his office and slammed the door in his startled secretary's face. There was little enough privacy in this one-horse town as it was. The last thing he needed was Florence telling the whole county—the whole state!—his business. Damn but he'd be glad to get to Jackson!

Turning, he pinned his sister with a fierce look. "Are you saying that that weak-kneed fool you married mortgaged the whole place? Every goddamn acre?"

Her eyes cold, Camille got up from her chair and brushed by Jack without replying.

"Come back here, Camille!"

She reached the door before turning to face him. "When you want to hear what Tom said, let me know, Jack—provided you keep your personal opinion of Pearce to yourself. He was my husband. He was sick for five years. He—"

"Sick! He pickled his liver with booze, Camille. The dumb jerk would still be around if he hadn't got drunk and wrapped himself around that bridge abutment."

She opened the door, but Jack slammed it shut again. "Okay, okay," he said, mastering some of his irritation. "I'll admit that he couldn't seem to stay away from the stuff. But to mortgage Willow Wind..." His angry, baffled look spoke volumes.

"I know." Camille shrugged helplessly. "Tom said it was a miracle the house itself hadn't gone on the auction block before now. He said—"

Jack swore, interrupting her. "Tom Pettigrew's a lawyer, not a farmer," he said in disgust. "Why didn't you say something to me before now, Camille? You knew I'd been trying to get a long-term option on the place from Pearce—all twenty-five hundred acres of it. But no, he was perfectly satisfied to let my manager run everything, make all the decisions, sweat all the sweat while he looked for the meaning of life in the bottom of a whiskey bottle." He slammed a fist into his hand. "Damn it! If he'd let me lease it along with Willow Wood, we wouldn't be in this fix now."

"He was sick, Jack."

Jack made a disgusted sound. "Sick, drunk, what the hell's the difference now?"

Camille pushed her fingers through her dark hair, sighing with weariness. "I didn't know he'd mortgaged it, Jack. It's as much a surprise to me as it is to you. Even Tom didn't know until it was done. Some lawyer in Memphis handled everything. Besides, the land was Pearce's to do with as he chose. Have you forgotten that?''

Jack didn't even bother to reply. "Who holds the paper? The bank?"

"No." She bent her head suddenly, searching in her purse for her car keys. "A corporation."

"A cor—?" He broke off, frowning. "Who? What corporation?"

She shrugged. "Something called Delta Star Enterprises, headquartered in St. Louis according to Tom."

He stared straight ahead, thinking, and then shook his head. "Never heard of it. Have you?"

She slipped the strap of her bag onto her shoulder. "No, Jack. Until today, I never heard of it."

He stopped at the window and looked out at the dusty street below. "Just like Pearce," he muttered. "Some of the biggest names in the state ready to bail him out and he goes to St. Louis for help. Who in hell does he know in St. Louis?"

Again he silently cursed Pearce Wyatt, carefully keeping his back to Camille. She was as silly as Pearce. After all these years, she was still as loyal as she'd been from day one. Loyalty, he thought with disgust, was a commodity he had never been saddled with. Twenty-five hundred prime acres at Willow Wind mortgaged by that booze-soaked fool to some remote corporation—probably some foreign outfit that would complicate his life royally when he tried to undo the damage. And just when he'd been so close to getting his hands on Willow Wind at last...

He cleared his throat. "Don't worry yourself over it, hon," he said, recalling his sister's presence. But by the time the words had left his mouth he was already dismissing her, thinking of people he knew in Jackson. Or maybe United Planters in Memphis... "I'll take care of it," he said thoughtfully. "I'll take care of it."

WITH A DISTRACTED SMILE at Florence, Camille crossed the thickly carpeted floor of Jack's outer office, feeling distinctly relieved. It was a false sense of relief, she admitted to herself. She'd merely postponed what was sure to be an unpleasant scene by keeping Linc's involvement in Willow Wind's future to herself. Once Jack had started ranting and raving, she'd suddenly realized she had no obligation to tell him anything. Pearce was dead. He might have had serious problems, but he had been her husband and she owed him some kind of loyalty. She didn't have to listen to Jack denounce him.

Closing the door behind her, she stopped for a moment, imagining how Jack would react when he learned the rest of the story. He couldn't possibly be more shocked than she had been. Lincoln Cantrell. She pressed her fingers against her mouth as if to keep her tumultuous thoughts at bay. Pearce had mortgaged Willow Wind's land to Linc. Her first lover. The man who'd rejected her and their love and finally abandoned her.

Why, Pearce? Why?

She drew in an unsteady breath and fought against the emotion welling up inside her. Blinking furiously to hold back the tears, she pulled herself together. She was no longer the impetuous seventeen-year-old who had fallen in love with Lincoln Cantrell. She'd lived through a lot of heartache since then. It hadn't been easy watching Pearce throw his life away. She'd been forced to stand by helplessly, smothering her emotions while single-handedly assuming responsibilities that other couples shared. She'd had to live each day with expectations that invariably came to nothing and then struggle not to let bitterness and resentment eat away at everything worthwhile and good that was left. With his death, she'd tried to forgive him.

Pearce, Pearce, how can I forgive this?

Camille steadied herself and stepped out into the glare of midmorning. What had made Pearce keep it from her? She had known his fragile state of mind, especially in the past year. Why had she left the management of Willow Wind to him, knowing how unstable he'd become? Even with Jack working the acreage along with his own, she should have taken a closer interest. *Especially* with Jack working the acreage.

Shielding her eyes against the bright sunlight, she thought back. It was doubly puzzling how Pearce had managed to keep his involvement with Linc a secret from Jack. Hadn't Jack been in on every decision that concerned the property? Until today, Camille had thought so.

Walking slowly, she absently dodged two boys on skateboards streaking past her. Deep down, she knew why Pearce hadn't confided in her. Months before Pearce died, Jack's manager had taken over the nitty-gritty details of running Willow Wind, and Camille had been only too glad to let him. She'd been caught up in her own responsibilities at Sunny Day, her kindergarten, the one thing in her life that had kept her going those last dark, demanding months of Pearce's life.

"Hello, little sister."

Deep in thought, Camille almost bumped into Christine Keating. Coolly confident in apricot silk and white linen, her sister-in-law gave her an amused look.

"Christine! What brings you into town on such a hot morning?"

Christine flicked a disdainful glance down the street.
"Jack promised me lunch at the club. My bridge group
was to meet this afternoon, but Dootsie Simpson had to
cancel. Which means I'm stuck with nothing to do for
the whole day. I'm so bored," she complained, wrin-
kling her mat-perfect nose.

She was strikingly beautiful, Camille thought. Even
with the mercury hovering at ninety, Christine looked
crisp and poised, as flawless as though she'd just stepped
from the pages of *Vogue*. Her blond hair was styled to
appear casually windblown, even though there hadn't
been a sigh of wind all day. Her earrings were large
beaten-silver disks inlaid with some kind of gemstone.
On Christine, they looked absolutely right. If appearance
alone counted for anything, she would make a stunning
first lady for the state.

"How did you get away from your kindergarten,
Camille? I don't know how you stand it. Cooped up
every day with those noisy, squabbling brats, never a
conversation with anyone over the age of five. Ugh!"

No reply was expected, so Camille said nothing.
Christine wasn't the only woman in the world who pre-
ferred a limited association with small children, she reminded herself.

Christine's eyes narrowed suddenly. "Did you finally
get around to seeing Tom Pettigrew?"

"Yes, I was just talking to Jack about it."

"Good. The sooner he gets everything straightened
out, the better."

Camille's eyebrow arched. "Who, Christine? Tom or
Jack?"

Christine looked impatient. "Jack, silly. Tom is only
a lawyer, after all. Just leave the management of the
Twin Willows to Jack now. You're lucky he's family,

Camille. You can keep on just as you are—burying yourself in your little school.''

Camille considered telling Christine the unsettling facts but decided to let it go. She had a feeling her sister-in-law would be no more pleased than Jack that Pearce had not done the expected thing and turned to the Keatings when he needed help.

Why hadn't he? It was a question that puzzled her, too.

"Oh, by the way…'' Christine had walked a few feet away, but now she turned, looking at Camille over her shoulder. "Guess who I just saw stopped at the red light as I was getting out of my car?''

"Who?'' Camille wondered at the almost malicious expression on Christine's face.

"Linc Cantrell.''

Camille's face drained of color.

"And he wasn't alone.''

I don't care. He can have all the women in the world with him and it won't matter to me.

"He had a little kid with him.''

Camille's heart screamed a denial. Suddenly she couldn't breathe. It was the heat. Summer was always like this. Hot and stifling. A little like hell. She had been to hell one summer seventeen years ago.

"A girl.'' Christine shrugged and twisted the knife. "Black hair, big eyes. She looked a lot like you, Camille.''

Camille turned blindly, bent only on escape. Her mind rocked with the bitter knowledge that Linc was back in town, that he had a child. Did he also have a wife? Had he come to take Willow Wind away from her and install his family in her home?

Pearce, Pearce, what have you done?

She already had her keys in her hand; otherwise, she wasn't sure she could have located them. She headed in the direction of her car, not responding when Dan Culpepper, Blossom's deputy sheriff, greeted her, not even hearing him. Oblivious now to the heat, she went right by Marilyn Clarke, one of her oldest friends, as she came out of Sears. Doggedly, she stared straight ahead, trying to hold back the past.

Christine's words rang in her brain like one of those distorted recordings reverberating with echoes on top of echoes. Did Christine know about her and Linc? Camille made a soft, anguished sound. She had only managed to bear the pain because no one knew. But that look in Christine's eyes…the malicious note in her voice…

Stumbling slightly, she reached the curb and started across the street. A loud honk startled her, and she waved a distracted apology to the driver. She never wanted to think about that summer when she and Linc had fallen in love, had *made* love. Pain shot through her like a hot knife. Then she'd gotten pregnant, and Linc had turned his back on her.

Pearce, Pearce, you don't know what you've done.

She was in her car on her way out of Blossom when she remembered her aunt. Abigail had come into town with her that morning. She was waiting at the ice-cream shop. Sighing, she turned around in the parking lot of the Sunflower Store, the closest thing to a supermarket in Blossom, and headed back the way she'd come.

CHAPTER TWO

"DADDY, CAN WE STOP and get some ice cream?"

Linc opened his mouth to refuse. Ice cream wasn't exactly what he had in mind for Nikki's meal, but she had already unfastened her seat belt and was standing up. They still had to locate the supermarket and buy groceries. Maybe an ice-cream cone would pacify her for a while. Then they'd find a place to eat a real meal.

"Please, Daddy…"

"Okay, punkin." Linc readily admitted that he hadn't learned to say no to Nikki yet. Hell, learning to say no was just one in a list of a hundred things he didn't know about parenting. Wasn't that the word nowadays? He wasn't even sure of the lingo. The only thing that came naturally, he'd found, was loving Nikki. He didn't have any trouble with that.

He pulled up in front of Brown's ice-cream shop and got out of the Bronco. Nikki scrambled across the console and over his seat. Closing his arms around her, Linc felt a rush of love and protectiveness so powerful that he couldn't move for a moment. She was so small, so dependent on him. Nothing, he promised silently, would ever hurt her again if it was even remotely in his power to prevent it.

Nikki squirmed with impatience, and he lowered her to the sidewalk. Then, holding on to her hand, he led her into the old-fashioned ice-cream shop.

"Why, it's Lincoln Cantrell!"

Linc's startled gaze shot across the room to the tiny, gray-haired woman primly seated at a small table. "Miss Abigail?"

"I'll declare, I thought I was seeing things when you came through that door, boy. Although I don't know why. I saw it in the tea leaves just a few days ago."

Urging a suddenly shy Nikki along, Linc made his way through the cluster of small round tables and curlicue chairs toward the old lady. She waited, her head to one side, as bright-eyed as ever, he noted with a smile. She'd always reminded him of a quick little sparrow.

"Welcome back to Blossom, Lincoln," she said softly. She might be petite and fragile-looking, but the hug she gave him was surprisingly strong, enveloping him in a cloud of lavender. Instantly he was assailed with memories of skinned knees and bound fingers, gingerbread and lemonade. Although Linc's mother had been the housekeeper at Willow Wood, Abigail Keating, the judge's sister, was the only mistress Linc could remember in the big house. She had always treated him with kindness and affection.

Bending slightly, she peered through her bifocals and smiled at Nikki. "And who's this young lady with you?"

Linc nudged Nikki gently forward. "This is my daughter, Nicole. Nikki, this is Miss Abigail Keating." Nikki resisted and ducked behind his long legs. Linc looked helplessly at the elderly woman.

Abigail didn't seem to notice anything out of the ordinary. She began rummaging in the depths of an old-fashioned tapestry purse. "I'm so glad you came in here, Nikki. I've been trying to decide what flavor of ice cream to choose, and I just can't make up my mind."

With a coin purse in her hand, she went to the counter. Frowning through her spectacles, she studied the array of ice cream behind the glass.

Nikki watched her for a minute and then ventured from her hiding place behind Linc. She gave him a beseeching look. Smiling faintly, he allowed her to grab a fistful of his jeans and pull him toward the counter.

Looking down at the dark-haired moppet, Abigail smiled. "I think I'll have mint chocolate chip, Nikki. What about you?"

Nikki looked first at the ice cream and then at the old lady, her wide blue eyes full of uncertainty and mute appeal.

"Can't quite decide, hmm?" Abigail began pointing out flavors. "Let's see now...there's strawberry, black walnut, rocky road, pralines and cream...." She glanced down and smiled as Nikki solemnly shook her head, rejecting all the exotic flavors.

"Well..."

Shyly Nikki lifted an arm and pointed.

"Vanilla?" Abigail exclaimed, raising her eyebrows above her spectacles. "You've decided on vanilla?"

Nikki nodded.

Almost holding his breath as he watched, Linc felt a catch at his heart. Since Joanna's death—with the exception of the woman who'd been his housekeeper in St. Louis and himself—Nikki had rejected everyone who tried to communicate with her. For the first time since making the decision to come home, some of his tension eased.

Abigail gave the amused clerk behind the counter an imperious look. "You heard that, Freddy. One mint chocolate chip and one vanilla."

"Coming up, Miss Abigail."

"Thank you," Linc said softly to the old lady a few minutes later when Nikki went back to the clerk for another napkin. She hadn't spoken, but she hadn't closed up inside herself, either, a habit that distressed Linc almost as much as her silence.

Abigail looked at him. "Don't thank me, boy. You've got a beautiful little girl there, and anybody with eyes to see can tell she's been through something terrible. Be patient and just keep loving her. One day soon, she'll be fine."

His mouth quirked. "Did you read that in your tea leaves, too?"

She lifted an admonitory eyebrow. "Humph. Still as skeptical as ever, I see."

"Well…let's just say I always wondered what brand of tea you used, Miss Abigail."

She chuckled. "Plain black tea, you rascal. And well you know it."

He leaned back, still smiling. "It's good to be home, Miss Abigail."

She patted his hand. "I was sorry to see you go, Lincoln, although I knew it was meant to be. Now I'm glad the time is right for you to come home."

Linc wasn't sure what to make of that as he helped Nikki back onto her chair. One thing he was sure of: although she was slightly eccentric, Abigail Keating had always been thoroughly honest, and he knew she wasn't just pretending to be glad to see him. He felt a rush of affection for the old lady and thought wistfully what a wonderful grandmother she would have made for Nikki.

"Tell me where you've been, Lincoln, and what all you've done."

"Well, I started out in Memphis after leaving State," he told her. "And then I went to New Orleans. But I ended up in St. Louis.'' He crossed a booted foot over his knee. ''As for what I've done, I guess I've dabbled in a little of this and a little of that.''

''Commodities, stocks and bonds, real estate, speculating for oil, just to name a few?''

He sat back, staring at her. ''More or less, Miss Abigail.''

''Don't look so shocked. I didn't read it in my teacup, son.'' She smiled softly and then added in a quiet voice, ''Pearce kept me informed.'' Her gaze went to Nikki, who had wandered over to the window and was taking in the sights of the small town. ''What about this child's mother?''

''She's dead.'' His tone was bleak. ''She died six months ago.''

''Oh, my.'' Miss Abigail's gaze returned to his face. ''I'm so sorry, Lincoln.'' Searching his eyes thoroughly for a few seconds, she nodded slowly. ''You've come home.''

He laughed harshly. ''I guess you could say that. But I still have…other responsibilities.''

''Pearce would want it that way.''

He gave her a startled look.

She was shaking her head, her blue eyes shadowed with regret. ''He never quite managed to conquer the devils that plagued him, you know.''

''I was at the funeral,'' Linc told her. ''I didn't stay. I couldn't. I had to get back to Nikki in St. Louis.'' He hesitated, recalling her nightmares, her terror every time he had to be away from her. ''I can't leave her, Miss Abigail. She's…''

''Still very fragile.''

He nodded. ''It's tough. About all I got out of the

psychologist was to be patient and show her lots of love."

The old lady's gaze went again to Nikki. "For such a lovely child, I'm sure you'll find an abundance of both," she said with a soft smile.

He cleared his throat, then asked, "How is Camille?"

"Very sad. Burdened with Willow Wind. Harassed by Jack."

Linc's breath escaped in a hiss. "Nothing ever changes with him, does it?"

She gave him a telling glance. "I'm expecting you to do something about that," she told him. "She needed you once a long time ago, Lincoln, but other forces were at work. Now, according to the leaves—"

Linc made a faint noise of protest. "Miss Abigail, I don't think—"

"There was something sinister afoot then, Lincoln." The old lady stared down at her ice cream as though the chocolate bits were tea leaves, and frowned. "I was never quite certain.... You and Camille were meant for each other. When you took off for God-knows-where, I was a little outdone with you, Lincoln. Your place was here, boy. Didn't you know that?"

Linc stared at her, wondering if the old lady had finally gone around the bend. Why was she talking about Camille and him like that? Didn't she know? She was living in the big house back then when it all started. She had known Linc all of his life, and even though his mother was the housekeeper, Abigail had been close to Kate. Surely Abigail Keating knew about his mother's affair with Joseph Keating. Why was she saying he and Camille were meant for each other? Didn't she know Camille Keating was his half sister?

He blinked when she reached over and patted his

hand. "It's good you're home, Lincoln," she told him again.

The bell tinkled above the door of the ice-cream shop as someone came in. Nikki instantly abandoned the window and scurried back to Linc. He pulled her close to his thigh and looked up as Miss Abigail made a happy, chirping sound. "Camille, just look who's here."

COMING IN from the glare outside, Camille took a second or two to get her bearings. The half smile she sent her aunt faltered as she recognized the man slowly getting to his feet beside the tiny table.

Dear God, I'm not ready yet.

Her heart rocketed in her breast and her breathing stopped. When it began again, it was shallow and uneven. At Pearce's funeral, she'd been dazed from heat and grief and sheer exhaustion. She hadn't allowed herself to really look at him. Today there was nothing to cushion the shock. She couldn't faint into oblivion again. She could only stare at him and try to endure the feelings coursing through her like molten lava.

The door brushed softly against her backside. Hastily, she took a step forward and then stopped in her tracks. There was nowhere to go except toward the table her aunt shared with Linc. He was as tall as ever. Seventeen years ago, he'd been twenty-one, slim as a reed and quick to smile, his features boyish. Now he was uncompromisingly mature. No less trim, but so much more powerful, broader and harder; quintessentially masculine.

His face... The years had not been kind. Lines were deeply etched beside his mouth. His chin was squared off, his jaw set. His eyes... If all eyes were blue or brown, then Linc's were brown. Whiskey brown, the color of the judge's favorite bourbon, so she'd always secretly thought. When he laughed, they'd lit up from the inside. Now, unwaveringly focused on her, they were guarded, almost wary.

"Hello again, Linc." Her voice was cool.

"Camille." His voice was deep and low. She stifled the sudden leap of her senses almost before it happened. She reminded herself that this was a man with no honor, no integrity. This was a man she had every reason to despise.

"Come join us, dear," Abigail said.

"No, I—" The refusal was automatic. She cleared her throat. "Not right now, thanks." Seeing the consoling look Abigail sent Linc, Camille wondered for the first time if her aunt knew of their shared past.

A faint whimper broke the tension. Everyone looked down at Nikki, who, sensitive to the slightest hint of distress, had pressed her face tightly against Linc's thigh. With a soft word, he bent and swung her up into his arms.

Christine was right, Camille thought, watching him tenderly stroke the dark, silky head. *Linc's child looks like me. She's the little girl we might have had. Instead...*

"What's the matter, Nikki honey?" Linc's tone was gentle, loving. Nuzzling Nikki's temple, he caught her chin and looked into her eyes. "Here's another lady I want you to meet, punkin. She's part of Miss Abigail's family, just like you're part of my family. Her name is Camille." At that, the little girl lifted her head and gazed directly at Camille.

"Hello, Nikki." Soft and ragged, the words seemed torn from Camille's throat. Watching Linc's arms enveloping the child, seeing the love in his eyes, hearing the tenderness in his voice struck her to her very soul. Linc, who'd never even considered the possibility that she'd been carrying *their* child, was adoring and indulgent with this little girl. Did he expect her to act as if she were any long-ago acquaintance meeting them casually? Dear God, was she expected to forgive and forget?

"Guess what, Nikki." Abigail Keating bustled around her chair just as Linc set Nikki back on her feet. "Camille is a kindergarten teacher, did you know that? She spends every day with lots of little girls just like you."

Camille gratefully directed her attention to the child instead of the father. She sank into a chair next to Nikki. "Have you ever been to kindergarten, Nikki?"

Nikki, wide-eyed, shook her head solemnly.

"Never?"

Another slow shake.

"How old are you?"

Nikki gravely held up four fingers.

"Hmm, four years old. I'll bet you can say your ABC's already." Camille raised her eyebrows in question.

Nikki nodded.

It was obvious that Nikki wasn't going to say a word, but she was willing to communicate. The professional in Camille recognized that the child had suffered some sort of trauma, but she wasn't going to get involved with Linc's child. Any close contact with Nikki would force her to deal with Linc. Not now. She simply couldn't. His involvement in Pearce's affairs was a complication that she planned to turn over to Tom Pettigrew.

Linc dropped a protective hand on Nikki's shoulder. As Camille rose, he met her eyes. "You're looking well, Camille."

"Thank you." The warm tone she had used with the little girl cooled noticeably.

He shook his head helplessly, dredging up a smile with difficulty. "I never know what to say in a situation like this."

Camille fixed her gaze on something outside the big bay window but said nothing.

He hesitated, searching her profile. "If there's anything I can do…"

"Thank you." She was barely aware of the words. All she could think of was how deeply and cruelly he'd hurt her all those years ago. Didn't he realize how much it hurt her to see him with the child of another woman? A woman he cared about, judging from his obvious love for the little girl.

What did that other woman have that I didn't have, Linc?

He expelled a slow breath. "Have you seen Tom Pettigrew?"

"Yes. I just left his office."

"We need to talk, Camille."

She faced him fully then, determined to be done with self-pity and recriminations. She'd had years to learn both were useless. He had destroyed her peace of mind once before, but she'd be damned if he'd do it again. "I assume you're referring to Willow Wind and your claim to it?" she inquired stiffly.

He nodded. "Yes…uh, well, not exactly." He gave her a look that was almost pleading. "I do want to talk to you about Willow Wind, but it's not like you think, Camille."

But Camille wasn't listening. She put a hand under Abigail's frail elbow and began ushering her across the floor.

"Camille—"

Holding the door, she waited while the old lady crossed the threshold. And then, before stepping out into the heat, Camille stopped and looked at Linc over her shoulder. "You can get in touch with Tom Pettigrew if you have anything to say to me."

HE HAD PLENTY TO SAY to her, but he didn't want it filtered through her lawyer first. As he shopped in the Sunflower Store, he rehearsed exactly how he would say it. But by the time he and Nikki were on the road out to the Twin Willows, he had accepted reality. He wouldn't be able to talk to Camille until she was good and ready. And who knew how long that would be?

It was midnight before he had Nikki settled. While Nikki explored the house where he'd grown up, he had unpacked and put away groceries, heated soup and made grilled cheese sandwiches, and then, after patiently introducing Nikki to every nook and cranny in Kate's Cottage, he'd finally managed to persuade her to choose a bedroom. She was now sleeping, her night-light glowing softly beside her bed.

With his hands folded beneath his head, Link stared unblinkingly at the ceiling. Everything was so damnably familiar. From the moment he'd made the turn at Keating's Corner and caught a glimpse of the first of the Twin Willows, ghosts of the past had been hovering at his shoulder.

At that hour—twilight—the stately lines of Willow Wood had been gilded in the rosy glow of the setting sun. The cypress siding, chosen for its imperviousness to Mississippi humidity, was painted snow-white. Through the leafy tracery of the trees, the mansion gleamed like a pearl. Without realizing it, he'd slowed the Bronco and simply stared, drinking in the perfect symmetry of the six Corinthian columns and the graceful sweep of the stairs that led up to the front door. It was a domain fit for a king.

Jack Keating's domain.

"Daddy, *that's* the Twin Willows, isn't it?" Wide-eyed, Nikki had whispered the question.

"Not the Twins, love." His own tone had dropped to a husky note. "Only one of them. That's Willow Wood. There, look." He gave the Bronco a little gas, slowly covering the scant half mile to a pond heavily fringed with weeping willows, their branches drooping low over the water. In the fading light, all was crystalline and still except for the twilight-loving insects skimming the pond's surface. Beyond the pond, shielded by its own screen of pecan trees was Willow Wind. He pointed to it.

"And that's Willow Wind."

Camille's home. Pearce's land. His now. Or as good as.

At the thought, he shifted restlessly on the bed, swung his legs over the side and sat up. If a stiff drink would help, he wouldn't hesitate to pour himself one. But he knew from experience there wasn't enough booze in the world to banish the devil that rode him tonight. He rested his elbows on his knees and buried his face in his hands, muffling a tortured sound.

Getting to his feet, he grabbed his jeans and pulled them on. He always had paperwork, and with any luck it would be enough to distract him. Without turning on any lights, he left his bedroom and made his way down the hall. He slowed at Nikki's door long enough to as-sure himself that she was still sleeping. Then, entering the living room, he stopped short.

Moonlight poured in through the oval leaded pane of the door, imbuing the satin brocade on the Victorian sofa his mother had so loved with a silvery sheen. But it wasn't his mother he saw sitting there. It was Camille. He flung himself down in a deep, soft chair and leaned his head back, closing his eyes. He thought of Camille as she'd been that night, before he learned the dark secret that had changed the course of both their lives.

THE JUDGE'S ANNUAL New Year's Eve bash was in full swing. Bored and restless, Linc stared at the glitzy crowd. Practically everyone who was anyone in the entire state appeared to be on hand to welcome in the new year at Willow Wood. The house itself was a major attraction, he supposed, because people sure seemed to love gawking at it. But the real reason people came was the judge himself. Joseph Keating was one of the most powerful men in the state of Mississippi.

"How soon before we can split to catch the score?" Pearce Wyatt grumbled, lifting a fresh glass of champagne from the tray of an impassive waiter. "I've got a hundred bucks on the Fighting Irish."

"Well, kiss it off," Linc told his best friend. "This year, the Bear is going to clean their clocks."

"Bull—" Pearce caught the eye of a matron who'd taught both him and Linc at Sunday school and hastily amended the expletive. "Bull-oney! You put your money where your mouth is and maybe I'll have some confidence in your predictions."

Linc leaned against the mantel and crossed his legs at the ankles. If he had a hundred bucks to blow, he wouldn't hesitate. Unfortunately, he didn't have an extra twenty-five, let alone a hundred. Not for long, though. Three more semesters and he'd finish up at State. With his education behind him, he'd step into the job he'd been groomed for since he'd been old enough to know a cotton boll from a soybean. The judge made no secret of his long-range plans. Jack Keating, his son and heir, would study law and go into politics. Linc would manage the Keating plantation. He was more than ready!

"Have you seen Cami yet?"

Pearce's question brought him back to the here and now. "Yeah, she's…"

"…not our little tomboy anymore."

Following Pearce's gaze, Linc found himself staring, too. He hadn't seen her in more than six months, and so he hadn't been prepared for the change in Camille. He had been standing at the fireplace underneath the huge picture of the judge when something, a ripple in the crowd, a sixth sense—he wasn't sure what—had drawn his eyes above the heads of the judge's guests and up the sweeping curve of the staircase. Everything inside him had stilled. There, at the top, wearing scarlet velvet and a wary, vulnerable look, was Camille.

Their eyes met, and she smiled. The impact of that smile had been far more potent than the judge's fine champagne.

A moment later Camille was claimed for a dance, and Pearce saluted her with his glass. "She sure is looking fine, buddy," he said to Linc. Over the shoulder of her dance partner, Camille's answering smile was warm and friendly. Then, catching Linc's eyes, she blushed and quickly looked away. Pearce swore without heat. "As usual, she can't see anybody but you, you son of a bitch."

Linc took a casual sip of his drink.

"So, is the feeling mutual?" Pearce asked, giving him a sidelong look.

Linc shifted so that he was no longer propped against the mantel. "Back off, Pearce." Tonight, for some reason, he was unwilling to reveal to anyone, even Pearce, his sudden, unexpected reaction to Camille. What was it? She still had the same face, the same stubborn little chin, the same dark, untamed hair. But when she'd looked at him through eyes as shadowy as Mississippi twilight, he'd felt as though he'd been kicked by a mule.

Pearce nudged his elbow. "Who's that she's with?"

Linc's jaw set. "One of those jerks from Jack's fraternity. Dwayne Archer. His old man is the state insurance commissioner."

Pearce grunted. "Figures. I saw him eyeing her before like he was thirsty and she was water. Jack introduced them and the next I knew, they were on the dance floor."

"Yeah. I noticed."

"She doesn't appear to be enjoying herself."

Linc scowled. He'd already arrived at the same conclusion. What the hell was Jack doing, pushing her at that bozo anyway? For a moment or two, Linc watched Camille's discreet efforts to keep Archer in line, itching to plant a fist in his fat gut.

Archer shifted suddenly and pulled Camille tightly against him. Even from across the room, Linc could see her struggle to put some distance between them. The hell with Jack; he was cutting in. He turned to place his glass on the mantel, but just as he stepped forward, the judge appeared at the door of his study and, catching his eye, motioned him over.

"Damn it!" He grabbed Pearce's shoulder. "Go over and cut in, Pearce. The judge wants me for something." He watched silently as Pearce threaded his way through the gyrating couples. Only when he saw Camille step gratefully into Pearce's arms did he turn away and head in the direction of the study.

WHEN HE CAME OUT, Camille had disappeared. The judge, holed up in his study with the former governor, had run out of Chivas Regal. Linc had been sent to fetch another bottle from the judge's private stock. He was frequently reminded of his real role at Willow Wood by little incidents like that. When you cut through the bull, he thought wearily, he was basically an employee. A hired hand.

Slanting a hand through his hair, he searched the room for a glimpse of Camille's dark head. The band was playing something slow, and the lights had been dimmed. Pearce was dancing with a long, leggy blonde balancing his champagne glass on the provocative curve of her derriere. Linc shouldered his way through the crowd.

"Where's Camille?" he demanded.

Pearce, feeling the effects of too much champagne, grinned. "I rescued her and then she said she needed some air."

"Where's Archer?"

Pearce blinked and searched the crowd. "I dunno."

Linc stood for a moment chewing on his lip. Would Archer follow her outside? Even if he did, would he be stupid enough to try anything? Camille was an innocent; anybody could see that. She'd had difficulty controlling Archer on a public dance floor. She'd be even more vulnerable outside. Suddenly he caught Jack Keating's eye. Jack looked self-satisfied. He had a smirk on his face, as though he were enjoying his own private joke.

Uneasily, Linc left Pearce and the blonde and headed for the French doors that opened to the courtyard. If Jack had set up one of his buddies with his seventeen-year-old sister, it proved what Linc had long suspected. He was a twisted, opportunistic snake who'd stop at nothing to further his own selfish ambition.

Hurrying, he crossed the back lawn and headed for the barn. When Camille was upset, she always went straight to those horses. She might be all grown-up and beautiful beyond anything he had expected, but he'd bet she hadn't changed that much.

For a second, when he wrenched open the door of the barn, nothing but flat silence greeted him. Then he caught a sound and began moving quietly down the shadowed corridor. A couple of the horses whickered and stamped restlessly. He started to call Camille's name, but another sound—this one harsh and masculine—made him go still, gripped with a cold premonition. He heard her anguished cry and then a ripping sound that tore through him like a hot knife.

No! Rage, raw and primitive, exploded in him. He charged blindly through the dark, all his instincts focused on getting to her. At the last empty stall, his brain registered everything through a red haze: Archer's massive body holding the struggling Camille against the rough wall, a thick leg shoved between hers. Her satin softness bared where her dress was ripped and gaping open. Archer's crude fingers violating her, desecrating her innocence. Her face—God, her face! It was deathly pale, her expression anguished.

Howling with outrage, Linc launched himself at Archer. Camille screamed piercingly. Linc's fingers clamped on the collar of the sleek black tuxedo and he gave a mighty yank. He felt a surge of savage satisfaction as the jacket ripped apart. Archer wheeled around in stunned surprise, just as Linc drove his fist into the beefy, slack-jawed face with all his strength, then followed it up with a punishing left to Archer's soft gut. The man's size exceeded his own by at least forty pounds, but surprise—and too much booze—gave Linc the edge he needed. That and the picture of Camille brutalized by Archer's obscene lust that was seared in his mind. Again he rammed his fist into thick lips, smiling dangerously at the gush of blood and saliva that spurted onto the barn wall and over the front of Archer's white shirt.

Archer came at him, swinging like an enraged ape. Lithely, Linc stepped aside and brought the edge of his hand down on the back of Archer's neck in a quick chop. It was enough to stun Archer, but he didn't go down. He reached blindly for Linc, intending to crush his assailant's ribs with his massive strength. Shifting again, putting all the force he had behind it, Linc slammed his fist into Archer's Adam's apple.

"Linc, stop! You'll kill him!" It was Jack Keating, and he was furious.

His chest heaving, Linc stood over Archer, watching him claw at his throat and struggle to breathe. "Then you'd better take care of him," he snapped without turning around.

The judge came puffing up behind Jack. His eyes widened when he saw Dwayne Archer sprawled on the floor of the empty stall. "What the hell's going on here?"

"It's Camille," Linc said, still lusting for Archer's blood.

"Camille?" The judge turned to look at his daughter, who was huddled against the rough boards in the shadows at the back of the stall. Caught in his gaze like a rabbit in a trap, Camille looked as though she wished the floor would open and swallow her up. Linc felt a

fierce protective urge to wrap his arms around her, to
shield her from the curious, intrusive eyes of her father
and brother. What was the matter with them anyway?
Didn't they have any normal feelings for their own
daughter and sister? Couldn't they see she was fright-
ened out of her mind?

"Well, what about Camille?" Jack demanded in a
hostile tone. "And it better be good, Cantrell."

Moving slowly, Linc turned reluctantly from Camille,
still shielding her with his body. Behind Jack and the
judge, he could see a crowd inching forward curiously.
"Keep those people back," he said. "I don't think you
want the details of this spread all over the state."

Jack muttered something, obviously hesitant about
leaving his buddy writhing on the floor. But at a curt
nod from the judge, he went to head off the crowd.
Standing tensely in front of Camille, Linc listened in
disgust as Jack gave some kind of laughing explanation
for the extraordinary scene in the barn. When he came
back, Jack shot Camille a hostile look before putting out
a hand to Archer to help him up. He brushed awkwardly
at the wisps of hay and barn dust that clung to the expensive fabric of Archer's tuxedo, frowning at the blood-
stains and jagged rip.

When he finished, he straightened and look at Linc,
his eyes furious. "Now, what happened here?"

Linc looked at Archer. "You want to tell them?" he
said softly. "Or shall I?"

Archer had finally regained his breath. "He's crazy,
do you know that, Jack? You got a crazy man hanging
around here."

"I don't hang around here, Archer. I live here."

Archer turned and deliberately spit on the ground.
"You're not family, Cantrell," he said flatly.

"Daddy—" Camille started forward, holding the bodice of her dress together.

Linc stepped in front of her, shielding her. "He tried to rape her, Judge."

The judge looked surprised, but before he could say anything, Jack laughed skeptically.

"Rape her?" He shook his head. "You *are* crazy, Linc. Dwayne wouldn't do a thing like that." He looked at Archer. "Would you, Dwayne?"

Archer adjusted his collar with a finger and gave one or two brisk tugs at his jacket to straighten it. "You know I wouldn't, Jack."

Linc's hands balled into fists. "You filthy, lying—"

"Linc!" the judge barked.

Linc swallowed the furious words he longed to say in Camille's defense. He would defy Jack, but not the judge.

His eyes hard, Linc stared at Archer. "Then how do you explain Camille's torn dress and her scream? Women don't scream for no reason."

Archer smiled at the judge and shrugged, extending his hands, palms up. "She's a little, uh…high-strung, Judge. My fault, sir. I guess I came on a little strong."

Jack gave him a hearty thump on the shoulder. "You see? A little misunderstanding, that's all it was." Grinning, he draped an arm around Archer. "A little too much Jack Daniel's, huh, buddy?"

"Yeah." Archer grinned at Camille. "No hard feelings, sugar?"

Camille stared at him without speaking.

"She's fine, Dwayne," Jack said. "Right, Camille?" He shot her a menacing look.

"Camille?" The judge waited.

"I'm fine." Shielded by Linc, she darted through the

stall door, lifted her skirt and fled through the darkened depths of the barn to the other exit.

Jack waited only until the judge and Dwayne Archer were out of earshot before venting his fury. "What the hell do you think you're doing?"

Linc, spotting a metallic glint on the stall floor, bent over. He brushed at some straw before straightening up, taking his time. "I'm picking up Camille's locket," he said, looking Jack straight in the eye. "What does it look like I'm doing?"

"Don't get cocky with me, Cantrell. I've had just about enough of you for one night."

"Then I'm one up on you," Linc said coldly. "I've had more than enough of you and your cronies."

"Do you know who Dwayne Archer is?" Jack demanded.

"Yeah, he's a sleazy bastard who brutalizes seventeen-year-old girls."

"His old man's the state insurance commissioner, you stupid hick! He's got his fingers in more money-making ventures than any other single individual in this state," Jack snapped. "That's who he is."

Linc stared at him. "And that gives him the right to rape your sister?"

Jack dismissed Camille with an impatient swipe of his hand. "She wasn't raped, for God's sake! She overreacted. She always overreacts."

"She didn't overreact, Jack! That animal was going to rape her! I was here. I saw him." Linc raised his eyes to the ceiling. What did it take to get through to this jerk? "Did you want me just to stand by and watch?"

"You didn't have to half kill him!" Jack roared.

"If you hadn't interrupted me, I *would* have killed

him," Linc snarled back. "He's scum, Jack. He's not fit to touch Camille's shoes."

Jack stared incredulously. "Who are we talking about here? Some little goddess? Give me a break, man. Camille's still wet behind the ears, a silly twit sashaying around tonight acting like she knew what it was all about. She asked for what she got! And you, you arrogant bastard, you were out of line beating up on an invited guest."

Linc lost his tenuous grip on his temper. "And you, you twisted son of a bitch, don't have a shred of decency or you'd come to the defense of an innocent girl whether she's your sister or not!"

A deadly look settled in Keating's eyes. "You listen here, Cantrell, and you listen good." He took a step closer until his forefinger almost touched Linc's chest. "Just who the hell do you think you are? You think because the judge feels some kind of misguided responsibility for you and your sainted mother that you have privileged status around here." His tone became low and menacing. "Not as long as I'm around, you hear? I'm warning you, if you don't stay in line, I'll get rid of you—and your mother—quicker than a bad habit. Now, you got that?"

The fat was in the fire now, Linc thought. Whether here at Willow Wood, at school or socially, he had felt Jack's hatred almost as long as he had known him. Jack would have been happy if Linc had announced his intention to pursue a career anywhere else but at Willow Wood after graduation. It had been a private thing, something both acknowledged without dressing it up in words. Until tonight. But there was Linc's deep love for Willow Wood, his obligation to the judge, to his mother.

And there was Camille....

Alone in the barn, he'd prowled around like a caged
tiger that night, wrestling with his thoughts, smarting
from Jack's threats, wondering how much the judge
could be relied upon if Jack really set his mind to getting
rid of him. Suddenly the answer to that had become
crucial.

There was Camille....

He had started looking for her then, almost panicking
before he finally tracked her down to Kate's Cottage.
She'd been alone in the dark, crying softly. Now,
slouched deep in the chair, he could see her curled up
on that brocade settee, and the seventeen years seemed
no more than the difference between going to bed one
night and waking the next day. Placing his head in his
hands, he pressed his eyes with his thumbs, wishing
the memory weren't so vivid. Wishing he could erase
the look of her, the feel of her, the taste of her from his
mind and never be cursed with it again.

But he knew better.

CHAPTER THREE

LINC WAS RUNNING OUT of patience. Pearce's death had created a sticky situation, but it had to be faced. It was something Linc wanted to deal with directly, just him and Camille. They didn't need some damned lawyer listening in, scrutinizing everything without having a clue as to Pearce's motives. The problem was getting her to see it his way. It was already a week now, and not a word from Camille.

Scowling, he poured himself a cup of coffee and took it outside. What he'd really like was to take matters into his own hands, haul himself over to Willow Wind and force her to see him, talk to him. But what he wanted and what he would do were two different things. He tasted his coffee, resigned. Meeting in Tom Pettigrew's office was probably the way it was going to be. But when? She couldn't put him off forever.

He started across the yard toward the fence. He understood why she wanted to avoid him, but recalling the shock and then disdain in her eyes at the ice-cream shop, he felt the sharp sting of regret. She despised him—and with what she believed was good reason. God, it hurt. He wasn't certain he could stand being around Camille knowing that she hated him.

He propped a booted foot on the fence and stared out over the east field. Cotton, as far as the eye could see. This particular portion of Pearce's place was producing a bumper crop. Pearce would be proud. With a short, hollow laugh, Linc tossed away the dregs of his coffee and turned to go back inside.

Then he saw her.

She was riding a beautiful little chestnut mare and going at a breakneck pace. He breathed in sharply. She still rode with the grace and style that had earned her dozens of ribbons and trophies before she was sixteen. As he watched, she sailed over a blackberry thicket. His heart pounded furiously, but she took the jump with ease. She checked the mare instantly, and Linc knew that she'd seen him. With a subtle command from her rider, the mare changed direction. He tensed, realizing she was heading his way. At last.

"Morning," she said coolly, reining in the excited, winded horse.

She looked like a queen peering down at him like that. But her blue eyes were turbulent, at odds with the cool sound of her voice and guarded expression on her face.

"Hi," he said, shaking his head, smiling faintly. "You still ride like the wind." The mare snorted and threw up her head. Reaching across the fence, Linc caught at the bridle and ran a palm over the horse's neck. "She's a beauty. Have you had her long?"

"About two years." She bent and stroked the mare's neck on the opposite side. "I call her Firefly."

Staring into her eyes, Linc forgot the mare. Gone was the seventeen-year-old innocent he'd left behind. In her place was a woman in the full blush of womanhood. And a thousand times more beautiful than she'd been at seventeen. The spirited run had put color in her pale cheeks. Her black hair was confined in a long French braid hanging down her back, but little wisps wet with sweat curled at her temples and low on her neck. Her mouth, bare of lipstick, looked vulnerable and all too kissable. He broke off that thought guiltily.

"I talked to Tom a few days ago," he told her, forcing himself to look beyond her to a stand of willows that crowded the banks of the pond between the two plantations. "He told me he'd get back to me when you were ready to talk."

She drew in a breath. "I know. I just haven't been able to manage it. I've been busy." Her hand clenched on the reins, causing Firefly to dance skittishly and toss her head. Camille soothed her in a low-pitched voice. "You look tired," she said suddenly.

He glanced at her. "I was up a couple of times in the night with Nikki."

She frowned. "Is she sick?"

"No, she's just…having a little trouble."

Camille nodded. "I can imagine. Strange house, strange bed, strange place."

"Strange sitters."

He thrust his hand through the side of his hair, feeling like a man nearly at the end of his rope. "I need somebody permanently, somebody really good, which appears to be a problem. I've been through three in just one week."

Camille didn't comment, but she looked suddenly wary.

"Do you know anyone?"

"No…. No, I—"

"I thought that since you deal with little kids all day you might be a good person to ask."

"I told you, I don't know of anyone."

Still holding the horse's bridle, he looked directly at her. "You may as well get down off that horse, Camille. We need to talk, and now's as good a time as any. As a matter of fact, it's just as well we waited until today. I've had time to look over the place and make some plans.''

"Plans?"

He drew in a deep breath. "Will you get down off that horse, Camille?''

Without another word, Camille dismounted and, walking alongside the fence, secured the reins on a low rail in a shady spot, giving Firefly enough slack to crop at the still dew-damp grass. With a quick twist of her body, Camille went through the boards of the fence. "Okay, talk,'' she said to Linc with a challenging look.

"Let's sit down,'' he told her, motioning toward lawn furniture that looked as though it had seen better days. Which, of course, it had. Although Linc had seen to it that the contents of Kate's Cottage were cared for, the grounds had been neglected. Still, the scent of wisteria and honeysuckle hung in the early-morning air, calling to mind other times when there had been no bitterness or secrets between the two of them.

Camille sat down on the edge of a wooden bench. Linc straddled one beside it, allowing himself just one long, pleasurable look at her. For days he'd resisted calling her, knowing he was the last person she'd want to see. But this meeting was necessary, he assured himself. She lifted her eyes, and for just a moment, the years fell away as morning-glory blue clung to whiskey brown.

"It's been a long time, Cami.''

Something flashed in her beautiful eyes. "Yes. Was that what you wanted to say?''

Up close, he was struck again by how much more beautiful she was now than she'd been at seventeen. At Pearce's funeral, she'd been pale and strained, as though she were made of glass and ready to shatter. Today there was a bloom to her skin, a fresh, feminine sweetness about her. Her scent, subtle and flowery, was the same. It was completely captivating.

"Linc—" Her tone was impatient and curt and brought him back from his reverie. "I have a lot to do this morning," she reminded him.

Realizing he'd been staring too long, he shook his head, smiling slightly. "'Scuse me. I was just thinking how lovely you are now." He jutted his chin in the direction of her long braid. "I see you're still fond of pigtails." Maybe if he treated her like a kid sister, he'd be able to think of her that way.

"I really have to run." She started up. Without thinking, he stopped her with his arm.

"No, wait—" What had he expected? Withdrawing his hand, he felt mired in guilt and regret. He'd been a fool to think he could wish away all that had gone before. Wearily, he settled back. "How much did Pearce tell you?"

"About what?"

"About his problems with Willow Wind. Did you know he'd been in trouble for more than five years?"

"Financially, you mean?" He nodded and she shook her head, looking faintly distressed. "No, not really."

"Wasn't that about the time he was first hospitalized?"

Camille closed her eyes, so vivid was the scene that flashed before her. Pearce in a hospital bed hooked up to tubes and machines, looking so vulnerable, so sick. Pearce promising he would never drink again. Pearce telling her he needed her love, not her pity.

"I'm sorry, Cami. I know this is hard for you."

She looked at him. "Why, Linc? Why did he do this?

He knew you would be the last person I'd want help from."

Their eyes clashed for a long second, and then he lifted one shoulder in a resigned gesture. "I don't know, Cami."

A spasm of pain crossed her face. "Stop calling me that!"

His hand rose as if in protest and then fell back to the table. "Maybe he knew he could trust me to take care of you."

She was off the bench in a heartbeat. "I don't need taking care of, Linc. Least of all by you. I don't want your charity, and I most certainly don't want your pity. I'm a businesswoman." She gave him a direct look. "A successful businesswoman. Sunny Day is the best preschool this side of Memphis. Pearce may have come crying to you when he got in trouble, but I don't need you. I'm not a silly teenager anymore."

Linc rose slowly, his mouth set in a grim line. "You're no farmer, either. Who's going to manage Willow Wind? Tell me that. The cotton's half-grown, but there's still defoliating, picking, ginning, marketing and accounting to be done. And that's not counting any unforeseen problems cropping up."

"Jack and I have already discussed this."

"Jack?" The name was repeated softly.

"Yes, Jack. My brother. His manager's been overseeing this season's crop anyway."

"Is anything in writing?"

"What?"

"A contract, Camille. Did Pearce formally lease the acreage?"

She put a hand to her forehead. "I don't think so."

She gave him a testy look. "Why should he? Jack is family."

"Right," Linc said dryly.

Camille's shoulders drooped. She sounded genuinely distressed when she said, "Why didn't Pearce turn to Jack?"

"Maybe he was afraid of being eaten alive."

"What?"

"Never mind, Camille. Just hear this. I hold the paper to Willow Wind. Forget leasing the land to Jack. I'll take care of notifying him and his people about the way it is."

She looked so upset that he almost told her she could do whatever she wanted, that she could hand the whole thing over to Jack Keating. Almost, but not quite. No, he owed Jack Keating a debt. With a few cruel words, Jack had destroyed his future, stolen his boyhood and his idealism, snatched from him his goals and dreams. And he had enjoyed it. At last Linc was in a position to make Jack squirm, and he wasn't passing it up.

"Camille—" He leaned forward. "The way Pearce arranged it, you need my consent for any major decisions, as I'm sure Tom Pettigrew told you."

"He told me no such thing." Camille pressed her hand against her stomach as though rebelling at the thought of a future coupled so intimately with Linc's.

"Before you get all bent out of shape, let me tell you what I've worked out."

She looked at him in silence.

"I've already got a pretty good idea of the situation as it is today. The field hands who've been with you and Pearce for years know the routine. They just need managing, someone to take over the job Jack's man has been doing. I can handle it, Camille. I—"

"What are you talking about? You've been wheeling and dealing in high finance, Linc, not raising cotton! This is not a stock-market takeover or one of your realestate deals. This is Willow Wind, my home, and the bread and butter of dozens of people."

She was pushing him, and when he made a short sound of impatience, Camille's heart leaped, sending a thrill all the way through her. She wanted to torment him. She wanted to hurt him.

When he spoke, his voice was surprisingly low and controlled. "Have you forgotten that for the first twenty-one years of my life I ate, breathed, slept and dreamed cotton? Have you forgotten that, Camille?"

"That was a long time ago."

"I can handle it, Camille. Trust me on this."

"Trust you?" Her voice was almost a squeak. "I trusted you once, Linc. I don't think I want to be that big a fool again."

He started to say something, but she held up a hand. "This discussion is pointless anyway. As you say, you hold all the paper, so you can do things your way. Fine." She turned sharply, sending her black braid flying.

Swearing, Linc started after her. "Camille—"

They both stopped short at the sound of a child's high-pitched wail. Linc turned abruptly. "It's Nikki."

"Daddy, Daddy!"

Camille halted at the rails of the fence. Straightening slowly, she watched as Linc's little girl appeared in the doorway of the cottage. She was sobbing, and she looked like a little lost waif in her flower-sprigged granny gown. The knuckles of her small fist rubbed at one eye; in the other hand she clutched a well-worn bunny. Spotting her daddy, she started across the porch in a fresh burst of weeping. Camille's heart lurched as the child reached the steps. If she didn't slow down...

"Nikki, wait!" Linc called out, but Nikki was beyond caution. She began to go down the steps, her short legs barely able to reach from one to the next. One bare foot caught in the ruffle of her nightgown and she started to tumble down the steps. But Linc was there in time, sweeping her up, gently cushioning her face against his chest.

"Baby, baby, don't cry," he crooned, nuzzling her soft, dark curls. "Daddy's gotcha. Did you have another bad dream, punkin?"

Another? Drawn to the two as though pulled by a magnet, Camille cautiously moved closer. The child seemed terrified or in pain, and neither emotion was something a four-year-old should have to bear, even in a bad dream. After a few minutes, Linc's voice, repeating nonsensical words in a low, reassuring tone, had stopped the tears.

"I was s-scared, Daddy." Snuffling, Nikki rubbed her nose against Linc's T-shirt. Camille struggled against her emotions. There was something about a man tolerating the indignity of a little kid blotting a runny nose on him.

"There was nothing to be scared of, punkin. I was right out here in the front yard." Linc lifted his head and looked at Camille. "I was talking to this pretty lady. We met her a few days ago when we got ice cream, remember?"

Using her bunny rabbit as a shield, Nikki, hiccupping, eyed Camille warily through its long floppy ears.

"Hello again, Nikki."

Nikki looked first at Camille and then beyond her, wide-eyed, to Firefly, who was placidly cropping grass at the fence line.

Seeing her interest, Linc said, "That's Camille's horse, Nikki."

Nikki gave Camille an awed look before turning her attention back to the mare.

Smiling, Camille asked, "Do you like horses?"

Nikki nodded. After a moment, she wiggled in a wordless demand to be put down. Linc complied, easing her to the ground. Holding on to his jeans at the knee, Nikki tugged him closer to the horse.

"Her name is Firefly," Camille volunteered.

"Firefly," Nikki whispered, blue eyes as big as saucers.

Camille heard the swift intake of Linc's breath. Looking up, she saw that he was staring intently at Nikki.

"He's big," Nikki whispered.

"He's a she," Camille told her. "A girl horse is called a mare, Nikki."

"A mare," she repeated, trying out the new word. She looked up at Camille, her small features screwed up in the bright morning sunshine and then turned her face in to Linc's thigh. "Her name's Camille," she whispered shyly, darting a quick look in her direction.

"That's right," Linc said, his tone unsteady. Reaching down, he swung her up into his arms again as though he needed to give her a hug.

Camille's gaze dwelt for a long moment on Nikki's dark curls nestled under Linc's chin. She felt as though her heart were being squeezed by a giant fist. A part of her was screaming to escape. Another was hopelessly ensnared. Linc's face, when she glanced at him, seemed to be carved in stone.

Nikki put one small palm on his hard jaw, making him look at her. "Is she gonna be my new baby-sitter?"

Her voice was hesitant. She sniffed, traces of tears still in her eyes.

Camille didn't wait to hear Linc's reply. "No, honey. I was just taking Firefly for a ride, and I stopped to talk to your daddy."

"I don't like baby-sitters." Nikki's voice trembled and new tears puddled, trapped by her long lashes. Snuggling even closer to Linc, she wrapped one small arm around his neck. "I like riding with you, Daddy."

Camille got a quick mental picture of father and daughter cruising the roads that crisscrossed the twin plantations. Had she been riding around all day with Linc in his vehicle? For heaven's sake! No father who knew anything about parenting would set that kind of precedent. But then, this whole thing was probably a lark to him. He'd be returning to St. Louis as soon as... As soon as what? Where was Linc's wife? Had Nikki been the innocent victim in a messy divorce? Were her nightmares the result of yet another modern-day tug-of-war in a courtroom?

Seeing the disapproval in Camille's eyes, Linc crouched and gently set Nikki on her feet. "Nikki," he began huskily, before clearing his throat, "why don't you show Camille our special secret?"

Looking at Camille, Linc held his breath, blatant appeal written all over him.

"Does she want to see it?" Nikki asked, leaning against Linc's knee.

Camille hesitated, ready to run. "A secret?" she heard herself ask weakly.

Standing with one tiny foot covering the other, Nikki wrinkled her nose as though considering. She nodded.

Camille smiled. "Okay."

Sticking close to Linc, Nikki pointed to a huge bank

of ligustrum bushes flanking the fence beyond the tree where the mare stood. She tugged at his hand, pulling him along. Glancing at him from beneath her lashes, Camille saw his mouth slanted in a half smile. But, meeting her eyes, he merely shrugged helplessly.

At the bushes, Nikki turned to Linc and lifted her arms. "Pick me up, Daddy."

Still smiling, he swung her up once more and held her as she leaned over and carefully pulled a branch aside. She glanced shyly back at Camille, but her blue eyes sparkled with anticipation. "Shhh," she said, putting a finger to her lips.

Solemnly, Camille rose on her tiptoes and peered through the dark leaves. There, tucked firmly in the crotch of a limb, was a bird's nest. Inside were three baby birds, their tiny beaks wide open, heads weaving back and forth on fragile necks.

"They want their breakfast," Nikki whispered.

"And what about you?" Linc demanded suddenly, suspending her in front of him with two hands beneath her arms. "Isn't it about time for *your* breakfast, young lady?"

Nikki giggled and kicked her feet, hampered only slightly by the pink-sprigged gown. Hugging her hard, Linc set her on her feet and gave her a soft smack on her little bottom. She giggled again and ran toward the porch. As she scrambled up the steps, tangling again in her gown, he gave a soft chuckle. Hearing it, seeing the expression on his face, Camille felt a bittersweet twist in the vicinity of her heart. Their interaction was all too familiar to someone like her who dealt with children daily. It was a mixture of indulgence and affection, the unique pleasure that a parent finds in his own child.

She said nothing after Nikki disappeared behind the

screen door. In the distance, on Jack Keating's land, a big tractor lumbered between evenly spaced rows, scattering a flock of startled doves. Overhead in a magnolia tree, a mama blue jay scolded the humans below for invading the confines of her nest.

"Sweet Jesus," Linc whispered, staring blindly across the field.

"What is it?"

He looked at her. "Nikki was talking to you."

Camille was puzzled. "She seemed shy in the ice-cream shop last week, but…" She shrugged. "It doesn't take most four-year-olds long to overcome that."

"Nikki hasn't spoken a word to another person besides myself and my last housekeeper in more than six months."

"Oh?"

"Yeah." His laugh was unsteady. "For a minute there I wanted to jump up and hug somebody—you, Nikki, that damn mare." He shook his head. "I don't know.…" His eyes held a suspicious brightness. "It's just that I was about at the end of my rope. I've done everything I knew how to do—experts, doctors, tests…you name it. Then, in two minutes, she's chattering away."

Camille said nothing.

Linc followed the progress of the tractor for a few seconds. Then, looking at her, he said simply, "Thank you."

"I don't think—"

"Camille…" He put out a finger, almost touching her lips. "Thank you."

A thousand questions clamored to be asked, but she wouldn't. *She wouldn't.* She wasn't going to get caught up in something that could rip the heart right out of her. Again.

His hand fell and he pushed his palms into the back pockets of his jeans. "I just wish I knew what to do about the nightmares."

She hesitated. "I guess it depends."

"On what?"

She made an indistinct sound. "On circumstances. Some children are just naturally high-strung. An upsetting incident at bedtime can do it. Too much excitement. Fatigue. Or, of course, trauma."

Linc took a deep breath. Making an effort to curb the emotion she'd unwittingly evoked with the word *trauma,* he raked a hand through his hair. "How long does it last?"

"That depends, too," she said, turning from him. What was the matter with her? If she didn't want to talk about Nikki, then where was this conversation going? She turned around to face him, intending to say another quick goodbye. He was thrusting his hand through his hair again, looking overwrought and vulnerable.

Camille closed her eyes and took a deep breath. "What seems to be the problem, Linc?"

He gave her a relieved look. "Nikki's mother died six months ago," he said gruffly, a muscle twitching in his jaw when he heard her swift, sympathetic sigh. "It was at Christmastime. They were out shopping, Joanna and Nikki. Joanna stepped off a curb, and a drunk driver came out of nowhere."

His gaze was fixed on the line of trees behind Kate's Cottage, but Camille knew in his mind he was seeing the horror all over again. *She* was seeing it. A shopping mall decked out for the holidays. Tinsel and carols, shoppers and Santas. And in the festive scene, one unsuspecting mother with a four-year-old finally calling it a day, more than ready to go home.

Linc looked at Camille, his mouth twisted bitterly. "You think it could never happen to you, right?"

Camille waited, pale and still.

"Well, it did. Joanna was dead on impact." He shook his head as though still disbelieving. "But somehow Nikki…Nikki wasn't touched. Not a scratch."

Camille pressed her hands against her trembling lips.

Linc blinked a few times before looking at her. "But she was hurt, Cami. Maybe even more than if she'd been struck, too, and knocked unconscious. Surely that would have been more merciful than watching her mother tossed like a rag doll for forty feet and then having to suffer the sight of Joanna's blood, the hysteria, the horror."

Camille simply looked at him, unable to speak.

Linc stared beyond her, shaping a thought. "So, now you know the reason for Nikki's nightmares and why she's retreated behind a wall of silence, why she's afraid to stay with a baby-sitter." He sighed, kneading the corners of his eyes with one hand. "And why I feel so inadequate sometimes trying to deal with it."

"You seem to be doing fine, Linc," she said.

"Yeah."

"It seems…unfair that both you and Nikki experienced the same childhood tragedy," she murmured after a moment.

"What?"

"Weren't you four years old when your own father was killed in that hunting accident with Dad?"

Linc glanced at her sharply, then away. "Oh, Robert Cantrell. Yeah, I was four when he died."

Something about his reply seemed odd, but she couldn't quite pin it down. "I'm so sorry, Linc. I…I don't know what to say."

He shook his head. "You don't have to say anything, but I'd appreciate anything you can think of that might help Nikki."

Camille put a hand to her throat. *Don't!* she wanted to cry. *Don't do this to me!*

"It was just so good to hear her begin to open up." His smile was slightly crooked, but his eyes were intense as they met hers. "It's no wonder your kindergarten has a reputation as the best, Cami. You seem to know just what to say, what to do."

She could feel a warm flush coloring her cheeks. More than anything, she wanted to get away from here, away from him before she said something or promised something that she would regret. "It's nothing special, Linc. Don't read anything into it that isn't there. I'm trained to deal with young children, that's all."

Even before she stopped speaking, he was shaking his head. "You don't learn how to reach a traumatized child from a textbook or a seminar, Camille. It comes from your heart. Nikki sensed it. She trusted you instinctively."

Camille stood up and began backing away. "She isn't going to be special to me, Linc. I won't let her be special. Your daughter is no different to me from the dozens of children that I teach every day."

For a moment, their eyes clashed in silent battle, but Camille wasn't finished. In a low, throbbing voice, she said, "How dare you come back here with your child, expecting me to open my heart to her? Yes, I'll be kind to her. Yes, I'll treat her with the care I give all children. But have you forgotten that when you left me all those years ago, you didn't even care enough to ask if the sex we shared might possibly have resulted in a child of our own?"

Hoarsely, Linc whispered her name. His eyes burning, he put out a hand to touch her.

"Don't!" Camille stepped swiftly aside. "Just... don't...touch me." She didn't think she could bear to feel the touch of Linc Cantrell's hands ever again.

"God, Camille, are you saying—"

"I'm saying I'll be good to your little girl while you're here in Blossom, Linc. But don't expect miracles."

Turning from him, she rushed through the fence rails and, blinded by a sudden gush of hot tears, fumbled with Firefly's reins. She didn't want to know about Linc's life away from Blossom, about Nikki's mother, about the tragedy that still haunted them. She didn't want to know anything that might draw her back into something that would surely destroy her.

She threw Linc one last, burning look. "Thanks to you, I don't believe in miracles anymore." Then, with a short command to the mare, she wheeled away and took off in a wild, desperate effort to outrun the past.

At the barn, Camille dismounted and automatically began walking her horse. After the headlong gallop away from Kate's Cottage, Firefly was winded, flecked with foam. Camille felt a prickle of conscience. She hadn't done that to a horse for a long, long time.

As if in a trance, she led the animal around the paddock, her thoughts still as turbulent as the unbridled pace of her ride. More times than she liked to remember, she'd sought refuge in her horses. But it wasn't going to work today.

Yes, she had once believed in miracles. The night that Linc finally noticed her, it had indeed felt like a miracle to Camille. The night of the judge's New Year's Eve party...

"CAMI? ARE YOU in here?"

Camille shrugged quickly at the tears on her cheeks and sank deeper into the corner of Kate's brocade sofa, curling her legs tightly beneath her. The coals of a spent fire glowed dully. "Umm… Here I am, Linc."

Linc came through the cottage door into the living room, frowning. Automatically he reached for the light switch. "It's dark in here, Cami. Let me—"

"Don't!" she said sharply. "Please."

He nodded, and then, after a second or two, started toward her. "You want some company," he asked lightly, "or is this a private party?"

"S-some party." She made a sound that could have been a laugh or a sob. The party she'd so looked forward to had turned into a nightmare.

He studied her intently in the soft glow of the coals and then sat down beside her. "Did he hurt you, Cami?"

She wasn't quite able to conceal a shudder. "No, but I was really scared there for a minute. Thank heaven you came when you did."

"I should have killed him."

She smiled shakily. "If you had, then I never would get to dance with you."

He was staring at his hands. At her words, he turned his head, looking at her sideways. "Did you want to dance with me?"

"I was dying to."

In the big house, the band began to play, the sound carrying easily in the December stillness. His eyes locked with Camille's, Linc got slowly to his feet. He put out a hand. "May I have this dance?"

Her eyes wide and very dark, Camille stood. It seemed the most natural thing in the world to step into his arms. She forgot that her dress was torn, that her nose was probably pink and shiny from crying, that the night had been more sordid than magical. As the music swelled softly, he urged her closer until they were touching everywhere, and forgetting that he was used to older, more sophisticated girls, Camille lost herself in the joy of dancing with Linc at last.

It was just as wonderful as she'd imagined it would be. He smelled good, sort of spicy, definitely masculine. When she sighed dreamily, he shifted and slid both arms around her waist, giving her no choice except to link her own arms around his neck. It gave her a delicious kind of feeling, nothing like the way that other—

Quickly she banished that thought. She wouldn't let anything tarnish these moments with Linc. They were too precious. She'd longed for just this from the time she'd wheedled permission from the judge to attend the party. She looked up at him and her heart tripped over itself—he was so beautiful.

It had been almost more than she could bear when he went off to college. That was more than three years ago, and all the summer fun, all the long evenings spent in his mother's cottage, all the give-and-take that she'd so cherished had come to an end. She'd been a child then, only fourteen. To be in his arms now, moving to the slow beat of the music, was thrilling.

Meeting her eyes, he smiled. And then the music stopped.

Almost reluctantly, it seemed, Linc released her. Her eyes downcast, she ran her palms awkwardly down the velvet skirt. "Thank you," she whispered.

He tilted her chin up with one finger. "I should be thanking you," he told her. "When you disappeared, I thought I'd missed my chance to dance with the most beautiful girl at the party."

"Oh, Linc." She was breathless. She'd longed so much to hear words like that from him.

"Here, you dropped this."

She looked up and then reached for the locket that dangled from his fingers. "Thanks," she whispered, and without looking at it, slipped it into a small pocket in her velvet skirt.

"Was it a Christmas gift?"

"What? Oh. Yes."

He frowned. "From one of those jocks who are always eyeing you at school?"

She gave him a startled look. "No. It's from Daddy."

He relaxed. "I thought it looked special."

"It's special because Kate has wonderful taste," Camille said bitterly. "He sent your mother to buy it. I can't ever remember getting a gift—birthday, Christmas, whatever—that the judge actually chose himself, Linc. He always sends Kate."

"Cami." There was sympathy and something else in his eyes.

"So does Jack."

He took her chin in his fingers. "It's been a bad night for you, hasn't it?" His tone, the cottage, the dying fire all had a caressing quality that made her want to turn into Linc's arms, to have him hold her tight, to hear him promise all sorts of improbable, wondrous things.

"Why don't they love me, Linc?" Her eyes, swimming in tears, searched his.

He sighed. "Don't say that, Cami. They do. How could they not? It's just that..."

She moved, sitting up straight on the sofa, shaking her head, and his hand fell away. "They don't and it's time I faced it." With her palms, she wiped the tears from her cheeks. "It's okay. I've known it for a long time—

I just never admitted it out loud.'' She laughed shakily. "When you know that your own father and brother don't really care whether you live or die, it's not something you want to dwell on, you know?''

"Camille—''

She smoothed a hand over the once-elegant velvet. "Now you're in for it, too.''

Linc laughed shortly. "You mean because I decked Archer?''

"That, too, but…'' She hesitated and then looked directly at him. "I heard what Jack said, Linc. He doesn't like it when you stand up to him.''

"Jack's an ass,'' Linc muttered.

"It's almost as though he's trying to drive you away,'' she said, looking troubled.

There was a small silence. "If he gave it a serious shot, he might not have too much trouble,'' Linc said slowly.

"Don't say that, Linc! You belong at Willow Wood as much as…as Kate or Aunt Abby.''

Linc was shaking his head. "Abigail belongs here, Cami, yes. She's a Keating. My mother, as Jack has already reminded me once tonight, is just the housekeeper. As for me, I'm only here because of the judge's charity.''

"But…but…''

He smiled. "Forget it, Cami. Jack's not running things yet. The judge still has a lot of good years left. Only senility would make him think putting Jack in charge of Willow Wood is a good idea. Jack's no farmer.''

"No…'' Camille thought for a second. "But even so, he's almost fanatical about Willow Wood.''

"Not as a producing plantation,'' Linc said. "He's

more interested in possessing the land than in cultivating it.''

''I know....''

Suddenly, noise spilled out of the big house. Linc caught Camille's hand, and together they went to the door of Kate's Cottage. He opened it to snatches of laughter and voices carrying across the lawn in the crisp winter night as the elegant guests climbed into their expensive cars and started them up. One by one, they began to pull out, negotiating the curving drive slowly, headlights arcing over the cotton fields, heading for the main road.

''Seems the party's over,'' Linc murmured.

Camille nodded, her free hand clenched at her breast to hold her dress together. ''I guess so.''

''You know something?''

She glanced at him quickly. Although it was dark, she could see the white curve of his smile. ''What?''

''I usually hate these things.'' He spread the edges of his tuxedo jacket wide. ''I feel stupid all rigged out like a penguin, making small talk with people I never see except at the judge's parties. Tonight I racked my brain looking for a way to get out of going.'' The smile he gave her sent her heart on a merry-go-round. ''However, now that I know the company's improved, it won't be such a chore next year.''

Camille's whole body flushed with happiness. She'd dreamed of this, but reality was a thousand times better than her dreams.

''I have to go back tomorrow,'' he said.

''I know. When will you be home again?''

''Not until spring break. Will you save some time for me then?''

"You know I will. You don't even have to ask."
When he grinned, she blushed and looked away.

"I'd better get you inside, little girl. It's late."

She put her hand on his arm. "Not yet. I mean, ah…"
She glanced down at her dress. "I want to be certain
everybody's gone before I go in."

He nodded, understanding, and the grim look was
back on his face. When she tried to pull her hand away,
he wouldn't let her. Instead, he made himself comfortable, leaning against the door. He pulled her against him
so that her hips nestled against his front, and crossed his
arms over hers, firmly securing her in his embrace. "You
want to know something else?"

She could feel his breath in her hair, hear the steady
rhythm of his heartbeat. Closing her eyes, she made a
wish that the moment could last forever. "What?"

"When I looked up and saw you at the top of that
staircase tonight, I couldn't believe my eyes."

"Really?" He dropped a kiss on her hair and she
shivered.

"You had grown up."

She laughed softly, breathlessly. "Isn't it about time?
You didn't expect me to stay in a single braid and braces
forever, did you?"

"I don't know what I expected." He nuzzled the side
of her face. His kiss was just a soft, gentle brush of lips
against her cheek, but it made her heart dip and reel
more than the most daring ride she'd ever been on at the
county fair.

"Linc…"

"You took my breath away, Cami."

She angled her head back so that she could look at
him. She was smiling and so was he. For a moment, that
was all they did—smile and look at each other. And then

Linc wasn't smiling. He was looking at her with something in his eyes that set her heart racing.

"You are beautiful, Camille."

"Am I?"

"So beautiful. Too beautiful. I have to do this...." He
bent and touched her mouth gently with his.

His lips were warm and firm, just barely brushing hers
at first. But then, as she shyly relaxed, he became more
insistent, persuasive. With tiny sipping motions, he
tasted her, softly nipping at her full bottom lip and
then—to Camille's amazement—licking her. Enthralled,
all her senses heightened, she delighted in the delicious
things he was doing. She didn't have much firsthand
experience, but she'd seen movies. He started to pull
back, but it took only her small whimper to change his
mind.

"You taste so good, Cami. Sweet...so sweet. I knew
you would." He opened his lips fully, covering hers with
a warm, sweet suction, using just enough finesse to
arouse her without alarming her.

Trustingly, Camille's lips parted and welcomed the
first feathery strokes of his tongue against hers. He was
breathing hard. She loved the sound, loved knowing that
kissing her did that to him. She raised her hand and
touched his cheek. His beard was rough, but she liked
the feel of it. Just as she liked the feel of his body against
hers. Being trapped in the hard muscularity of his arms
made her feel small and defenseless. Her femininity was
new and untried, but it blossomed sweetly now in response to his strength and virility. Pressing a little closer,
she lifted her arms and wrapped them around his neck.
The move brought her body close against his. Unconsciously, naturally, she moved her hips.

Linc drew in a sharp breath as he felt her softness all

along his chest and thighs. Soon his palms were skimming along her rib cage, grazing the swell of her breasts. Camille arched a little, offering herself. Linc's fingers were unsteady, fumbling, as he encountered the smooth, rich velvet. And then he felt the raw edge where it was torn. When he pushed her away, his voice was ragged.

"What the hell am I doing?" Groaning, he reached up and caught her wrists. "Cami, we can't do this."

Dragged abruptly back to reality, Camille could only stare at him at first. And then she turned crimson with shame. She started to turn away.

"Wait, Cami, I didn't mean it like that." Tugging gently, he pulled her back against him. Resting his chin on her head, he searched for words to explain. "You've had one bad experience tonight, Cami. I would be taking advantage of you if I went any farther. That would make me no better than Archer."

"No! Don't say that. Don't even talk about yourself and that…and him in the same breath."

Still enclosing her securely, he held both her hands in his, tucked against his chest. Her head bent, she thought how right and good it had seemed being held by Linc, kissed by Linc. It was nothing like what had happened with Dwayne Archer.

"Besides," she whispered, torn between shyness and her deep hunger for him, "it wouldn't be taking advantage."

He hugged her, smiling against her temple. "It would, Cami. You're only seventeen, just a kid. I shouldn't even be out here with you tonight, let alone kissing you, touching you."

"I'm not a kid anymore, Linc. In just a few months, I'll graduate from high school. Some of the girls in my class are already married," she said earnestly. "Some of them already have babies!"

Suddenly he held her at arm's length. "That may be, but it doesn't change anything I've said. You're not like them, Camille." His tone was husky. He cradled her cheek in his palm while his thumb stroked her bottom lip hypnotically. "You're special."

Her eyes searched his. "You mean that?"

She could see the smile that danced into his eyes even before it touched his mouth. "I swear it on red creek mud and Twin Willows blood."

She giggled. It was the honor code she, Linc and Pearce had used as children when there was a need for secrecy. She punched him playfully on the arm. "I'm all grown-up now. I draw the line at smearing mud on me and sticking myself with a pin!"

He tweaked her nose. "Then I guess you'll just have to trust me."

She looked at him, her heart in her eyes. "I do, Linc. You know I do."

WHAT A FOOL she'd been. Camille leaned her head against Firefly's side and blinked furiously to hold back her tears. From that moment on, and throughout the rest of the year while Linc was away at school, she'd fantasized about what they would do, where they would go when summer came. And when it did, and Jack went out of his way to keep Linc so busy that he wouldn't have any time left to be with Camille, she'd gone to ridiculous lengths to circumvent Jack. Sneaking a moment together in the barn, she and Linc would laugh, kiss, glory in the wondrous feelings that grew and grew with each passing day. She'd shamelessly revealed her love for him. Truly that summer, he'd been the very air she breathed.

Closing her eyes, Camille let the tears fall. Once, she had indeed believed in miracles.

CHAPTER FOUR

LINC PUT DOWN the phone and punched a few numbers into the computer. He studied the screen, altered a column of figures and then tapped the command for a complete printout. With the assistance of his computer and the telephone, it had proved simple to conduct most of his business from Kate's Cottage. Glancing at his watch, he saw that it was almost eleven. As usual, once he'd started crunching numbers, the time had gotten away from him.

Standing up, he stretched, then rolled his shoulders to work out the kinks. His stomach growled, reminding him he'd forgotten dinner again. Sighing, he pinched the skin at the bridge of his nose. Tomorrow, top priority was finding a housekeeper/sitter. Nikki needed something besides chicken noodle soup and peanut butter and jelly. That was no way to treat his child.

His child.

As they had all day, Camille's words came back to him the instant his mind was free. It couldn't be! She couldn't have been pregnant when he left, could she? There had been only that one time without protection. Wiping a hand over his face, he muffled a groan. Whom in hell was he kidding? He wasn't a teenager. Many unplanned pregnancies happened the first time a couple had sex. He bent his head, closing his eyes. She would have told him, wouldn't she?

Walking to the kitchen, he didn't bother turning on a light. He opened the refrigerator and took out a beer. It was ice cold, the taste sharp and satisfying. He focused on that small physical pleasure, pushing away the dark, guilty memories.

He lifted the can just as a loud pounding on the front door startled him. Beer sloshed over his knuckles. Groping in the dark, he managed to locate paper towels and rip off a handful. He hadn't heard a car. Who could want him at this hour?

"Cantrell! I want to talk to you!"

Frowning, he strode over to the front door and yanked it open. Jack Keating had the screen door open, ready to bang again. "Keep your voice down!" Linc whispered. "I've got a little girl sleeping in here."

"I'm coming in, Cantrell. We've got business to discuss."

Linc planted himself firmly on the threshold. "Not in here, we haven't," he snapped. "Not at this hour. If you've got something to say to me tonight, it'll be out on this porch or not at all."

After a second or two, Keating grudgingly removed his hand from the screen door and stepped back. Linc came out onto the porch, quietly closing the front door behind him.

"What's on your mind, Jack?"

"I just got the skinny on Delta Star Enterprises."

Linc crossed his arms over his chest. "No kidding."

"I know now it's you holding the paper on Willow Wind. I'm here to make you an offer."

"I'm not interested."

Keating bit off an oath, controlling his temper with difficulty. "I've lined up some people. We'll give you a good price."

"I'm not selling, Jack."

Keating exploded. "What the hell do you think you're doing, Cantrell? That's Keating land. Pearce is dead, and now it's Camille's by right."

"Camille and I have already discussed this. She understands."

Jack's eyes narrowed suspiciously. "She told me she'd never heard of Delta Star."

"It was the truth. She had never heard of it until Pearce's lawyer mentioned it."

Jack eyed him skeptically.

"If you're worried about Camille, don't be," Linc told him. "She has the big house. That'll never change."

"Son of a bitch." Jack was shaking his head, his tone incredulous. "You're still sweet on her! Jeez, that's rich. That's too much."

"Get off my property, Keating." His tone menacing, Linc clenched his fists, holding his arms at his sides. Jack took a hasty step backward but he was still riled. Cantrell had legitimate title to Kate's Cottage, which was practically in Jack's own backyard. It was a stark reminder of how easily the land could get away from him. A little piece here, a little piece there, like that forty acres the judge had turned over in a fit of generosity. But not another acre would be lost. By God, he would see to that.

"I don't know how you snookered Pearce," he told Linc, "but I'm going to see to it personally that no court in this state upholds the paper he gave you."

Linc shrugged. "You can try."

"He was a drunk! He didn't draw a sober breath the last five years of his life. If that's not incompetence, I don't know what is."

"Interesting," Linc drawled. "You've become a politician since I left, but I didn't know you'd passed the bar, too.''

Jack's eyes were mere slits. "You always did have a smart mouth, Cantrell, but it won't cut any ice in this state. Not now. You're not taking Willow Wind away from Camille, not the land or the house. I'm going to see to that.''

"Away from you, don't you mean?" Linc retorted softly.

"Camille is family. She knows I'm looking out for her interests. I don't care what she tells you. That's the way it's going to be.''

Linc snorted. "Yeah. Well, you give it your best shot, Keating. Maybe she'll be as easy for you to manipulate now as she was when she was seventeen. But I wouldn't count on it.''

"You just remember this—" Jack's voice vibrated with rage "—I got rid of you once, Cantrell. I can do it again.''

Linc's mouth was a grim line as he watched Jack stride off across the stretch of ground that separated Kate's Cottage from the rear area of the big house. For a long time, he stared into the black night. Then, spinning on his heel, he went back inside.

His beer was lukewarm. Grimacing, he emptied the can in the sink and tossed it into the trash. He opened the refrigerator, intending to get another. In spite of his attempt to ignore it, Jack's threat zinged around in his head like a hornet on a hot day. He stood there, bathed in the soft light of the refrigerator, seething with hatred. Some things might have changed in Blossom, but Jack Keating hadn't. He was still the same ruthless manipulator he'd been seventeen years ago. He still thought he could jerk the strings and Linc would dance....

"The judge is dead."

Standing in the half-open door of his dorm, Linc stared into Jack's pale eyes. He'd expected it. The judge had been in a coma for nine weeks. Still, it was…hard.

Jack's lip curled. "Jeez, you look surprised. He's been brain-dead for more than two months. Did you expect a miracle?"

No, no miracle. Linc's mother had been killed outright in the same accident. She and the judge had been traveling back from Jackson after visiting Abigail in the hospital. Somehow, they'd gone off the road and plunged down a steep embankment.

Shock, grief, loss, regret—he'd lived with them all for weeks. His mother had been everything a mother should be. And the judge—well, the judge's influence had been larger than life on everyone within his sphere. Linc was no exception. Linc, especially, was no exception. Joseph Keating had been like a father to him for as long as he could remember. More, he'd been teacher and mentor, dictator and disciplinarian. Now he was dead.

With an impatient oath, Jack shouldered past him. Linc stepped back to let him in, too shocked to react with his usual spirit. Jack gave the room a quick, disdainful survey before crossing the cramped quarters and leaning casually against the old-fashioned radiator.

"This isn't exactly luxury living, is it?"

Linc looked around. He'd had the same dorm room the entire four years he'd been in college, paid for by the judge. Which, of course, was Jack's point. "I manage."

Jack laughed. "Yeah. Good thing my old man was so generous."

Because of the judge, and his debt to him, Linc didn't plant his fist in Jack's sneering face. With his arms stiff at his side, fists balled, he took a deep breath. "When did it happen, Jack?" he asked.

Jack shrugged. "They pulled the plug a couple of hours ago."

Linc turned, unwilling for Jack to witness his reaction. After a few seconds, he reached blindly for his shirt and began to fumble with it.

"You won't need that," Jack said.

Linc glanced up. "What?"

"I said you won't need that." Jack straightened to his full height, his gaze locked with Linc's. "You won't be going back to Willow Wood."

"What are you talking about, Jack?"

"The judge is dead, Cantrell. Your free ride is over. Your days as the fair-haired boy have ended. My house is not your house anymore. In fact—" his lips stretched into a slow, evil smile. "—after you hear me out, I don't think you'll even *want* to go back to Blossom again."

Linc slowly lowered the shirt in his hand. "Don't talk like an ass, Jack. I don't live in the big house and I don't want to. Kate's Cottage is my home. We can discuss all this another time, for God's sake. The judge has just died, and nothing's going to keep me from his funeral."

"I wouldn't bet on that."

"Come on, Jack. The judge was like a father to me. He—"

"You don't know how right you are."

"What?"

Jack reached for a chair and sat down, straddling it with his arms resting on the ladder-back. He motioned with a nod of his head to the bed. "You might want to sit down to hear me out."

"Cut the bull, Jack. Just say what's on your mind."

"Robert Cantrell wasn't your papa, Linc."

Linc stared. "Excuse me?"

Jack smiled, showing a lot of teeth. He was enjoying himself. "This gets complicated, I'm afraid. Robert Cantrell, the manager of Willow Wood, was married to your mother, but when she got pregnant with you, Cantrell wasn't the proud papa."

Suddenly Linc surged up out of his chair, his eyes wild. His voice, when he spoke, vibrated with outrage. "Your father has just died, Jack. Because of that, I'm not going to punch your teeth in, you miserable bastard."

"Bastard?" Jack lifted both eyebrows and made a show of leaning back without getting up out of the chair. "I think you have it wrong, *Cantrell*. I'm not the bastard—you are. And as for defiling the name of your saintly mother, don't look at me. Uh-uh. I think when you start clearing out the skeletons in that cottage she squeezed from my old man, you'll find that our darling Kate wasn't quite so saintly after all. She—"

Linc didn't wait for more. He lunged at Jack, who leaped up and back, knocking over the chair. It hit Linc in the knees, throwing him off balance. Jack scrambled backward into a desk, sending books and a lamp, pencils and papers to the floor. Blind with rage, Linc kicked the lamp out of his way, ignoring the crash as the glass base splintered. He had his hands on Jack's shirt when a loud knocking sounded on the door.

"What's going on in there? Hey, y'all keep it down. People are trying to sleep, damn it!"

His chest heaving, Linc dragged Jack up close, his arm pulled back, ready to strike. Everything in him yearned to pound Jack's sneering face to pulp. "You're lying, goddamn you!"

Jack stared back. "I'm not."

Linc blinked once, breathing hard. Then he uncurled his fist and pushed savagely, sending Jack staggering against the radiator. Disgust and rage swirled together, disorienting him momentarily.

"It was the judge," Jack said softly.

Something else, a harsher, more excruciating feeling washed over him. For a second he thought he might die from it. His knees suddenly felt too weak to hold him up. Moving carefully, like an old man with brittle bones, he went to the bed and sat down.

"You're lying," he said again. But even as he spoke, the words lacked force. He felt his world shattering. Even Jack, small-minded, avaricious, jealous-hearted creep that he was, wouldn't make up something like this.

"See for yourself." Jack tossed a book on the bed.

Linc picked it up. It was some kind of journal. He opened it, frowning. Katherine Keating's journal. Jack's mother. His hand shook, so he balanced it on his knee to read the page marked with a large paper clip. In the last entry, the judge's wife wrote of her intention to leave Willow Wood because she'd learned of his affair with Kate Cantrell.

"Where did you get this?" he asked Jack.

"It was in the judge's things. I've been going through his stuff...." At the fierce look on Linc's face, he shrugged cynically. "Hell, we knew he was dying. I was going to have to do it eventually, wasn't I?"

Linc was silent.

At ease again, Jack relaxed against the radiator and extended his legs in front of him, crossing them at his ankles. He motioned to the book with a sly expression. "A real stunner, isn't it?"

Linc closed the journal with unsteady hands. His stomach churned. He was going to throw up. No! Not in front of Jack. Never, he thought, grinding his teeth. Never in front of Jack. But, God, he could hardly take it in. "How do you know this is true? Maybe your mother—"

"Get real, Linc. It explains everything." Jack scooped up the journal. "The judge and Kate were always close. Long ago, he gave her the cottage and the land it's on. Hell, that's why he gave you that forty acres." He looked away for a moment as though putting it all in perspective. Shaking his head, he said with a satirical smile, "You know, I've got to hand it to the old man. He had her right where he wanted her. He put her up in that damn cottage and let her keep her job. But if she'd been stupid enough to make any demands, he'd have turned her out—" he snapped his fingers "—just like that. No job, no reputation, no nothing. Yeah, he was something else, my old man."

"It's not true!" Linc cried. "You don't know what you're talking about."

Jack looked at him in disgust. "Why the hell are you bitching? He paid for your education, didn't he? And he made no secret of the fact that he was grooming you to manage Willow Wood."

"He did that out of respect and friendship for Robert Cantrell," Linc argued hotly. "You know he always felt obligated because he was hunting with my father when they had that accident."

"According to my mother," Jack stated with a smirk, "he was definitely obligated."

Linc plowed his fingers through his hair. "It can't be true—"

"Why else would my mother leave? Why would she simply walk out on the judge? On two kids?" Suddenly there was something else in Jack's tone. Viciousness. "I was only six years old. Did you know that? Things were never the same after she left.''

Linc studied Jack's face for a minute, but Jack's scars weren't the problem just now. He was still trying to take it all in....

"And then there's Camille.''

Linc's heart stopped. Camille. God, Camille. If what Jack said was true, then he and Camille... Suddenly he was hit with the full impact of the revelation. He lurched to his feet, turning his back to Jack.

"Like I said—'' from behind him, Jack's tone was mocking "—this gets complicated.''

Linc didn't even hear. He was too caught up in the insanity that had been set in motion. His brain reeled as he tried to sort it all out. Camille couldn't be his half sister! There was no way. He couldn't feel about her as he did if that was true. It would be— He couldn't even say the word.

"I know you two've been messing around.''

Linc whipped around. "Shut up, Jack! This is nothing to do with Camille. Whether there's anything to this crazy story you've come up with or not, Camille is innocent. She—''

"I don't think she's too innocent anymore,'' Jack said.

Linc was suddenly still. "What does that mean?''

Jack's expression was sly. "Well...leaving aside nasty stuff like incest...''

"What, then?'' Linc demanded, his eyes hot.

"She's seventeen, buddy.'' Jack raised both eyebrows meaningfully. "You can be nailed for statutory rape.''

Linc released a quick, furious breath. "You rotten son of a bitch! You twisted creep!''

Jack didn't blink. "And don't think I won't press it,

Cantrell. The time for having things your way is over. You messed up royally by screwing around with Camille.''

Linc stared hard into Jack's face. "I think I'm beginning to see where all this is going.''

Jack bared his teeth in a sneer. "Well, just in case there's still doubt, here it is straight. I don't want to see you in Blossom again. Or even in Mississippi. If you do show up, even for the funeral, the sheriff will be waiting with a warrant.'' With that, he turned and walked to the door. Then he stopped.

"I'm not bluffing, Cantrell. I don't think you want Camille's reputation destroyed, but I'll do it if you force my hand. I've spent a long time trying to figure out a way to get rid of you.'' He gave a short laugh. "In the end, you handed it to me yourself.''

Just before closing the door, he stuck his head back in and called, "Thanks.''

EVEN NOW, seventeen years later, Linc could still taste his rage, his shock, his disbelief as he'd struggled that night trying to make sense of the crazy puzzle—the pieces simply wouldn't fit. If Jack had spoken the truth, then it meant everything Linc had believed of his mother—that she was good and honest and virtuous— was false. Joseph Keating, instead of being a caring mentor and generous benefactor, was a defiler of women, an unprincipled bully. Ever since Linc was four years old, the judge had been like a father to him. But to discover that Joseph Keating actually *was* his father was devastating. In a fifteen-minute encounter, Jack Keating had taken everything from him—his future, his mother, his respect for the judge. Linc could almost taste the bitter pain of that night. The sense of betrayal had not lessened with the years.

But his worst memories were of Camille and what he'd done. He had agonized over that, tried to push out of his mind, to erase from his memory, the times they'd spent together. The phone call he'd finally made to her had been the single most difficult act he'd ever performed.

A cold beer in his hand, he wandered through the dark house and out to the front porch. Leaning a shoulder against one square beam, he looked out over the land. His mother had always impressed on him the importance of owning land. Well, now he had it, a lot of it. Where was the satisfaction he should be feeling? Where was the sense of accomplishment he'd believed lay in success? Where was the peace that came when a man finally made it? When was he going to feel that?

But it was Jack Keating's land that surrounded him. Willow Wood land. And directly in front of him sat the big house. It was a cloudy night, but he could make out the white line of the fence that divided the two plantation houses, and beyond that the silver surface of the willow-draped pond. On the other side of the pond was Willow Wind. Unlike Jack's place, which was always lit up like a circus, Willow Wind could barely be seen. Soft light glowed in two downstairs windows. Upstairs, no light burned at all. Everything appeared dark and serene. Apparently Camille was not haunted by the past. His features harsh and brooding, Linc downed the rest of his beer and, with a crunch, crushed the can.

The sound was empty and harsh. Like his soul.

IT WAS DARK. And hot. Her body moved in perfect harmony with the horse's smooth strides, deriving pleasure

from the undulating, almost sensual rhythm. A deep, rich
carpet of grass cushioned her ride, muffling all sound
except the rush of wind whipping through her hair. The
fence line was a few yards in front of her. It loomed
suddenly, stark white in the moonlight. She prepared
herself for the jump. Beneath her, she felt the horse's
powerful muscles bunch. He was up...up. Her heart
lurched in sudden terror. It wasn't a fence. It was a cliff.
Suspended in midair, she looked down on jagged rocks
and broken trees with grasping appendages that looked
like skeletal arms clawing upward...reaching for her.
There was blood everywhere. She screamed....

Camille jerked upright in her bed, her heart pounding
in her chest. Still in the grip of terror, she covered her
face with her hands, her whole body quaking. Tears
streamed from her eyes as she struggled to banish the
macabre images. She needed to turn on a light, but her
limbs felt leaden and numb. Drawing in a deep, uneven
breath, she rested her head on her knees and waited.

She hadn't had the dream in a long time. When she'd
first married Pearce, it had come often. Back then, she
would actually scream out loud, still half-asleep. Pearce
would put his arms around her and hold her close, rocking her back and forth, back and forth, in their bed,
crooning meaningless words until she came awake fully
to find herself crying.

Camille fumbled for the lamp and turned it on. Even
with air-conditioning, her bedroom seemed hot and
close. She heard a distant rumble of thunder. At the same
time, a limb from a tall cedar tree outside her window
scraped against the screen. Shuddering, she threw aside
the sheet and got out of bed. Still off balance from the
nightmare, she swayed slightly.

How wonderful it would be to lie down and sleep

peacefully all the night through. She couldn't remember
how long it was since she had been able to do that. She
bent her head and rubbed her temples wearily. Why had
the nightmare come back?

Delayed stress. She'd been running on adrenaline forever, it seemed. Pearce had begun drinking excessively
five years ago and had been seriously ill the last eight
months of his life. She'd borne the brunt of that. And
now the plantation and all the problems that came with
it were on her shoulders. And, of course, running a kindergarten required energy and a lot of creative planning.
Otherwise a day spent with four- and five-year-olds de-
teriorated into chaos. Juggling her responsibilities had
obviously taken a toll.

Linc was back.

Camille buried her face in her hands in shame. It
wasn't Pearce and his dreadful ordeal or her stressed-out
life-style that haunted her sleep tonight. It was Linc. If
she'd needed proof that he could still turn her life upside
down, the recurrence of that old nightmare proved it.

She got up and walked over to the window, pulling
the curtain aside. A storm was coming. The willows on
the pond were twisting and thrashing in the wind. Willow Wood, as usual, was lit up like a Christmas tree.
Jack always kept several spotlights artfully concealed so
that the elegant house and its landscaping were dramat-
ically detailed. Behind it was Kate's Cottage. Linc's
now. Standing there, idly stroking the sides of her arms,
Camille was suddenly assailed by memories.

One summer, the judge had paid Linc to paint the
cottage. Even then, innocent as she'd been, she'd responded to the look of him shirtless in faded cutoffs,
braced on a tall ladder wielding a paintbrush and grinning down at her. She'd been a willing gofer, running

and fetching for him while he issued orders in a way that seemed natural. Even Pearce jumped when Linc said the word. Pearce, easygoing and gentle, was simply no match for forceful, decisive Linc.

Linc and Pearce and me. Her heart turned over. Oh, that time had been sweet. Isolated on the two plantations, they'd only had one another for most of their childhood. The only discord they'd ever had, Jack had usually instigated. But mostly the judge had encouraged Jack's interests in matters that didn't concern the younger ones. She, for one, hadn't missed him. But oh, how lonely she'd been when Linc and Pearce had finally gone off to college. She had literally lived for summer.

But it was never the same. From then on, when Linc was home, he'd worked from daylight to dark, thanks to the judge. Pearce, wealthy and idle for the most part, had spent this time junketing around the country.

Camille leaned her forehead against the windowpane. Their lives had all been mapped out. Pearce, whose real love was writing, was going to become famous and pay someone to run Willow Wind. Linc was going to manage Willow Wood. And Camille... She had stupidly assumed that her future was intertwined with Linc's, especially after that first time they made love.

It was her idea, she had never denied that. From that first kiss at New Year's, she'd fallen wildly, madly in love. Linc had known she was too young, and to his credit, he had tried to keep their ever-growing desire for each other under control. Maybe Jack had suspected something, because he seemed to invent ways to keep Linc busy. Linc had confided to Camille one afternoon when they'd seized a few minutes together, that in a way he was glad Jack did so, because their kisses were getting more and more out of control.

It had happened one night at the pond. Camille knew that Linc sometimes cooled off with a swim after dark. Nude, she suspected. When she joined him that evening, after his initial surprise and a few futile words to discourage her, they'd ended up making love. Afterward they talked about marriage, but she was still only seventeen. Linc had reminded her that he was basically penniless, dependent on the future planned for him by the judge. He'd pointed out that it was unlikely Camille's family would welcome her marriage to a hired hand. On top of that was his obligation to the judge. What if he refused to accept him as a son-in-law?

In her naiveté, Camille had brushed his doubts aside, and they'd had one more long, golden month—thirty days filled with laughter and loving—before the accident that killed his mother and sent her father into a deep coma. He had given her a gold charm engraved with her initials entwined with his, telling her he wished it could be a ring. Then he had kissed her and pledged his heart and his love forever.

"Camille?"

At the sound of her aunt's voice, Camille dropped the curtain and turned quickly from the window as though she'd been caught doing something dishonorable.

"Abby, you shouldn't be up at this hour."

"Why not?" the old lady returned. "I've been lying in bed awake for the past thirty minutes."

"Thirty minutes?"

"About the time you woke from your nightmare."

Camille had long since ceased to be amazed at Abigail's inexplicable ability to sense her moods. "I'm sorry I woke you," she said, shivering a little at a streak of lightning. "It's the weather. I think we're in for a storm."

"Yes," Abigail said serenely, coming across the room. She didn't seem to notice the lack of light. "But it won't be bad. Here, have some of this." She held two brandy snifters. Without asking, Camille knew they each held a splash of Southern Comfort, Abigail's prescription for anything that ailed, provided it was past sundown. Before that, tea was the panacea. Smiling softly, Camille accepted hers and then together they stood at the window, sipping silently. Again her eyes were drawn to Willow Wood and Kate's Cottage. All the windows in the cottage were dark except one.

Was Linc sleepless and tormented, too?

"Want to talk about it?" Abigail's tone was gentle.

"It was just...a nightmare." Even in the dark, Camille shifted under the scrutiny of Abigail's gaze. "Actually, it was Red Devil again."

Abigail sighed. "That horse was too much for you. I told Joseph that when he bought it. He was bound to throw you one day. Lucky for us, you survived it."

Camille shook her head, feeling pain in her heart. "Red Devil was beautiful and well trained. I was the reckless one. I killed him, Abby." *And my baby.*

Silently sympathetic, Abigail slipped her arm around Camille's waist and gave her a warm hug. The scent of lavender drifted up in a cloud, and suddenly Camille's eyes flooded with tears. Abigail Keating was the only mother she had ever known. Other girls' mothers had driven about in station wagons, played bridge and golf at the country club and shopped in Jackson and Memphis, while Abigail had stayed at Willow Wood, painting touchingly beautiful watercolor scenes, drinking tea and then reading the leaves. She was a mixture of eccentricity and practicality, and Camille loved her dearly. Her throat tight, she squeezed her aunt's hand. What would she have done all these years without Abigail?

"It's time to put the past behind you, Camille."

"I'd love to," Camille said, once more leaning her head against the windowpane. "Any hints on how to do it?"

"Pearce is gone, rest his soul. You were a good wife to him, Camille."

"He thought I didn't love him, Abby."

"I know."

"That's why he drank," Camille said, her voice breaking.

Abigail shook her white head. "You weren't responsible for Pearce's addiction, Camille. No one was but Pearce himself."

"You don't understand, Abby." She put her hand to her throat. "I really didn't love him." In the dark, it was almost a relief to admit it.

"You didn't love him in the way a woman loves a man," Abigail said gently. "But you did love him, Camille."

"Only as a friend. For Pearce, it was never enough."

"Where is it written we all get our heart's desire? You must put it behind you and get on with your life."

"I don't know if I can," she said, blotting her eyes with a tissue.

"Why? Because it might open a door to something beautiful and good for you?" Abigail twitched at the long fold of her robe and sank into a rocking chair beside the door. "Guilt and remorse make very heavy burdens, Camille. How will it benefit poor Pearce if you continue to carry them around? How long will it take for you to earn absolution?"

"Abby—"

"You talked to Linc."

Startled, she and Abigail exchanged a long look in the dark. Then Camille nodded.

"Good."

With one finger, Camille slowly traced the top of her glass. "All these years, Linc and Pearce never lost touch."

"They were the best of friends, after all," Abigail said, rocking gently.

"Closer than we ever imagined," Camille said. "For years Linc has been subsidizing Pearce, and I didn't know a thing about it. Now he's holding mortgages on Willow Wind."

"What goes around comes around," Abigail said obscurely.

"What?"

Abigail finished her drink without replying. "What do you think about Linc's little girl?"

The southern Comfort burned going down. "She's a beautiful little girl," Camille said after clearing the huskiness from her throat.

"And very attached to her daddy."

"I'm sure he's a conscientious father," Camille said stiffly.

"Loving, indulgent and patient, yes," was Abigail's reply. "But not very experienced, I think."

Camille finished her drink and collected Abigail's empty snifter. "It's late, Abby. We need to get back to bed. I'll take these glasses downstairs."

Abigail stopped rocking and, for a long moment, simply looked at Camille. "That could be one of the doors you might try opening." Then she got out of the chair. "Good night, dear."

CHAPTER FIVE

"JACK SAYS you and Linc have been talking." Christine blew the smoke from her cigarette sideways, her eyes on Camille. It was Saturday, a day her sister-in-law usually spent in Jackson or Memphis indulging her passion for shopping. Among other things. Why she had decided to pay Camille a visit Camille had yet to discover.

"I took Firefly out one morning and Linc was outside on his porch." Camille shrugged. "We talked, yes. I was bound to run into him sooner or later."

"Uh-huh, sooner or later."

"Is there something unusual in having a conversation with an old friend?"

Christine laughed, but it had a malicious sound. "Is that what he is, an old friend?"

Camille gave her a straight look. "I think that describes him, yes."

Christine leaned back and crossed her legs. Although Camille had offered her coffee, she'd taken diet cola. With a long, manicured nail, she stroked the icy wetness on the tall glass. "You and Pearce and Linc were always close."

"People who grow up together usually are," Camille said, taking her time stirring cream into her coffee. Whatever Christine was getting at, she wished she'd get on with it.

"Yeah, a real tight group," Christine said with a

touch of sarcasm. "A 'magic circle.' That was the way Jack put it."

"We were kids, for heaven's sake. And isolated out here at the Twin Willows. We were forced to spend a lot of time together, Jack included."

"That's not the way Jack remembers it."

"How exactly does Jack remember it?"

Christine smiled as she tasted her drink. "He was never in the magic circle, he says, and Pearce was kicked out about the time you began to shed your tomboy image."

Camille set down her cup carefully. Long ago she'd learned not to let herself be rattled by her sister-in-law. But a cold knot had settled in her stomach. She didn't want to discuss anything about Linc with Christine.

"We all grow up eventually," she said, glancing at her watch. "I have a couple of errands, Christine. I—"

"Jack knows Linc Cantrell was more than a buddy to you that summer."

Camille stood up and took her cup over to the sink. "What is the point of all this, Christine?"

"He thinks you and Linc were sleeping together."

Camille turned on the water and squirted liquid soap. "Really this is all ancient history. Linc and I—"

"Jack thinks you had an abortion."

The cup slipped from Camille's hand and hit the old-fashioned ceramic sink, shattering loudly. She stared at the broken pieces, stricken. An abortion! Even the word itself was too vile. Was that what they all thought?

"Don't worry," Christine said flippantly. "Actually, it was a good thing."

"A good thing?" The words came out faint and shaky.

"Yeah." When Camille failed to look enlightened,

Christine added with exaggerated patience, "He was after you because of Willow Wood, Camille."

"You don't know what you're talking about, Christine."

Christine ignored that. "Unfortunately for Linc, Jack wasn't about to sit around and let that happen." She laughed. "Linc couldn't wait to get out of the county after Jack put the fear of God in him."

Camille's lips parted, but it was a second or two before she was able to ask, "What, exactly, did Jack do?"

Christine lit another cigarette and crossed her long legs. "Threatened him with statutory rape." At Camille's expression, she smiled with sly enjoyment. "You were seventeen, sugar. Jailbait. The thought of serving time cooled Linc's ardor, I'm afraid."

Camille stared. "You mean Linc actually believed Jack would do such a thing?"

Christine laughed. "Jack would have, sugar. In a New York minute. There was a lot at stake." Her tone hardened. "Jack wasn't going to stand by and watch some nobody slice off half of what was his."

Camille leaned back, stunned. Now, seventeen years late, she finally knew the reason Linc had abandoned her. Without her having a chance to do a thing about it, her brother had taken it upon himself to change the course of her life. She felt shaken by the force of her anger. She felt betrayed, cheated. Who had given Jack the right to play God?

"The way things turned out," Christine said, jiggling the ice in her glass, "Jack would probably have pushed for the abortion anyway."

Repulsed, Camille turned away. Christine's insensitivity was amazing. Even if her facts had been right, how could she talk so callously about something so personal and private? So painful?

"I've been wondering," Christine said, thoughtfully tapping her bottom lip with a forefinger. "Who paid the bill? It couldn't have been the judge. He was lying in a coma in the hospital. And it wasn't Jack. Abigail? No, she's too morally upright to ever condone abortion."

"Christine—"

She snapped her fingers. "Pearce! Of course. It's perfectly logical. According to Jack, he always had the hots for you. As evidenced by his hasty proposal the minute Linc was out of the running."

Camille had had enough. "Christine, there wasn't any—"

She broke off as Christine closed her fingers around her upper arm. When she spoke, her tone was hard. "Linc's trying to worm his way into your life again, Camille. You're crazy if you let him do it."

Camille pulled free. "He's in my life whether I like it or not, Christine. Every acre of Pearce's land is mortgaged to him."

"Your land, Camille! Don't forget that. With Pearce dead, all that land is yours now."

Camille took a deep breath. "I'm not sure I even want it."

Christine gave her arm a little shake. "Don't be a fool! Jack is standing by ready and willing to buy him out. So far, Linc has refused outright. He's hiring extra help, pouring money into new equipment, but he doesn't really care about Willow Wind, Camille. He didn't bail Pearce out because he cared about him. He did it to spite us, to spite the Keatings. Don't make the same mistake twice, Camille. Don't trust him."

Later, Camille stared at the shards of her broken cup

in the sink, her feelings too mixed up to identify. Trust
Linc? Hardly. She wouldn't make that mistake ever
again. Linc had run away because Jack threatened to
have him arrested. Finding that out should bring her a
measure of peace. Instead she felt only empty and bitter.
Even the threat of prison was no excuse for abandoning
her without giving her any say in his decision. He could
have asked her to go with him. She would have, without
a second's hesitation. But he hadn't given her a chance.

Tears blurred her vision as she picked up the broken
pieces of the cup, one by one. Her life had been shattered
by the events of that night, the night her father died.
Even now she could recall her anguish when Jack decided to withdraw the life support. After weeks of waiting and hoping and praying, the judge was suddenly
gone. Jack had driven her and Abigail home from the
hospital and then immediately disappeared. Abigail,
fragile herself after a long illness, had needed her. She'd
settled her aunt finally and then retreated to her room.
Never had she felt so alone. When the phone rang and
she heard Linc's voice, for the first few seconds, it had
been everything she needed....

"WHEN CAN YOU BE HERE, Linc?" Her throat ached
with the need to cry. First Kate and now her father. Both
were gone forever. She could bear it, but only with Linc
by her side.

"Camille..."

Closing her eyes, she leaned against the wall. Just
hearing him speak her name made her feel better. "Can
you leave tonight, Linc?"

"Camille, I can't come. I'm sorry."

She was still for a heartbeat, certain she'd misunder-
stood him. "What did you say?"

She heard the rasp of his breath as he inhaled. "I have to go away, Camille."

"Go away?"

"Yes, I—" His voice broke, and he cleared his throat. "Something important has happened, something that I have to take care of right away. I have to leave tonight."

"No." Blindly, she put out a hand. "Linc, you don't understand. You can't go away. You have to come home. Daddy just died. Nothing's more important than that. He—"

"I know, Camille. Jack was here." He hesitated. "I can't come."

"Let someone else do whatever it is you're talking about, Linc. You have to come home!" Tears she'd managed to hold back overflowed and poured hotly down her cheeks. "Don't you understand? You have to!"

"I wish I could, sweetheart." His tone was husky. "More than you'll ever know, I wish I could. But I can't."

Even in her grief, Camille realized something was wrong. A protective hand went to her abdomen. "What is it, Linc? What's happened? Tell me."

He was silent. Then, "It's something…private, Cami. Something I can't discuss with you."

"We love each other, Linc. There's nothing we can't talk about together." She turned so that she faced the wall. Lowering her voice, she said urgently, "You have to, Linc. There's something—"

"I'm sorry, Camille. I'm sorry."

"Linc…" She was sobbing, panicked now. "I have to tell you something. I—"

"I love you, Camille. Remember that. I'll always love you."

He sounded so final. Her voice shaking, she said, "When will you be back, Linc? When will I see you again?"

There was another long silence. "We can't, Camille." Again his voice broke. "This is goodbye. We can't ever be together again."

The line went dead.

She stared at the receiver in her hand. Linc wouldn't just hang up like that. Her fingers trembling, she quickly dialed his number. It rang and rang, but there was no answer. She played over in her mind what he'd said.

We can't ever be together again.

For a moment, she was overcome with a wave of dizziness. Nausea rose in her throat. That had happened a couple of times in the past few days. She knew the reason. She hadn't been to a doctor, but she knew. Jack might suspect, too. Just last night at the hospital, she'd felt queasy suddenly and had run to the bathroom. Jack had eyed her sharply when it was over.

Carefully, she tried Linc's number again. It began to ring. She wouldn't panic. There had to be some explanation. Again there was no answer. Finally, an hour later, his roommate answered and told her Linc was gone. He'd packed his things and cleared out. He wouldn't be back.

The next hours were forever unclear in Camille's memory. Dazed, she headed straight for the barn. With shaking fingers, she saddled Red Devil and mounted him. Her throat ached as she remembered Linc cautioning her about riding him at night. Big and powerful and eager to run, he leaped at the touch of her hands, leaving the house and grounds behind in a blur.

It was a wild ride, but she was beyond caring. Her face set, her heart numb, she went blindly, not caring which direction she took. Red Devil's hooves flew over the land. In minutes, he was at the crossing of Red Creek, taking the short jump easily in a shower of pebbles and mud.

She didn't realize she was crying until she passed beneath a low-hanging willow that raked across her face. One hand left the reins just as a rabbit darted out of a hollow log. Red Devil leaped to the side and went down in a tangle of powerful horseflesh, and Camille went with him. She rolled quickly, but not quickly enough. There was a sickening crack as the horse's foreleg snapped. Then one of his flailing hooves caught her in her abdomen. The deep, fierce pain made her cry out. For a second, she lay trembling and remorseful at the destruction of the magnificent horse. But then she felt warm, sticky blood between her legs.

That night, alone in her bedroom, she lost her baby.

WHY WAS SHE CRYING again?

It was a long time ago—the surreptitious visit to a doctor, the judge's wake, the funeral, three endless days. And all the while, her secret despair over Linc's rejection coloring her whole world empty and gray. The memory was buried deep like a thorn embedded in flesh, needing only the slightest pressure to bring it achingly alive. Now that she knew Jack's role in the whole sordid mess, she ought to let go of her resentment of Linc. Instead, what she felt was a new hatred for Jack adding to her bitterness. He had been so clever, his machinations so skillfully planned. Even her marriage must have been part of his plan. After the judge's funeral, he'd certainly pushed her and Pearce together. And in all these years, she had never suspected.

Her mouth twisted with renewed anger and old, old

pain. If she hadn't been so young, so distraught and so overwhelmed by the loss of her baby and Linc's abandonment, maybe she would have seen through him. He had manipulated them all—her, Linc, Pearce. And he had gotten away with it.

She placed the last of the broken pieces of china in the garbage and washed her hands. She had news for Jack. And Linc. She was through being manipulated.

"THE CHILDREN ARE DRIVING me crazy today."

"I noticed." Jessica Perkins, Camille's assistant at Sunny Day, tacked the last example of morning artwork on the board and climbed down from the stool. "Let's have some iced tea while we can. The little darlings will be inside clamoring for lunch in about ten minutes."

Smiling wryly, Camille went to the window to check on her charges. Outside, twenty-three preschoolers were busy letting off steam. The "little darlings" had been no more boisterous than usual this morning, but for some reason, she had a headache. It had been a dull throb when she woke up, but now it threatened to develop into a full-fledged killer.

"I don't know why you talk about them like that," she told Jess, watching one of the aides break up a quarrel between Bobby Phillips and his best friend. "You know you love every little grimy-faced urchin out there."

"Sure." She handed Camille a tall glass tinkling with ice. "No doubt about it, I love them best out there."

Camille laughed and took the tea. "Thanks."

They sat down, neither one talking, enjoying a rare moment of peace. Taking on Jess Perkins as a partner in her business had been one of Camille's best decisions. She was patience itself, kind and down-to-earth, and the kids loved her. With her curly brown hair, slightly plump figure and twinkling blue eyes, she even looked maternal. With four children of her own, there was hardly any situation Jess hadn't already encountered and mastered. Some people managed life so effortlessly, Camille thought, staring into her iced tea.

Noticing her abstraction, Jess smiled. "Miss Abigail would surely find a message in there somewhere," she said, amused.

"True, but I'm not sure I want to hear it," Camille said. "To be honest, Jess, I'm not sure about very much lately."

"Would this mood have anything to do with Lincoln Cantrell?"

Camille took a deep breath. "I saw him this weekend. I needed to talk to him about Willow Wind and what he planned to do."

"That sounds reasonable."

"He's going to stay on here and manage the farm, at least through this growing season. Maybe longer."

"Well, that's not all bad, is it? You need help with the place, and he definitely has a stake in it now. And experience. After all, he was raised at Willow Wood, wasn't he?"

"Yes."

"Then what's the problem?"

Camille hesitated. Her life was so full of complications lately that it was hard to know where to begin. Jess had been a mainstay through the most trying times in Camille's marriage, but she didn't know very much about Linc. Nobody did, not even Abigail. Or so Camille had assumed all these years. After Christine's visit, she wasn't sure how much of her private life was still private.

"It just…bothers me," she murmured with a helpless shrug.

"The two of you share a lot of history," Jess pointed out reasonably. "You can't expect to react to him the same as you would a total stranger."

"I know one thing—it's terrible being indebted to Linc, of all people."

"Do you think he'll take advantage of you?"

"Yes! No." She shook her head and almost winced with pain. "I don't know, Jess. That's just it. I don't know anything anymore. I've spent a long time hating Linc Cantrell. Seventeen years. Suddenly I'm not sure what I feel."

"Seventeen years is a long time to keep hatred alive."

"Maybe." Camille laughed shortly. "But I thought I'd managed it until…" She got up suddenly, turning her back on Jess's too perceptive gaze. Her head ached abominably and she rubbed both temples wearily. "I can't explain it, Jess. It just bothers me—knowing he's running things at Willow Wind now, making decisions, underfoot all the time, seeing him, seeing…"

"His little girl," Jess added perceptively, her tone gentle.

Her words made Camille's heart jump, spawning images of Nikki's small face, the way she'd looked in her granny gown, clutching her worn rabbit. "Yes," she conceded softly, "seeing his little girl."

"You like her." There was understanding and sympathy in Jess's expression. She knew how much Camille had longed for a child of her own.

Camille stared down at her hands. "Who wouldn't?"

Jess was smiling softly. "What does she look like?"

"Tiny," Camille replied instantly. "She's very petite. And black-haired with these big blue eyes that seem to hold all kinds of secrets.... And she does have secrets, Jess.'' Then, wrapping her arms around herself, she told Jess about the tragedy that had taken Linc's wife and traumatized Nikki.

"My God!'' Horror and compassion mingled in Jess's voice.

"But I think she's come through it fairly well. Except for the nightmares and some separation anxiety. Linc said that she wouldn't talk to anyone until just recently, which is probably understandable.''

"Did she talk to you?''

Camille's gaze strayed beyond Jess, seeing Nikki looking wide-eyed at Firefly, hearing her sweeping condemnation of all baby-sitters, recalling her small face as she animatedly surveyed the nest of baby birds. "Yes, she talked to me.''

Jess's eyebrows rose at the expression in Camille's eyes.

"But I don't intend to get involved, Jess.''

SIX O'CLOCK was considered the rush hour at the Magnolia Café, the only place in Blossom even remotely resembling a fast-food outlet. Camille went inside, undecided whether to order something and take it with her or to find a table. Either way, she'd be eating alone, and she'd had enough of that lately.

"Hi, Camille.'' Mavis Potts, the Magnolia's only waitress, gave her a friendly smile. "How've you been, honey?''

"Fine, Mavis. And you?'' In the tiny dining room, several people recognized her and nodded, smiling. Alton Jenkins and his wife, Barbara, waved. Camille waved back. She could see they were almost finished. Sue and Tatum Hollis motioned her over, but she smiled, shaking her head. "Thanks anyway," she mouthed. She would have just a burger to go.

"Mavis, I think I'll have—" The door opened behind her. She turned and was suddenly looking into Linc's whiskey-brown eyes.

"Camille." He nodded, pulling off his dusty Stetson and brushing it against his thigh. No power on earth could keep her eyes from roaming the full length of him. He was rumpled and travel stained, his boots caked with red delta mud. He looked tired—no surprise, since his days now began at dawn. At his side, hugging his other thigh, was Nikki.

"Hi, Camille," she said, offering up a shy smile.

Camille smiled at the little girl. "Hello, Nikki." Her eyes then met Linc's. "Hello."

For some crazy reason, she felt an urge to walk to him, take Nikki's hand and find them a table in the café as though they belonged together.

"Y'all want a table?" Mavis inquired, obviously assuming the same thing.

"No, I—"

"No, we—"

For once, they agreed on something, Camille thought. Linc didn't want her joining them any more than she wanted to. A week had passed since she'd made it clear to him how she felt, and she was happy to see that he was taking her at her word. It was bad enough being in his debt and having him managing Willow Wind. Complications would abound if she didn't keep her distance from him and Nikki. As she'd told Jess, that was just what she intended. So why was she feeling just a tiny bit rebuffed?

Tearing her eyes from Linc's, Camille turned her gaze to Nikki, and really looked at her for the first time. A fine film of dust covered her from her dark curls to her small pink Reeboks, but her hands and face were clean, obviously freshly washed. She looked exhausted—an appealing little waif in a skimpy, ketchup-stained T-shirt and shorts twisted at the waistband. Camille felt a pang in her heart, thinking of Nikki having to manage alone. Daddies weren't allowed in a public ladies' rest room, which she guessed had been the last stop for these two before they got to the Magnolia. "How've you been, Nikki?"

Big blue eyes stared unblinking into Camille's identical ones. And then Nikki's shy smile spread slowly across her face. "Okay."

Helpless to do otherwise, Camille reached out and fluffed the dark curls. "Are you still keeping watch over those baby birds?"

"Uh-huh." The toe of one small Reebok made a grimy mark on the floor. Her small face turned up to Camille. "Know what?"

"No, what, honey?"

"Daddy says I can have a kitty."

Camille flicked a glance at Linc. "Wow, that's really neat. I'll bet you can't wait."

"I have to wait till the baby birds are all grown-up."

"Oh. Good idea."

"Daddy says kitties are the best pets for little girls. Is Firefly your pet?"

"Well…in a way, I guess she is."

"When I get big, I betcha I'll have my very own horse, too." She turned her big eyes on Linc. "Can I, Daddy?"

Linc raked a hand over his mouth, replying with an indistinct mutter. He shot a look full of appeal to Camille, and she felt an aftershock of emotion ripple through her.

Nikki cocked her head to one side, studying Camille. "Are you having a hamburger, Camille?"

Camille hesitated. "I was, but now I've changed my mind, I think. Maybe I'll go home and have some soup and fruit instead."

She looked at Linc with disapproval. It was one thing for adults to grab fast food after a long day, but a growing child needed better nutrition.

Ruddy color climbed up his cheeks, and he dropped a protective hand on Nikki's shoulder. "We need to make a trip to the grocery store, but somehow the time got away from me."

"We rode all over today," Nikki announced expansively.

Again Camille's eyes went to Linc's. Had he dragged the child around with him in his vehicle all day?

"I haven't been able to find anyone to leave Nikki with yet," he explained, sounding defensive. "I had a long day. We planned to break some new acreage but discovered most of the equipment couldn't be used. Then I had to drop everything and go into town for spare parts." Twirling his Stetson round and round in his hands, he looked like a man almost at the end of his rope. "Everything that could go wrong did."

"I'm hungry, Daddy."

"Okay, baby. We're gonna get something right now."

Camille sighed, feeling caught in a flood tide that was sweeping her into something she was going to regret. "I think I know somebody who might be the kind of sitter you need for Nikki."

For a few seconds, they simply stared at each other. "Thanks," Linc said huskily. "I really appreciate it."

"She's the grandmother of one of my students. She's a widow, so it's possible that she might consider living in. I think I've got her number." She rummaged inside her purse for her address book. "I'll give it to you and you can take it from there."

She opened the small black book, but her hands seemed all thumbs as she flipped through it. "I'm sorry, I don't have it," she said, frowning. "I'll have to get it from my files at Sunny Day."

"Thanks," he said quietly, meeting her eyes. "I appreciate that."

Somehow, the address book slipped from her fingers. She made a grab for it, and Linc's hand went out at the same time. Camille's heart stumbled at the tiny jolt. From his touch? Or that look? Both? To cover her reaction, she bent her head to search for her keys.

How long had it been since she felt that special something? That delicious thrill that promised—Whatever it promised, it wasn't worth it, she reminded herself, as memories rushed in. If she'd learned anything seventeen years ago, it was that she was the only one likely to be affected by the attraction between them.

But it was hard to make her heart believe that. Her fingers closed around the keys as if they were a lifeline, and she turned to leave, almost bumping into someone coming in. She drew back quickly, hearing the jangle and thump as the keys fell to the floor.

Before either Camille or Linc could get at them, Nikki had them in her hands, turning them over curiously. Camille reached out, her heart suddenly racing.

"Nikki, let Camille have her keys." Linc put out his hand, but Nikki backed away, her attention fixed on a round gold charm on the key chain.

"You heard me, Nikki." Linc's tone was meant to be

obeyed, but Nikki seemed fascinated. She turned the charm over and over, frowning at the elaborately engraved initials. "This isn't reg'lar ABC's, is it, Camille? What does it mean?"

Camille didn't answer because she couldn't. A thousand times she had started to throw the charm away. She watched Linc catch Nikki's wrist gently to take the keys. But when he saw the charm, his eyes flew to Camille's. The past was suddenly alive between them. Memories, intense and uncontrollable, were like shock waves undulating from one to the other.

I can't give you a ring yet, Cami, but it won't be long. Will you wear this until I can? His kiss as he slipped the gold chain around her neck had been bold and sweet, full of heat and promise. *See, a C for Camille and an L for me. One day it'll be a ring, Cami.* The charm had been cold between her breasts, but then his mouth had warmed it, warmed her. *I love you, Cami.*

"What does it mean, huh, Camille?"

"Nothing, Nikki." Camille drew a deep breath and took the keys from Nikki, who gave them up without a word. Her face pale, she looked directly into Linc's eyes. "It means absolutely nothing."

CHAPTER SIX

"OKAY, EVERYONE GET ready to clean up." Camille clapped her hands, and ten four-year-olds stained with bright-colored finger paint tumbled out of their chairs and away from the long, low table. "Remember our rules! Let's make a big caterpillar. We don't want to get paint on one another, do we? Joey, don't tease Tracey! You know you wouldn't want purple paint in your hair." She put a restraining hand on Joey Thigpen's shoulder and thwarted his attempt to usurp Tracey Perkins's place in the line. She pretended not to see when Tracey gleefully retaliated by sticking out her small pink tongue at Joey. "Now, let's go. Ms. Perkins is waiting at the sink."

Tracey, looking like a blond, blue-eyed angel, gave a mischievous toss of her curly head and dashed toward the sink, leaving the squirming body of the "caterpillar" to make its way behind her.

To Linc, appearing at the door of Sunny Day Kindergarten, the scene was one of colorful, childish chaos. Four- and five-year-olds were everywhere. To him, it seemed impossible that the group of finger painters, draped in men's discarded white shirts worn backward, could ever be cleaned up again. Another group in a far corner of the room reminded him of ants crawling in, out and over an elaborate plastic maze that had half a dozen entrances and exits. He was aware of noisy kid sounds—squeals and laughter, bumps and yells.

Nikki shrank against his thigh, her little hand clenched in his. He wanted to scoop her up and reassure her, but he resisted the impulse, knowing she needed to be around other children. He breathed a prayer that he was doing the right thing.

With his eye on Camille, he waited while she turned the finger painters over to a woman at the sink. She said something to a towheaded boy, who grinned at her and proudly displayed two purple hands. She looked perfectly at ease with two or three dozen kids milling around her. Why didn't she have kids of her own? he wondered, then frowned because the thought of her having some other man's baby was painful. The thought of her having *his* baby had been with him since she'd made that incredible remark, but it was too dark and terrible to examine. She was smiling as she turned from the children and looked directly at him. With a feeling of regret, he watched her smile disappear.

"Camille." He nodded to her, not sure what kind of reception he'd get. He was prepared for anything except an outright order to get off her territory, at least until she'd heard him out. But she wouldn't reject Nikki. He was counting on that.

"Ouch, Daddy."

He glanced down at his daughter and realized he was squeezing her hand. "Sorry, punkin." He looked back at Camille, who was coming slowly toward him. "I hope this is not a bad time for you," he said, casting a helpless look around the room. He felt too big and too awkward among so many small people.

"We don't get many unscheduled visitors."

He clapped his Stetson against his thigh. "I guess not."

Not many men came inside the classroom at Sunny Day. Surrounded by the scaled-down chairs and tables and other paraphernalia of the kindergarten, he seemed so tall and broad, so thoroughly masculine.

Camille's eyes dropped to Nikki, and some of Linc's tension eased as he watched the strained look on her face fade. "Hello, Nikki."

Without replying, Nikki sought the familiar refuge of her daddy's long legs. Camille lifted her gaze to Linc. "I have the name of the baby-sitter I promised you. It's at my desk."

She turned and headed for the hallway leading to the rear area of the building. Linc hesitated and then followed, urging Nikki along with him. Again, he was struck by the grace and femininity that had blossomed in Camille. Once she'd been all coltish limbs, girlish and sleek. Now, in her soft cotton blouse and flowing pants, she was still as trim as ever, but her woman's body was enticingly curved, the line of her waist flared into a softly rounded and definitely tantalizing bottom. He smothered a curse as he felt an answering tightness in his own body. Forbidden or not, Camille was still the most desirable woman he'd ever known.

She entered a small office and immediately stepped behind her tidy desk. No surprise, Linc thought. Camille herself was neat and tidy. There was a shiny red apple in a place of prominence on the desktop. Behind her, some kind of huge green plant flourished.

She sat down and reached for a rotary card file. Then, flicking through, she found what she was looking for. Quickly, she wrote down a name and phone number. "Maybelle Franklin will take the job, I think. If you like her, that is. She raised a big family, but they're all grown and gone now. And from what she told me a couple of weeks ago at Church, she'll enjoy feeling useful again.'' She stood and pushed the slip of paper across her desk to him.

Here's your hat and what's your hurry? The message was loud and clear. Taking the note, Linc folded it and slipped it into his shirt pocket. Then, ignoring her unsubtle hint, he sat down. Nikki slipped between his thighs and snuggled close. He patted his pocket. "Thanks for your help, Camille. If this woman will come, it'll be a lifesaver. But that isn't the reason I came here today.''

"Oh?'' She didn't sit down.

For a moment, staring into the morning-glory blue of her eyes, the words he'd rehearsed eluded him. Instead he thought of all the unspoken reasons she had for refusing anything he might ask of her, especially anything to do with his child. His and Joanna's child. He stared down at the complicated pattern on his hatband and wondered at his audacity in asking Camille for anything.

Nikki shifted against his thigh and trustingly laid her small dark head on his knee. His love for her was an ache in his chest. Nikki was the reason he was here, he reminded himself. He took a deep breath. "I wondered if you might have room for one more little kid at Sunny Day, Camille.''

Something flickered in her eyes before she sank slowly back into her chair. "There's very little emphasis on educational skills in the summer session,'' she said.

He stroked Nikki's dark hair with one hand and chose his next words carefully. "That doesn't matter. In fact, it's probably best. There are other things more important right now." He hesitated, unwilling to say much in front of Nikki.

"Excuse me a second." Standing, Camille left the security of her desk and went to the door. Nikki lifted her head, her eyes watchful. "Tracey, will you come into my office, please?"

Instantly, the little girl with the yellow curls appeared in a flurry of giggles and vivid energy. Spotting Nikki, she stared with the frank curiosity of one child sizing up another. Nikki, staring at Tracey with equal curiosity, backed a little more securely into the haven of Linc's body.

"Hi," said Tracey without a hint of shyness. "What's your name?"

Nikki stared back, mute.

Undaunted, Tracey turned and pointed through the door to the wall of windows on the opposite side of the classroom. "We've got some newborn gerbils. Four of 'em! Come see."

Linc, looking in the direction Tracey indicated, saw a row of aquariums and cages beneath the windows, each containing a different variety of animal life.

Tracey walked right up to Linc and put a confident hand on his knee. "You know what color baby gerbils are, mister?"

It was apparent *Nikki* didn't, and she waited wide-eyed to find out. Linc grinned lazily. "No, what color are they, Tracey?"

"Pink!"

Still silent, Nikki shook her head slowly but emphatically.

"Uh-*huh!*" Tracey looked insulted.

Camille spoke. "Tracey, why don't you show Nikki the baby gerbils?"

Nikki looked torn.

"I'll be right here, honey," Linc said, giving her shoulder a reassuring squeeze.

"We'll leave the door open so you can see your daddy," Camille promised, smiling as Nikki took the first hesitant step away from Linc.

Assuming the matter was settled, Tracey marched to the door. "They are so pink, you'll see!" She glanced back to make certain Nikki was with her. "You know what? We had to take the daddy away from the babies because..." She paused with the exquisite timing of a born actress. Nikki waited, her eyes as round as saucers. "Because daddies *eat 'em up,* that's what!"

Watching them head for the wildlife area, Linc shook his head. "What happened to sugar and spice and everything nice?"

Amused, Camille shrugged. "Jane Fonda and others thought of a better way."

His mouth quirked in a rueful smile. "I'm not so sure."

Camille moved back behind her desk and sat down. "I don't have a lot of time during the mornings, Linc. Why are you here?"

He straightened in the chair and rested his ankle on one knee. Now that Nikki was gone, he felt less confident, as though he'd accidentally discarded his ace in the hole. "I do my best with Nikki, but I think she needs to be around other people besides me. Don't you think spending time here among some ordinary kids would be good for her? I came to ask if you would take her, Cami."

In a flash, she was out of her chair and at the window, her back to him. It was a bright summer day outside, a beautiful day. Birds sang, the sun was shining, flowers bloomed. Scattered over the kindergarten grounds was the newest in preschool playground equipment. She'd personally selected every item with care. Nothing but the best for Sunny Day had been her creed, because Sunny Day was all she had. She had no child of her own, no marriage. And the reason a kindergarten had become her whole life was sitting in a chair behind her calmly asking her to make a place in *her* school for *his* child. Nikki needed someone, and Camille filled the bill.

Camille's whole body tensed as he silently came up behind her. "I know it's a lot to ask, Cami."

She felt the heat of him, caught the scent of his after-shave. He smelled like sunshine and warm male. He smelled exactly the way he had seventeen years ago. Her heart began beating heavily. She felt as if somehow she were caught in a time warp. Or a nightmare.

She turned quickly, refusing to look into his eyes, and once again sought the refuge of her chair. "I don't know if it would work out, Linc."

Don't ask me to do this.

He twisted his Stetson round and round in his hands. "I thought…just for a few weeks, Cami."

"Oh, Linc, I don't know."

I can't, I can't.

"If it's me—" He shifted abruptly and turned to stare at the broad, flat sweep of hot, sun-washed delta framed by the window in her office. "You won't have to worry. I'll drop her off and pick her up. That'll be the extent of it. I know how you feel about me, Cami."

You know I loved you so much I thought I'd die from it when you left me? You know I made a mockery of my marriage because of my feelings for you? You know that I had to beg Pearce's forgiveness at his graveside because of my feelings for you, Linc?

God, no. And if there was any justice in the world, Linc would never know. She heard his sigh.

"I'm not asking for myself, Cami. I'm asking for Nikki."

Defeated, Camille realized she wasn't going to be able to distance herself from Linc's little girl or from the man himself. Thanks to Pearce, Linc was destined to play a major role in her life. As for Nikki... Already Camille was drawn to Nikki as to no other child in her care.

She cleared her throat against the huskiness that wouldn't go away. "When did you plan to start her?"

"I thought...tomorrow?"

She braced herself against the raw appeal in his voice. Still it swept over her nerve ends, much as his hand had once stroked her skin.

"I'll need some information," Camille said, pulling the side drawer of her desk open and taking out a couple of forms. "Even though Sunny Day is a private school, I'm still required to maintain certain records. What is her full name?" When he didn't reply immediately, she looked up.

"Nicole...uh, Nicole Camille," he said finally.

Camille clenched the pen tightly. Suddenly she stood up, unable to bear another moment. "Take these home with you," she told him, thrusting the forms at him as he got to his feet. Her mind whirled with a thousand thoughts. Emotions long buried in a far corner of her heart spilled over as though released from a sealed vessel that had irreparably shattered. How much was she expected to tolerate? How could he reject so totally the love they'd shared, drop so completely and finally out of her life and then turn around and christen his child with Camille's name?

"Cami, you don't understand...."

"Fill them out," she said distantly, ignoring his words and avoiding his hand, which had involuntarily reached for her. "I'm not a psychologist. Nikki exhibits some signs of trauma. If in a few days she doesn't appear to adjust to the school and the other children, you'll just have to pull her out." The expression in her eyes was a mixture of defiance and pain. "I'm sorry, but...there it is."

He said nothing, then nodded once. "I understand. Thanks again."

"Daddy..."

At the touch of Nikki's hand on his thigh, Linc glanced down. Tracey, at her side, wore an expression of smug triumph. He dropped to his haunches, his hand curving over the shape of Nikki's small, dark head. "Hi, baby. What did you find out? Are baby gerbils really pink?"

Nikki nodded solemnly.

"I told her so," Tracey stated. "Rabbits, too."

Linc's smile was indulgent. "Is that a fact?"

"Can we stay a little longer, Daddy?" Nikki's whisper was for Linc's ears only.

Linc looked trapped. "Today?"

"I'll be her Best Friend," Tracey volunteered. "Everyone who's new has to have a Best Friend. It's someone to show them where to get a drink of water and how to put up their things and where to go to the bathroom." She looked at Camille. "I know all of that, don't I, Miss Camille? So can I be her Best Friend? Can I?"

"Can I, Daddy?"

Linc hesitated, torn. "I don't know, sweetheart."

He glanced once at Camille, but that one look was enough to make her brace herself. She could almost read his thoughts. For Nikki to ask voluntarily to stay without Linc was a major step. A brief visit today might pave the way for tomorrow morning, when he would have to leave her for the whole day.

Still squatting beside the two little girls, he looked up into Camille's eyes. "What do you say, teacher?"

"Yeah, teacher, what d'ya say!" Tracey cried, jumping up and down. Nikki shyly gazed at Camille and then quickly ducked behind her daddy's shoulder.

"It's…fine," Camille said faintly, refusing to look at Linc again. "Tracey, take Nikki over to the Sesame Street house and show her how to make Big Bird talk."

"Okay! Come on, Nikki."

Linc gave Nikki a reassuring smile. She hesitated and then slowly released her hold on his blue chambray shirt. "Will you come back and get me, Daddy?"

He used his Stetson to give her a loving swat on her tiny behind. "You know I will, punkin. I'll be here waiting in the truck when school's over for the day."

"You won't forget?" Her blue eyes looked anxious for a moment.

"I won't forget. Cross my heart."

"Come on, Nikki!" Tracey, her fists propped impatiently at her waist, stamped her foot.

Nikki, after one last fleeting look, went.

Linc got slowly to his feet. Camille, watching the muscles of his thighs flex, felt crowded suddenly.

"I really appreciate this, Cami."

Camille swallowed, her throat dry. "Please be on time," she requested, her tone as neutral as she could make it.

He looked as though he'd like to say more, but after a few long seconds, he put on his hat and touched it politely in an endearingly gallant gesture. And then he was gone.

"YOU'RE RIGHT, Camille. There's a man it would be difficult to hate."

Jessica Perkins stood beside her at the window of Camille's office and watched Linc climb slowly into his vehicle. One hand was on the wheel, but instead of starting up and leaving, he bent his head suddenly and rested it on his arm. There was something about the set of his shoulders and his tight fist on the wheel that made him seem vulnerable, and somehow...needy.

Camille turned abruptly and sat down. "I don't think there was ever any doubt that Linc loves his daughter and that he's concerned about her." Her tone turned bitter. "In fact, the more I'm around him, the more I'm convinced that Nikki is his whole life."

Something in Camille's tone made Jess turn. There was unfinished business between Camille and Linc Cantrell, she knew, and she prayed it would all work out happily. She and Camille had been friends for ten years. It hadn't been easy for Jess and her husband when they'd moved from Nebraska so he could become principal of the high school. They'd been transplanted to the deep South without a clue as to how things were done "delta-style" and had needed someone to smooth the way.

Jess would always feel grateful to Camille and Pearce Wyatt for accepting them in spite of their "Yankee" ways, for opening their hearts to two strangers, advising them subtly and tactfully when they messed up. Jess had jumped at the chance to help Camille when she'd needed a partner at Sunny Day several years later. Since then, she had watched the sadness and pain mount in Camille's life. If ever a woman deserved happiness, it was Camille.

Studying the rigid way she stood at the window watching a man she professed to hate, Jess wondered suddenly about Camille's marriage to Pearce Wyatt. She had always sensed something missing in their relationship. For the most part, she'd attributed it to Pearce's alcoholism. Now she wondered if Camille had ever loved Pearce. If not, why had she married him?

"I've asked myself that question a thousand times," Camille murmured, and Jess looked startled before realizing she'd spoken her thoughts out loud. Camille laughed, but there was nothing warm or humorous in the sound. "Maybe a million times."

"You must have been very young."

"I was seventeen and traumatized by a miscarriage."

Jess's eyes widened. "My God." Her oldest daughter, Jennifer, was seventeen. The most responsible behavior she exhibited was cleaning her room once a week. The thought of her pregnant and scared twisted Jess's heart. Then to miscarry…

"I've thought about it a lot," Camille said, slowly taking a seat behind her desk. "My father died that year. He'd been in a coma for more than nine weeks after a car accident. Kate Cantrell, Linc's mother, was with him, and she was killed instantly. That was at the end of August. Linc and I had spent that whole summer together. I was in love and I thought…" Camille's mouth trembled. She caught her lip between her teeth and then shrugged. "I miscarried the night my father died…after Linc told me he wouldn't be seeing me again."

Jess frowned. "Just like that?"

"Just like that. He didn't even do it in person. He called me on the phone, can you believe that?"

Shaking her head, Jess said nothing.

"Right away Jack began encouraging me to date Pearce. I wasn't interested in dating anyone, but Pearce and Linc and I had always been close. Being with Pearce was comfortable, *comforting*—you know what I mean? I knew my feelings for him weren't the same as the passion between Linc and me, but by then I was pretty suspicious of passion and its consequences."

She bent her head and kneaded a spot between her eyebrows. "Jack kept pushing, Pearce kept pushing. Everyone seemed to push. It was such an ideal match— the Twin Willows, joined again. I felt like a doll being yanked around by a bunch of bullies. Two weeks after my eighteenth birthday, I found myself married."

In the small office, Jess's sympathy was a tangible thing.

"As you know, it was a disaster," Camille said with rueful honesty.

There was a long pause. In the silence, both women were thoughtful.

"You know," Jess said slowly, "Linc just doesn't strike me as a man who would abandon his responsibilities and people he cared about without a good reason." She hesitated, and then spoke with real puzzlement. "It doesn't seem to jibe with the man I met today."

Camille was absorbed in her own thoughts. "I had a very strange visit from Christine this past weekend," she said in a low tone. "She told me something about Linc that helps explain why he disappeared so suddenly that summer."

"Really?"

"Jack threatened him. I think he suspected that Linc and I were...involved, but I can't believe he knew everything. Surely he couldn't have realized what he was doing." She went very still for a second, frowning. "At least, I don't think so."

Jess lifted one eyebrow. "Just how far did he go, Cami?"

"According to Christine, he threatened to bring a charge of statutory rape against Linc if he didn't leave, get completely out of my life."

Jess looked shocked. "Oh, Camille! Even for Jack, that's pretty ruthless, isn't it?"

"He believed Linc was interested in me only because of who I was. If we had married, he would have had a share in Willow Wood."

"And what do you think?"

Camille stared unseeing at a scene outside the window. "It's possible, I suppose." She shrugged. "Not that it matters. It was all so long ago."

Jess leaned forward and said gently, "I think it does matter, Cami. In a way, Linc was forced to run for his life. To a college student without the support of a family, the threat of prison must have been terrifying."

"I can understand that," Camille said. "But don't you think he could at least have explained? Considering our relationship then, shouldn't I have been told? Shouldn't I have been given a choice whether to go with him or not?" She paused to take a breath. "Maybe what Jack said was true. Maybe what he really wanted was a piece of Willow Wood."

Jess studied her for a long minute. "And if what Jack said wasn't true?"

"Then I just don't know." Camille sighed. "As I've been saying to everyone who'll listen, it was all so long ago that it simply doesn't matter anymore."

Jess thought of Linc Cantrell's hard features and the bleak, empty look in his eyes and felt a deep concern for both Linc and Camille. She knew Camille as well as anyone in the world. Her feelings might be under strict control right now, but Camille was still subject to the same strong feelings that had driven a seventeen-year-old girl to give herself without reservation to the man she'd believed was the love of her life. She had been through hell. She was emotionally fragile. It would take only a small spark to ignite the embers of the wild, sweet love of her youth into a conflagration that could destroy her. Jess prayed that Linc would save some of the sensitivity he lavished on his small daughter for Camille.

CHAPTER SEVEN

ON HIS SEAT on the porch swing, Linc nursed a cold beer, his eyes fixed on the mass of clouds and color in the western sky. With the vast flat expanse of delta land setting the stage, the sunset fanned out in streaks of vivid orange and crimson, mauve and melon. He had always loved this hour when, with his work done, he could finally stop, draw a deep breath and enjoy the quiet fading away of the sun and another summer day.

It was good to be home again.

Pushing gently with one foot, he relaxed on the swing, enjoying the thrum of night sounds and the fragrant sweet-tart scent of an ancient sweet olive that had probably been planted in another century. In the distance, he could hear laughter and the occasional burst of music from the cabin of one of the field hands.

He leaned back, slouching. He was tired, worn out in fact. At best, farming demanded a lot of a man. And this situation was hardly the best. He had returned to Jack Keating all equipment not owned by Pearce—which turned out to be almost everything in working order. What was left still kept breaking down. He'd ordered new stuff, but only half of it had come in. His people were used to working under the slapdash supervision of Keating's manager. It had taken a couple of weeks before they'd begun to accept new rules, new authority, new ownership. Still, there was nothing he'd rather be doing, no other place he'd rather be.

He looked at the pond and thought longingly of a swim, but with Nikki inside sleeping he couldn't take the chance. If she woke from a nightmare, she shouldn't be alone. Not that she'd had a nightmare lately. She was sleeping as soundly as a little rock. In the mornings, she didn't make a peep when he dropped her off at Sunny Day, and every other word from her seemed connected to the school and her new friends. Thank God Camille had agreed....

The squeak of the old gate in the side yard brought his head around abruptly. Squinting into the dusk, he recognized Abigail Keating coming up the path, making her way carefully through his mother's old flower garden. By the time he'd set his beer on the floor and got to his feet, she was at the bottom of the steps.

"Miss Abigail! Here, let me help you." Catching her fragile arm, he eased her up the steps. "I heard the sound of that old gate and for a minute I thought maybe a ghost had come to call."

"I might be old enough to be a ghost, Lincoln Cantrell, but I'm still flesh and blood, as near as I can reckon." With a satisfied little sound, she sat down in Kate Cantrell's rocking chair.

"Surely you didn't walk all the way over here in the dark, Miss Abigail?"

"Well, I don't drive anymore, and I haven't been on a horse in thirty years," she retorted, "so I must have."

He grinned. It was surprisingly easy to imagine Miss Abigail Keating on horseback, seated sidesaddle, of course. "Yes, ma'am. I just meant that it's easy to take a fall walking alone at night."

She reached out and patted his arm. "Don't worry,

Lincoln. I manage to get around just fine, even after dark.''

He hovered a little uncertainly. ''Can I get you something to drink? I don't think I have any tea, but—''

''Thank you, no.'' She began to rock gently. ''I noticed you relaxing in the swing. Do sit back down. I waited until you got little Nicole settled before coming over.''

Puzzled, Linc sank back on the swing and reached down for his beer. Abigail's visit would have made a lot more sense had Nikki been awake. She hadn't made any secret that she liked the old lady. A couple of times when Abigail was out walking the grounds of Willow Wind, Nikki had hung on the fence, watching. Once she brought in a bunch of daisies that had come from Abigail's garden.

''I thought I might offer my services as a baby-sitter,'' Abigail said.

''Ma'am?''

''Camille tells me you have Maybelle Franklin keeping house for you now, which is good news. A man with your responsibilities can't do all the little things necessary to see to a child's welfare, and Maybelle Franklin will do just fine.'' She nodded her white head. ''Just fine.''

Linc cleared his throat softly. ''She seems to be working out.''

''Nicole likes her?''

''Yes, ma'am.''

''Good, good.'' She continued to rock gently. ''And how about you, Lincoln?''

''I like her too, Miss Abigail.''

She made a tiny impatient sound. ''Don't tease, Lincoln. You know very well what I mean. How are you settling in? Never mind the old saying that you can't go back home. I think you have, and I think it's working out fine." She stopped rocking suddenly and gave him a shrewd look. "Isn't that so?"

He crossed an ankle over his knee and rested his beer can on his boot. "It's a good year for cotton," he said cautiously. "I have a few problems with equipment, and the men, too, occasionally. But nothing serious. They're beginning to fall into line. Things seem to be coming together."

"Hmm." Abigail nodded and rocked. "How about you and Camille?"

Thinking she was referring to their forced partnership at Willow Wind, he said, "Everything's fine. At least I think everything's fine. Once she got over the shock of her situation, she seemed to be willing to make the best of it. She hasn't said much, one way or another. I don't know why Pearce chose to handle everything the way he did, Miss Abigail. Keeping her in the dark."

"Pride, I suppose," Abigail murmured. "Or what was left of it. Only the Lord knows now." She appeared lost in thought for a moment, then she said, "But that's not what I meant when I asked about the two of you, dear. The leaves are saying wonderful things, but I know Camille. She won't take the first step. It'll have to be you, Lincoln."

Some of his beer went down the wrong way. Clearing his windpipe, he leaned sideways to put the can on the floor, wondering what to say. Abigail Keating had been in Blossom all her life. She'd been a part of the judge's household when he brought home his bride, Katherine. She'd been a young woman when Kate and Robert Cantrell had first arrived. Even as a boy, he'd been aware of the close friendship between his mother and Abigail. She would surely know the truth.

"That's why I thought I'd offer to sit with Nicole in the evenings," she went on, as though unaware of his dismay. "I can see you're more or less tied to the house in the evenings. So unfortunate that Maybelle Franklin can't live in right now, as I'd hoped. It's that peculiar son of hers, Freddy. "You remember him, Lincoln? He just separated from his wife. She locked him out again. Maybelle always takes him in. It never lasts long, a few weeks at the most." She paused, looking at him. "Is that what she told you?"

"Uh, something like that."

She nodded once. "She'll be able to devote herself to you and Nicole totally once Freddy's back at his own house. In the meantime, when you want to visit Camille, I'll stay with Nicole. I don't know why I didn't think of it before."

"Thank you, but—"

She waved one fragile, blue-veined hand. "You don't have to thank me, Lincoln. I'm happy to do it for you. And Camille. You were made for each other. I've always known it."

"Miss Abigail, Camille and I—" He looked up, meeting her guileless expression. "That was so long ago, Miss Abigail. I don't think—"

"You aren't going to let Jack interfere again, are you?" she demanded in a stern tone.

He gave her a startled look, wondering if anyone else realized that Jack had had a hand in his disappearance.

"If only you'd said something before you ran away that summer, Lincoln." Her hands moved restlessly on the arms of the rocker. "It was such a shock to Camille.

Mercy, she looked like a ghost for weeks. She loved you, boy,'' she said, gently reproving.

She began to rock again. ''It was clear to me when Jack began pushing Camille and Pearce together that he favored an alliance between them. It was all wrong, and I would have stepped in—I did speak to Jack of my misgivings—but I landed back in the hospital with my gallbladder, and by the time I'd had my surgery and was on my feet again, the wedding was over.'' She brushed at a mosquito in front of her. ''Jack works fast when he's bound and determined on something.''

Abruptly, Linc left the swing and went to the edge of the porch. Nothing Abigail said about Jack's interference in their lives surprised him. What baffled him was Abigail's implication that there had once been a future for Camille and him. She knew the truth, didn't she? Abigail, of all people, would surely know.

''Miss Abigail, why are you saying all these things?''

''All what things, dear?''

He stared upward, as though seeking an answer. ''About Camille and me. A…uh, a relationship between Camille and me.''

''Because it's right, Lincoln,'' she said simply. ''It's meant to be.''

He faced her suddenly. ''My God! How can you talk like this? You know we can't…I can't…''

''You can't what, Lincoln?'' she asked, watching him.

He swallowed once, hard. ''You and my mother were good friends.''

''We certainly were. I loved Kate like a sister.''

''And Katherine Keating, you were close to her, too.''

There was a tiny pause. ''Not really close. She was Joseph's wife, and for his sake, I tried. But it was difficult. She was…troubled.''

Linc turned, fixing his eyes on the big house. "And my mother? Did she and Katherine, ah, the judge's wife, get along?"

"Everyone got along with Kate," Abigail said, her tone changing, lightening. Linc sensed her smile. "Kate was the kindest, most tolerant person I ever knew. Her goodness extended even to Katherine Keating."

"She and Katherine were friends?"

"Katherine didn't have any friends. Didn't want any. But I don't think she would have lasted as long as she did if it hadn't been for Kate. 'Buried down here in hell' was the way Katherine used to describe life in the Mississippi Delta. Her folks were from the bluegrass region of Kentucky, you know. Raised Thoroughbreds. She spent as much time up there as she spent here." Abigail gazed at the pale peach glow on the horizon. "Joseph indulged her shamelessly, hoping she'd come to accept Willow Wood, I suppose. A lost cause, as it turned out."

Linc closed both hands on the porch rail, trying to make sense of it. His mother and Katherine Keating were friends. Why would Katherine accuse Kate of adultery in her diary?

"Miss Abigail, what did you mean, she was 'troubled'?"

"I meant just that—high-strung, moody. At times, she was downright unreasonable. For instance, she used to be wildly jealous of Joseph."

Linc went still. "Did she have reason? Was the judge unfaithful?"

"Never. He never looked at another woman while he was married to Katherine."

A dozen questions suddenly crowded Linc's mind. If what Abby said was true, everything in his world was changed. He felt a sudden rush of joy. And then a fierce, bitter surge of outrage. He didn't even want to think about Jack Keating. Not yet. First, he needed to make sure....

"Katherine Keating kept a diary," he said.

"I don't know." Abigail rocked gently. "She might have."

"Jack showed it to me once."

She clicked her tongue in disapproval. "Shame on you both. A diary is a private thing."

"It was the night the judge died. It was in his things."

Her sigh was tinged with sadness. "Sounds like Joseph, keeping her diary. He never wanted anyone to know how much he loved her, how much it hurt when she left."

He swallowed, hating the necessity to say the words. "She wrote that my mother and the judge had been lovers."

Abigail gave a soft snort. "How utterly ridiculous, Lincoln," she said, not even raising her voice.

"It isn't true?"

"No, indeed not. Kate loved Robert Cantrell with all her heart. There isn't the slightest possibility that she would have done such a thing. As for Joseph..." She shook her head. "Never. He respected Robert Cantrell too much. And Kate, as well. Besides, he was absolutely besotted with Katherine."

The porch rail under Linc's hands felt warm, satiny smooth from the hundreds—no, thousands—of times his mother must have stood there. And his father. Robert Cantrell. Not Joseph Keating. The turmoil in his chest seemed to build until he felt he would explode. He wanted to lash out, kick the rail into splinters, bellow in rage.

There was a buzzing in his ears. Abigail's voice

sounded as though she were speaking through a wind-storm. "What in the world made you believe such a thing?"

He rubbed his hand over his face. "It was written in Katherine's diary," he said hoarsely. "I saw it."

Abigail snorted again. "Lies! Pure and simple. Just another attempt to torture Joseph."

Linc was shaking his head. "But why?"

"To make him release her. To let her go." She sighed and began to rock again. "Finally, after she had Camille, she didn't bother trying to persuade him. She just packed up and went."

For long seconds, Linc stood at the railing. It was dark now. Straight ahead of him, the big house was lit up. Light blazed from the windows, upstairs and down. As he watched, a figure passed in front of a window. And then again. And again. He realized it was Jack pacing back and forth, talking on the phone. Doing what he did best. Wheeling and dealing. Manipulating. Playing God.

Whose life was he turning upside down tonight?

Suddenly, deep in his gut, Linc felt a raw, burning rage, a fierce lust for the feel of Jack's throat in his hands. By God, the man had a lot to answer for! Who in hell did he think he was?

"Miss Abigail—" His voice rasped as though he'd just come through a fire. He blinked to clear away a haze and tried again. "Miss Abigail, would you mind staying a few minutes with Nikki?"

"You're going to Camille?" she asked, pleased.

"No ma'am." He stepped off the porch steps.

"Who—"

"Jack Keating. We have unfinished business."

CAMILLE MADE a final notation in the ledger and then closed it. She always felt a sense of satisfaction and—

she admitted it—a little smugness at the end of the month when all the numbers were plumbed and Sunny Day showed a nice profit. It had been that way almost from the first month of operation. At this rate, she could manage her personal expenses. She turned toward the French doors, where the rest of Willow Wind could be seen stretching flat and green toward the setting sun. Her personal expenses were all she could manage. Her profit wasn't enough to carry the whole plantation.

Why wasn't she more worried about that? Was she the world's biggest fool to sit by passively while Linc took over? She stood, her satisfaction suddenly ruined. What was the use of rehashing everything? It wasn't as though she had other options. Everything was going along exactly as Pearce had arranged it. Linc had total control.

Why, Pearce? For the thousandth time, why?

She tilted her head and massaged the stiffness in her neck. It was getting more and more difficult to sustain her anger at Linc. He painstakingly informed her of every management change. He consulted her on every new purchase. And once business was done, he wanted to know every detail about Nikki at school. How could you hate a man like that? How could you hate a man who was so obviously out of his element rearing a child, but was so conscientiously determined to do it?

A noise at the French doors brought her head up. Silhouetted against the backdrop of the soft patio light was a man, tall and broad-shouldered, his head turned, his profile harshly delineated. Linc. For a moment she didn't move. He rapped again. She went quickly to the door. Gathering herself, she opened it.

"I need to come in," he said.

She gave him a sharp look. "What's wrong? Is it Abby? She fell, didn't she? I told her—"

"It's not Abby."

She looked closer, trying to decipher what it was about him. He seemed tense, almost vibrating with emotion. But it was controlled. Bottled up.

"What's wrong?" she repeated, stepping back, unconsciously inviting him in.

The instant he was inside in the light, she gasped. "Your shirt…" The pocket was almost ripped away and the tails were out. Buttons were missing; one hung by a thread. A huge tear started beneath his arm and ended at his jeans, as though someone had grabbed at it. At him. An angry, red mark stretched across his ribs.

He glanced at himself and laughed mirthlessly. "It's nothing. You should see the other guy."

"My God, what have you done?" she whispered, her fingers pressed to her mouth.

"What I should have done seventeen years ago," he said in a voice as dark as night. "It was crazy and I'll probably have to pay for it, but it felt so damn good I'd do it again given half a chance." He met her eyes. "How about a drink? Or is Pearce's stock all used up?"

"Bourbon?" she managed. "Is that okay?"

"Yeah, fine."

She went over to a cabinet. Opening it, she found a glass, poured bourbon into it and then looked up at him.

He nodded once and took it, tossing most of it down in one gulp. "Thanks."

"What happened, Linc? You've been in a fight!" she said, her voice rising with the sheer absurdity of it. "What…? Who…?"

"Your brother."

"Jack? Jack!"

"Yeah, my old buddy, Jack." He finished the drink and wiped his mouth with the back of his hand and then set down the glass on her desk. He began pacing. "Camille, you are not going to believe what I just found out tonight." Shaking his head, he seemed at a loss for words. He stopped and looked at her for a few long seconds. "God Almighty..." His eyes dropped from hers and he plowed a hand through his hair. "I swear I don't know where to start."

"Is it...? Are you...?" Curling her hands, she pressed them tight against her middle, her voice almost a whisper. "Are you going to have to leave again?"

"Leave?" He gave her a sharp look and then laughed shortly, mirthlessly. "Hell, no! Not this time."

She relaxed a little. "Then, what—"

"He lied to me, Camille. He's a miserable son of a bitch and a liar to boot!" He slammed a fist into his palm. "I can't believe he did it to me. To *us!*" He started pacing again, and the words came pouring out. "I've been a few places, Camille, and I've seen some things that would make your hair curl, but I swear to God, I've never known anyone like Jack Keating." He stopped, turning to her. "You know something? Your brother's a manipulative, sleazy lowlife, and this state will be in deep trouble if he's running things. I can't believe he's related to you. The judge would turn over in his grave if he knew—"

"Linc!" She cut him off. "I'm trying to figure out what's set you off, but so far all I've heard is a disjointed tirade aimed at Jack. Please get to the point."

Looking at her, Linc put a hand over his mouth and jaw and held it there for a moment. "You're right. I guess I was so damn mad that he could destroy my whole life and then turn around and act like it had never happened...." He shook his head. "I guess it just got away from me for a minute."

"What did Jack do, Linc?"

He reached for her and guided her over to a sofa across the room. "Let's sit down first. This might take some time." He hesitated, staring at her with an intensity that left her breathless. All at once, she was seventeen again, inexperienced and wildly in love, her senses so attuned to his that she could almost read his mind. Scared suddenly, she scooted back, away from him, tucking one leg beneath her.

"You're not going to believe this," he said again.

"Please—"

"Camille—" he leaned forward and picked up her hand "—for seventeen years, I've thought...I've believed that you were my sister."

She stared at him in utter amazement. *"What?"*

"I know it's crazy...." He gave a short laugh, his thumb stroking the back of her hand. "At least, now I know it's crazy, but I thought the judge..." He cleared his throat, looking helplessly into her eyes. Then he said, "Jack told me the judge was my father."

"No."

"It's true. I feel stupid and furious and cheated and manipulated. You name it, I feel it. But it's true."

"What are you saying!" She pulled at her hand, but he wouldn't let go. With a strangled sound, half sob, half curse, she yanked her hand free, and curled herself into a tight ball. Without looking at him, she said, "This is ridiculous. Jack wouldn't—"

"He would," Linc said bitterly. "He did. With that one lie, he took everything that mattered to me, everything. Nothing remained the same. I could no longer think of Robert Cantrell as my father. Worse, he made me think that, instead of being the decent human being I always believed him, the judge was a bully, a coward, a man without the courage to acknowledge his bastard son. A man who had forced my mother to keep their shameful secret. Jack said if she'd made any demands, she would have been thrown out of the cottage, left to make her way however she could with her reputation ruined.''

Linc caught Camille's shoulders, forcing her to look at him. His eyes were dark with frustration and rage. "Can you imagine how I felt when I thought of my mother? To me, she'd always been everything good and wholesome, a virtuous woman, the ideal I measured all other women by. Jack took that from me. He stole my mother, my father, my future and the girl I loved.''

Bewildered, she took a deep breath. "But why?''

"Oh, Cami, don't you know?'' he said, shaking his head.

She did know. Ugly as it was, she knew. With Linc out of the way, Jack hadn't wasted any time throwing her and Pearce together. And with her heart broken, her baby lost, her self-esteem at rock bottom, she'd been easy to manipulate. More than easy.

"Fate played right into his hands,'' Linc said bitterly. "And there was no one to stop him.''

"How? What did he say to make you believe him?''

"He showed me your mother's diary.''

"My mother's…'' She frowned. "My mother doesn't have a diary. I've never seen a diary.''

"He brought me your mother's diary the night the judge died, Camille, knowing that your mother had only written those things to justify her leaving. He knew the truth, Cami. He admitted it!''

She sucked in a quick breath, the memories of that

night tearing through her. She looked at him, her own eyes now wide and dark with remembered pain. "Was that why you called? Was that why you couldn't bear to see me again?"

In a heartbeat, he was up off the sofa. He began to pace, a hand pressed against the back of his neck. "He wouldn't let me see you," Linc said, forcing the words through his teeth. "I wanted to come right home that night, but he threatened me. He told me—"

"I know what he told you," she said, but without sympathy. "Christine was only too eager to enlighten me a couple of weeks ago. I know he threatened to have you arrested because I was underage." Her eyes were hard meeting his. "But you still owed me an explanation. When you called, you could have explained."

He whipped around. "Explained what? That you and I had the same father? We had been to bed together, Camille! There's a name for that. I didn't want to hurt you any more."

"Hurt me any more?" She stood up. "I was pregnant, Linc. Did you think leaving me without a word of explanation didn't hurt?"

"God, Camille—" He reached for her, but she twisted away.

"You didn't even ask."

"I…" He shook his head. "I don't know what to say. I never once thought you might be pregnant. It was just that one time that we didn't use anything. After that, I was so careful. I—"

"Once is all it takes, Linc. You should know that."

"I'm sorry," he said, his voice and eyes bleak. "Will you ever be able to forgive me?"

She sighed. "Don't worry about it now. I've put it behind me. You should do the same."

"You didn't answer me, Camille."

"I've given you all the answer you're going to get."

He met her gaze but was able to sustain it only a second or two. Turning slightly, he stared down at his hands. "I should go." He started for the door. "I—"

"Wait. You're bleeding." Camille put out a hand and touched his cheek. He jumped as though he'd come in contact with a live wire. She leaned close, frowning. "Beneath your jaw. I didn't notice it before."

Gingerly, tilting his face, Linc touched it and then looked at the blood on his finger. "It's nothing. It'll be okay after a shower."

"I don't think so. It's cut. I've got some butterfly bandages. I'll clean it first and then put one on." She turned, heading down the hall.

He followed reluctantly. "It'll just come off again in the shower."

She went into a powder room and found a small box under the sink. "No, it won't. I use these on the kids. The adhesive is better than superglue."

When she turned, he was standing in the doorway, his broad shoulders filling the frame. She glanced once into his face, then quickly away, but the look of him was seared in her brain. Rumpled and bloodstained, his ruddy skin scraped and bruised, there should have been nothing appealing about him. So why was her heart suddenly thudding?

"You'll have to sit down," she told him, her voice husky. She put the lid down on the toilet. "I can't reach you otherwise."

He shouldered past her and sat, wincing slightly.

"Your ribs?" she asked.

He shook his head. "Just too old for this sh—stuff."

"Here, this might sting a little." She put one hand

alongside his jaw and with the other began to clean the wound gently. Only after he closed his eyes did she allow herself one long look at his face. Her breath caught in her throat. What was it about him that did this to her? Surely what had been between them was over long ago.

"If you look like this," she said, grasping for any distraction, "how about Jack? I think he's scheduled to do a TV spot tomorrow."

"Don't worry, I didn't mark him. At least, not much. He might be a little stiff getting out of bed in the morning, but he had it coming."

"I wasn't worried. And you're right, he had it coming." Linc sucked in a quick breath when she dabbed on disinfectant. "Who's with Nikki?" she asked.

"Abigail. That's how I found out." He held still while she put the tiny bandage in place. "She came over to tell me she would stay with Nicole in the evenings if I should just happen to want to visit you." He shook his head. "I didn't know what to say because I thought she, of all people, would know why I could never have that kind of relationship with you."

Camille leaned against the sink. "Please tell me you're kidding," she said faintly.

He gave her a wry smile. "What? About her fixing us up? Come on, Cami, you know that's what Abigail has always wanted."

"Well, it's ridiculous. She'll have to get the notion out of her head."

"Yeah, but how about her teacup?"

She popped the box back into the cabinet and closed the door with a bang. "Don't encourage her, Linc. It's...it's..."

"Ridiculous. Yeah, I know."

She took a deep breath and moved around him to get

out of the small room. It was tiny, but it had never seemed as cramped as it did that minute.

He was on her heels as she walked out, heading for the foyer. "Could we just talk about this for a minute, Cami?"

"Why? What's the point?"

He made a helpless gesture. "Maybe none, I don't know. But we can't just blow this away as if it didn't mean a damn thing. I won't keep you long. I promise." He searched her face, his eyes dark. "I've thought of you so long as my half sister that I hardly know what our relationship should be now."

"Exactly as Pearce defined it," she said stiffly. "You're running Willow Wind and I'm here on sufferance."

"Damn it, Camille! That's crap and you know it!" He shoved a hand through his hair. "Anyway, I don't want to talk about this place—or Pearce. Not tonight. I want to talk about what happened to us, to you and me."

"What is there to say, Linc? Do you want to hear how after you left, I felt like an empty shell? That I was so devastated I almost didn't graduate? Or how I couldn't stand even going to the barn because that's where we'd spent all those hours in the loft planning our life together." She held his gaze defiantly, her eyes too bright. "Oh, yes. Kate's Cottage. I couldn't go near there because that's where you kissed me for the first time. And when I finally got on a horse again, I couldn't ride by Red Creek or sit by the pond anymore, because that's where we made love.

"You want to talk about what happened?" she demanded, tears glistening in her eyes. "I wanted to die, Linc. That's what happened." She turned from him, her chin up. After a few moments of charged silence, she spoke, her defiance spent. "You were gone and my baby was dead. So I wanted to die, too. That's what happened."

My baby was dead.

Across the room, Linc closed his eyes helplessly and let the bitter truth wash over him. There had been a baby. God, what had he done? He could hardly breathe with the weight of Camille's pain and his own regret. How could he ever make it up to her? He searched for something to say, knowing all along there was nothing. Words wouldn't change a damn thing. His hatred for Jack Keating boiled up again. And with it, his vow to have his revenge. Jack would pay. By God, he would pay.

He crossed the room slowly and hunkered down in front of her. "Camille?" His tone was intense, low, almost a whisper. "If I could, I'd erase all the pain of that time for you. I can't. I failed you and I'll have to live with that." His eyes clung to hers. "But don't shut me out now, Cami. I wasn't there for you then, but I'm here now."

"You don't owe me anything, Linc. Just—"

"Hush." He put a finger on her lips. "You said the baby was dead. How far along were you? How did it happen? Was it the stress of it all? I want to know, Cami."

After looking at him a long moment, she shook her head. He frowned. "What? What does that look mean?"

"You didn't jump to the most natural conclusion of all."

He was puzzled. "Which is?"

"Abortion."

He stared. "Abortion? I know you would never do that."

"Oh, Linc." She closed her eyes, shaking her head sadly. "Thank you for that."

"What happened, Cami?"

"I was crushed after you called that night. I couldn't think straight. Nobody knew about the baby, so there was nobody to turn to. Abigail was ill, everyone else was caught up in Daddy's death." She picked numbly at a thread on the sofa. "I went to the barn—" She lifted her eyes to his. He waited tensely. "I know it was crazy, but I saddled Red Devil and tore out of there as though I could outrun the pain, the bewilderment…everything."

He reached for her hand and brought it up, holding it against his heart.

"We took a jump at the creek and…" She frowned as though seeing it all again. Her mouth trembled. "It was so quick. He stumbled and I hit the ground hard. It stunned me. When I came around, I was bleeding."

"Camille. Oh, Camille…" He swallowed hard, his eyes dark and luminous.

"They had to put Red Devil down," she said in a dull voice. "I killed him, too."

"Too?" His eyebrows rose. "You're assuming all the responsibility for the miscarriage? All the guilt?"

"Who else?" She turned her face away from him, but not before he saw the anguish in her eyes. "No one forced me to take a wild gallop in the dark."

"What about me?" He rubbed her hand gently against his cheek. "There's blame to share here. If I hadn't made that call, you wouldn't have been on that horse." His eyes roved over her face, caressing each feature. "It was an accident, Cami, a sad, tragic accident. Take your own advice and let it go."

For a long, long moment, their eyes held. In the foyer a clock began to chime the hour, the sound distant and lonely. Her hand clasped in his trembled, and Linc's body reacted with quick arousal. For the first time in years, he was free to touch Camille without the taint of guilt and shame. Holding on to her, he straightened up slowly and then eased them down on the sofa.

"This feels so good," he murmured, leaning back and rolling his head to look at her.

"What?" she asked, brushing at her tears.

"Being here with you." He lifted their linked hands. "Touching you, knowing it's okay, knowing that if I want to kiss you, it's okay, too." He held on when she tugged to free her hand, and gave her a quick, lopsided grin. "Knowing if you slap my face and chew me out, I only have to feel regret and disappointment and a good, healthy intention to try again another time. But, thank God, I don't have to feel guilty anymore."

Camille stared down at their hands. When she spoke, it was almost a whisper. "I'm not ready for this, Linc."

"That's okay, too. I'm still trying to take it all in, myself."

She raised her eyes to his. "How could he, Linc?"

"Jack?" He shook his head. "Who knows? But he won't get away with it, Cami. He went too far playing with our lives as though we were pawns in some chess game. I'm not a penniless kid dependent on the mighty Keatings anymore. It may take me a little while, but he's going to pay."

Camille looked troubled but said nothing. His expression cleared as he released her hand and sat up suddenly. "I need to get back to the cottage. I imagine it's past Abigail's bedtime."

But neither of them moved. Again, they became lost in each other's eyes. Linc reached over and touched the side of her face, savoring the smooth, velvety texture of her skin. Her hair was a dark cloud framing her face. He was close enough to inhale the scent of it. Of her. His heartbeat changed, became heavy and deep. Desire rose like a tidal wave. The attraction he felt for her was an irresistible force. Even when she'd been forbidden to him, he hadn't been able to banish her from his mind. He'd still lusted after her in secret. Even while married to Joanna—

He was off the sofa before that thought could be finished.

"I've got to go," he told her.

Looking a little confused, she stood, too. "Well…"

"Don't worry about Abigail. I'll walk her back over here."

"Thank you."

He pulled the front door open. Turning, he allowed himself one last, long look at her face. The urge to kiss her was so powerful he could almost taste it. Would she be as sweet and willing as she had been all those years ago? Beside them, the clock ticked loudly. Somewhere in the distance, a dog barked. He drew in a deep, reluctant breath.

His voice, when he found it, was colored with the strength of his emotion. "I'll see you tomorrow," he said.

"Good night," she replied after a moment, and then softly closed the door.

On the other side, Linc stared at it for a few seconds, not moving. Then, turning, he walked across the porch and down the steps, making his way thoughtfully across property that now, technically, belonged to him.

LYING SLEEPLESS in his bed long after midnight, Linc stared at the ceiling. With Jack's treachery exposed, the barrier that had kept Camille from him was down, and he was stunned at what he felt. As long as she had been off-limits, he had been able to deny his feelings, blank out the memory of that summer. With a groan, he threw an arm over his eyes, but nothing blocked the vivid, heated flashes that surged through him. Like quick clips from an erotic film, images danced before his mind's eye. Sensual, explicit memories of fierce passion, long, hot nights, slow, sweet sex. In spite of Jack's interference that summer, they had laughed and loved and played the time away, reveling as much in each other as in the newly discovered physical pleasures of their bodies. How could there be anything left after all these years?

What was he going to do about it?

Nothing, damn it! Rolling over in the warm bed, he kicked the sheet away. He couldn't have Camille. It was as simple as that. He already owed her a heavy debt for running out and leaving her pregnant and alone. His plan to destroy her brother was already set in motion. When the deed was done, she would never be able to forgive him.

Besides, when he'd done what he'd set out to do, he wouldn't deserve forgiveness.

CHAPTER EIGHT

"WAIT A MINUTE, Camille. I want to talk to you."

Camille looked up, her keys out, ready to unlock her car. Jack, in sunglasses and casual khakis, was striding across the lawn toward her. Since his campaign had gotten under way, he was usually outfitted in a suit and tie, even at this hour.

"Hi," she said, eyeing him curiously.

"Where is that crazy son of a bitch?" he demanded. "Nobody answered the door when I tried it just now at that run-down cottage. And don't play dumb, Camille. The two of you are thick as thieves these days."

"Are you talking about Linc?"

"Yes, I'm talking about Linc," he mimicked sarcastically. "Where is he?"

She stared at him for a second or two before asking, "Do you know what time it is, Jack?"

"What the hell does that have to do with anything?"

"It's not seven-thirty yet. How would I know where Linc is at this hour? He doesn't live here."

His lip curled. "Not yet maybe. But it's damn sure in his plan, little sister, you can bank on that. That is, unless you come to your senses before it's too late."

She sighed, looking away from him. "What's on your mind, Jack? As you know, I have to get to Sunny Day early."

"You're telling the truth? You haven't seen him?"

"Not this morning, no."

He studied her, but with the mirror lenses in his sunglasses, she couldn't read his expression. "Was he here last night?"

"Yes, he was."

"Do you know what he's done?"

She gave a bewildered shrug.

He reached up with a curse and whipped off the sunglasses. Camille made a choked sound, something between a gasp and a giggle. Jack's left eye was swollen shut, the skin around it a lurid blend of purple and green. High on his cheekbone was a cut that looked as though it would leave a scar.

"I was scheduled to do some television spots today," he said between clenched teeth. "I had to cancel the taping session. Do you have any idea how expensive that was?"

She covered her mouth. "What happened, Jack?"

"I was assaulted by that…that maniac," he sputtered. "He busted his way inside my house last night raving about crap that happened so damn long ago, I could hardly remember it. Next thing I knew, he started swinging."

"Are you all right?"

"Do I look all right?" he snarled. "That's not all. He threatened me." Jack drew himself up, tapping his chest with his fingers. "Me. Can you believe that, Camille? Threatening me in my own house like I was some damn field hand. I'll tell you, this time he's gone too far. This time—"

"That's exactly what he said about you," Camille put in softly. "The lies you told altered both our lives, Jack. That was the 'crap' Linc was so upset about. Did you think you could play around with other human beings as though they were…livestock or something?''

"God almighty, Camille! That was a hundred years ago. It's water under the bridge. Besides, things worked out, didn't they?'' He indicated the big house with a jerk of his head. "You've got this place. The land's back in the family. It's Keating land again and—''

"Will you listen to yourself, Jack! What do you mean, things worked out all right? My marriage to Pearce was a travesty of what marriage should be. I was unhappy and I made him unhappy. So much so that he drank himself to death. Both of us were cheated.'' She shook her head, unable to believe he could be so blind. "As for Willow Wind and all the headaches that go with it, I couldn't care less. I don't even want it now.''

"Damn you, don't say that!''

"I will say it! I don't want it, Jack. I never did and I don't care if Linc takes it over and thumbs his nose at you across that fence every day for the rest of your life!''

Jack grabbed her arm. "That's stupid talk, Camille. You've let Cantrell twist your thinking. He's weaseled his way into your life again, just like before. He doesn't care about you, you little fool. He just wants your co-operation while he figures out how to steal this place right out from under us. And if you don't believe it—''

She snatched her arm from his grasp. "I guess you didn't hear me, Jack. I'm not the passive teenager you manipulated seventeen years ago. What you want and what I want are two very different things, so you may as well accept that right now.''

He stared at her, visibly wrestling with his temper. "This is serious, Camille. This could go beyond a simple dispute over the Twin Willows. Do you know what he's done now?''

She refused to look at him. "I don't care what he's done."

"He wants to see the books all the way back—five years."

She shrugged. "So?"

He drew in a breath. "I don't want him getting his hands on those records, Camille."

"Why not, Jack?"

He swore again. "It's not a good time to call attention to my personal finances, for God's sake! I'm solid in the polls. I don't want anything screwing that up."

"Would your business dealings with Pearce reflect poorly on you, Jack?"

"Jeez, Camille…" He turned from her, rubbing the back of his neck.

"Yeah, Jack. I've been wondering that myself."

Camille whipped around at the sound of Linc's voice. He stood at the edge of her porch, one shoulder propped against a massive column. In a blue Western-cut shirt and worn jeans that outlined every bump and ridge of his masculinity, he looked both sexy and intimidating. He stepped down, removing his sunglasses, and began to walk her way. As he moved lazily across the short space between them, his boots crunched the pebbles on the driveway. He looked into her eyes with a smile that scattered her thoughts and stampeded her heartbeat before he turned to Jack.

"How long have you been standing there?" Jack demanded.

Using his thumb, Linc pushed his hat brim up a scant half inch. "Long enough, Jack. Long enough."

"What Camille and I are discussing is confidential, Cantrell. Keating business. So butt out."

Linc stared directly at Jack. "You don't give me orders now, Jack, especially when you're standing on Willow Wind land.''

Jack sent him a black look before turning to Camille. "Now do you believe me, Camille? Do you see what he's doing?''

Camille sighed. "Jack, why don't we talk about this later?''

"After he's had a chance to soften you up?'' Jack rammed his sunglasses back on his face. "Wake up, Camille. He'll have you back in the sack before you know it, and you'll be just as starry-eyed over him as you were—''

"That's enough, Keating!'' Linc took a menacing step forward, looking as though he'd like to finish what he'd started the night before. "If I were you, I'd be very careful before I said another word. What's between Camille and me concerns us and no one else. On the other hand, the matter discussed last night is between you and me. And I'm warning you, leave Camille out of it. If you try dragging her into the middle to save your political ass, you'll wind up losing more than an election.''

"I'VE NEVER SEEN anybody face Jack down like that before,'' Camille murmured, watching her brother stalk across the lawn in the direction of the big house.

"He's used to calling the shots and having everyone jump," Linc said harshly. "It's time he learned he can't always have things his way.''

"I guess so.''

"Don't worry about him, Cami. He's more than able to take care of himself.''

"I'm not so sure about that.'' Her mouth quirked and she giggled. "Did you *see* that shiner?''

"What shiner?" he asked innocently. When she looked, his mouth was twitching, too.

"You told me you didn't mark him."

"I lied."

Suddenly acutely aware of his closeness, she looked down at her hands. His scent was heady in the morning air—after-shave and soap and warm male. She'd spent the night vowing to keep him safely at arm's length, but at the first sight of him, she was almost trembling. Her legs threatened to fold under her any minute now.

"We forgot something," he told her in a low, husky tone.

"What?" The pulse in her throat was beating like a wild thing. Reaching out, he captured her jaw, and she had the crazy notion that he was going to kiss her. Right out in broad daylight. Before God and the Twin Willows. Anticipating it—wanting it—she almost ceased to breathe.

"We didn't even say good-morning," he said softly, his eyes trained on her face.

"Good morning," she whispered.

With a finger, he softly traced the bruised-looking area beneath her eyes. "Did I have anything to do with this?"

He had everything to do with it. After he left, she'd tossed and turned until the wee hours trying to sort out her tangled emotions, not the smallest of which was guilt. How could she be attracted to Linc when Pearce had been gone only a month? She'd also been consumed with curiosity. There were a thousand questions she wanted to ask about his marriage, his work, the intervening years.

But every instinct advised caution. People didn't really change. He'd abandoned her once, and it had been total abandonment. He had never looked back. Was she willing to take that kind of risk again?

"I didn't sleep very well," she said.

"Neither did I."

For a few long moments, they did nothing but look at each other. He still held her jaw, while with each second that passed, something intense and compelling grew. He brushed a thumb over her lips. "I kept wondering and wondering...."

She shivered as lightning streaked down her spine. "Wondering what?"

As though catching himself, he looked away quickly, his expression suddenly guarded. "Nothing. It's nothing."

But it was. She stared at him, her eyes dilated with remembrance. The passion they'd shared throbbed between them. He had felt it, too. She'd seen it in his eyes, felt it in everything he didn't say. But she remained silent, hesitant to take the step that would bridge seventeen years.

"Nikki's in the Bronco," he said, his eyes drifting to her mouth.

"Nikki?"

"I have to go to Memphis." He reached out and caught a flyaway strand of her dark hair, then tucked it behind her ear. "For spare parts."

"Oh," she murmured, openly staring at him.

"For one of the tractors."

"Tractors." Her eyelids felt heavy as his fingers, warm and a little calloused, began rubbing the side of her neck. Suddenly he rested his forehead against hers with a muffled groan. Her hands went to his waist and anchored there, her fingers sinking into shirt and man. He was all lean, hard muscle. Warmth and substance.

She closed her eyes, tempted to find out if pain and regret could be erased this way. Oh, if only they could. She'd been cold and empty for so long.

"You still smell the same," he said, his voice ragged.

She took in a deep, unsteady breath. So did he.

His lips skated sideways to her temple and skimmed the curve of her cheekbone, then dipped lower to her neck. His breath on her skin aroused her starved senses. Her head fell back, inviting more. He braced one palm against the car and found the pulse in her throat, closing his mouth over it with growing urgency. She felt the rapid rise and fall of his chest and realized her own breathing was just as wild. He turned his face into her hair, burying his nose in it.

"If you're going to stop me, Cami—" he inhaled the scent of flowers and pushed his hips solidly against hers "—now's the time."

Stopping was not what she wanted, Camille realized with dazed surprise. Instead, her senses clamored for more. Against his chest, her breasts were tight and aching. With a murmur, she turned her face to taste the skin of his neck. It was musky and damp, a little salty. She drew the smell of him deep into her lungs, awakening a host of sensory memories.

"Camille…"

She lifted her face to his, giving a glad cry when his mouth closed over hers in a ravenous kiss. Her arms rose and circled his neck tightly. Her fingers curled through his hair, heedlessly knocking his hat to the ground. She was no longer an inexperienced, passive girl. She was a woman with a woman's hunger. When her mouth opened in eager welcome, his arm curled around her waist, propelling her against the car, holding her there with the weight of his body as his hand captured her jaw to keep her just where he wanted her. His tongue was wild and frenzied as it explored the warm, inviting depths of her mouth. His knee moved between her legs, pressed against the aching mound of her femininity. She strained closer as desire escalated.

With a strangled groan, he left her, only to angle his head a new way. Threading his fingers through her hair, he sucked on her lip with fierce hunger, stroked the soft underside with his tongue. His need desperate, he held her as though he would never let her go. Camille's heart soared in joyful welcome.

Then suddenly she was free.

She swayed, putting out both hands, bumping against the car. Her arousal had been so complete, so mindless, that for a minute she was disoriented. With her fingers over her mouth, she stared at him from wide, smoky eyes, her mouth still dewy with his kisses.

"I'm sorry," he said, looking away, his jaw clenched. "I didn't mean to do that. I know you don't want... I was just going to—"

"Kiss me a little?"

He was bent over, picking up his hat, but something in the way she said it compelled him to look at her.

"I didn't mean to kiss you at all," he admitted quietly.

"Why not?"

He clamped a hand against his neck. "Camille—"

"I'm free and you're free," Camille said, determined to sound as sophisticated as any woman of the nineties. If he didn't want to acknowledge that something significant had just happened, then she wouldn't either. He'd humiliated her once, years ago. Only a fool would let him do it again. "We had an affair a hundred years ago. You weren't the only one wondering whether there was anything left." She gave him a bright smile. "No problem."

Linc scowled, his expression fierce.

"Daddy!"

They both turned at the sound of the childish voice. Nikki, in tiny red shorts and a Winnie-the-Pooh T-shirt, scrambled off the porch, rear end first, and dropped to the ground.

"What's taking so long?" she demanded, looking at her father. "I'm tired of waiting. Did he ask you, Camille?" She transferred her attention to Camille. "Is it okay?"

"Hi, Nikki." Camille darted a glance at Linc and found him looking as discomfited as she felt. Lord, what if Nikki had appeared one minute earlier?

"Since Sunny Day's in the opposite direction to where I need to go, I told Nikki she might be able to ride to school with you," he explained in a low tone. "That is, if you wouldn't mind."

"I don't mind." Camille managed a smile for Nikki while trying to pull herself together. She put a hand to her hot face. One question was answered; they were still dynamite together. And from Linc's reaction, she didn't have to wonder whether the feeling was mutual. What she did wonder was where they were going from here.

"Nikki, go get your things out of the truck," Linc said in the gentle tone he used with his daughter.

"Okay!" Nikki dashed off, pausing at the corner of the house to say, "Wait for me, Camille. Don't leave me!"

"I won't."

Linc turned to Camille. "I'll try to be back before school's out."

"It doesn't matter. If you're not, I'll bring her back

here with me. You can pick her up when you do get back." She reached for the car door.

Linc was quicker. He pulled at the handle. "I appreciate this, Camille."

"Okay, I'm ready!" Nikki was back, laughing. Her schoolbag hung from an overlong strap on her shoulder, bumping awkwardly against her legs with every step. Her attention was fixed on a yellow squash carefully balanced on her palm. The squash had been decorated as a goose, using peas and orange peel and a few chicken feathers. "See my veg'table project, Camille? Me and my daddy thought and thought yesterday, and this is what came out. Is it good?"

"It's very good," Camille said, resisting the urge to scoop her up in a hug. Unlike her feelings for Linc, which were a complicated and confused muddle, what she felt for Nikki was love, pure and simple. She had surrendered to her completely, just as she had suspected she would from the first time she'd looked into Nikki's face. She gave the dark curls an affectionate ruffling. Who could resist such a child? "Here, I'll hold it while you get inside."

Linc held the front seat forward as Nikki scrambled into the car. When she was settled with the "veg'table project" wedged protectively between her small knees, he stepped back and closed the door.

"Thanks again, Camille."

She got in and started the car. "It's nothing. I—"

"I know," he said gruffly, keeping his voice down so Nikki couldn't overhear. "It's nothing special. You'd do it for any one of your thirty students."

She looked at him then, one quick flicker of a glance. "Yes."

He hesitated as though he'd like to say more. But after

a moment, he stepped back without speaking and Camille backed out. Settling his hat firmly on his head, he watched her drive off.

LINC WAS STILL AGITATED as he approached Main Street in Blossom on his way to Memphis, which probably accounted for the fact that he drove through town at a speed well above the limit. Only the fact that, at seven-thirty in the morning on a Wednesday, Main Street in Blossom was usually devoid of traffic as well as most other forms of industry, saved him from an unscheduled stop by Deputy Dan Culpepper. At that moment Culpepper was occupied with breakfast at the Magnolia Café and didn't look up in time. Wiley Dawson, chatting with Sam Byrd over coffee and the newspaper in the next booth, did.

"Who the devil was that?" Sam asked, glancing up from an analysis of the upcoming election in the *Clarion Ledger*.

"Linc Cantrell, I do believe," Wiley informed him, thoughtfully taking in the cloud of delta dust in Linc's wake.

"Seems in a hurry."

"Probably gettin' a head start on the traffic to Memphis," Wiley opined. "He's been makin' a lot of trips lately tryin' to fix up that broken-down equipment of Pearce's."

Sam nodded. "Got his work cut out." He went back to his paper.

"I heard there was a little skirmish over at the Twin Willows last night."

Sam glanced up. "Oh yeah?"

"Uh-huh." Wiley stirred his coffee. "Little difference of opinion between Jack Keating and Linc."

"You don't say." Sam put his paper down.

"Seems Linc found out something Jack had done 'way back. Ticked him off so bad, he went so far as to get physical over it. Jack got up this morning with a black eye and a disposition to match."

"Well, what d'ya know?"

"Had to cancel an important date with some TV people that had to do with his campaign," Wiley said. "Mad as hell over it, too, I heard."

Sam began to polish his glasses. "Got that from Clarence, I guess?"

Wiley nodded. Wiley's yard boy, Clarence, was one of the eight children of Jack Keating's top equipment operator. Nothing happened at the Twin Willows that wasn't fully reported by Clarence. Both men looked out of the Magnolia's window where Linc had just passed.

"I wonder what's going on out there at the Twin Willows," Sam mused.

"We'll just have to wait and see," Wiley said. "One thing, though. I get the idea Jack's not too happy with Linc returnin' from the past like he did. Those two never saw eye to eye even when they were boys."

"Now that both are powerful men, we're bound to see the fur fly." Sam's eyes lit up with anticipation. "My money's on Jack. The Keating name's powerful, Wiley. You can't deny that."

"No, but…" Wiley leaned back, squinting down the road where Linc had disappeared minutes before. "Lincoln Cantrell's shrewd and smart, too. Always was. I'm not callin' this one yet, Sam. I'm gonna wait and see."

"OH, DEAR, WE'VE GOT company, Camille."

Something in Abigail's tone sent Camille's eyes to the window just in time to see Christine Keating's BMW swing around the curve that led to the front door of Willow Wind. Nikki made a tiny sound, as she always did when faced with the prospect of meeting a stranger.

Abigail reached for her hand. "Nicole, let's you and me take a walk in my garden. I want to show you some funny flowers that have a little bulb on them that pops open and spills out lots and lots of small black seeds."

Nikki trustingly placed her hand in the old lady's. Nikki never spoke a word to Abigail, but she seemed to like being with her. Watching them leave the room together as the doorbell pealed, Camille suspected the feeling was mutual.

"Christine!" Camille's eyes widened at the sight of her sister-in-law without avant-garde jewelry, designer clothes or her usual poise. She looked as though she'd slept in the wrinkled, oversize shirt and flared shorts she was wearing. Even more astonishing was the complete absence of makeup.

"Well, are you going to let me in?"

Camille moved hastily, murmuring an apology, then stepped to the threshold to see if Christine had come alone. Her car was empty. She looked beyond to the big house across the way, but Willow Wood appeared deserted. Puzzled, she closed the door and studied her sister-in-law. She couldn't remember ever seeing Christine looking so...frazzled.

"I need a drink," Christine said abruptly, raking at strands of her blond hair that had strayed from a once tight chignon.

"Christine—"

"Bourbon, gin, I'm not choosy." She turned into the spacious sitting room off the foyer and dropped into a chair, rubbing her forehead with unsteady fingers. "Abigail still prefers Southern Comfort, doesn't she? I'll take that."

Camille went to the liquor cabinet and poured the potent drink into a brandy snifter. Without a word, she handed it to Christine, who studied it with a bitter twist of her lips. "Southern Comfort," she said humorlessly, then swallowed most of it in one gulp. "Let's see if it lives up to its name."

"What's wrong, Christine?"

Christine stared at her silently for a moment. Then she set the glass carefully on a small cherry wood table and buried her face in her hands. "He's going to ruin everything, Camille."

"What are you talking about? Who? Who's going to ruin everything?"

"Linc Cantrell, the bastard. He's setting it all up so shrewdly, so damned cleverly, that Jack doesn't even see it. He keeps saying Linc's no threat, Linc can't touch him, can't really harm him...." She raised her eyes and gave Camille an imploring look. "But he can, Camille. He's smarter than Jack thinks. He's not the redneck kid Jack ran out of town seventeen years ago. And he's furious over what happened back then. He's successful and powerful now. Consequently, he's dangerous. You should have seen him last night." Suddenly her voice dropped, vibrating with emotion. "We have a snake in our midst, a serpent in our beautiful Twin Willows, Camille, and its name is Linc Cantrell. Don't you see it?"

Camille felt a small shock. There was a wild look in Christine's eyes that made her feel uneasy. She shouldn't have given her the drink. "Why don't I see you back home Christine? Jack will be back soon. It's about that time."

"You don't see it either, do you?"

"You're exhausted, Christine. It's the stress of the campaign. Why don't—"

"If you don't get rid of him, Camille, there won't be any use in continuing the campaign. He's going to destroy Jack."

"Destroy—" Camille's patience ran out. "Christine, how could Linc destroy Jack? The campaign's going very well. He's solid in the polls—he told me so just this morning."

Christine settled back against the sofa and stared into her empty glass. "Jack has secrets, Camille," she said softly. "To get where he is, he's had to do things that the voters wouldn't understand. He's vulnerable, don't you see that? Just a whiff of impropriety would be a disaster right now."

"What secrets? What improprieties?"

"Just…things, Camille." Christine shook her head. "You don't want to know."

Camille studied her in silence for a long moment, wondering if what she'd said was the result of too much liquor or if there really was something to her fears. Christine badly wanted to be Mississippi's first lady. Had her desire become an obsession? Was she imagining threats where none existed? Jack had other competitors, any one of whom wouldn't hesitate to crucify him publicly if there was ammunition to do it. Why was Christine centering her fears on Linc? Even though Linc had reason to hate Jack, he wouldn't deliberately wreck Jack's campaign. Or would he?

"I saw him dump his little kid on you this morning," Christine said, getting off the sofa and beginning to pace back and forth. "That's how he's going to do it."

"Do what, Christine?"

"Win you over." Her eyes gleamed. "That's how he's going to get around you. He knows you always wanted children. He has a kid, and he's not above using her to serve his own ends."

Camille got up abruptly. "I'm driving you home, Christine." She glanced around, looking for the keys to the BMW. "After a little rest, you'll feel better. I know you were upset over what happened between Jack and Linc last night. Since you seem to know Jack's secrets, surely you can see how Linc would be angry enough to lose his temper. They needed to clear the air, and they did. It's over now, Chris."

Christine, unconvinced, looked at her sadly. "It's not over, Camille. It's just beginning."

Helping Christine down the steps and into the BMW, Camille reminded herself that her sister-in-law was one of the most cynical people she'd ever met. Linc wouldn't do anything to jeopardize Jack's campaign whether Jack deserved it or not. For one thing, Linc was basically too decent and honorable to stoop to Jack's level.

Christine was imagining things.

CHAPTER NINE

AT THE SOUND of a car, Camille dropped the magazine she'd been flipping through without interest and walked quickly to the door. It was Linc. She pushed at the screen and stepped outside onto the porch. She didn't want to be in the small living room alone with him. If it could be called alone, she thought, running a nervous hand down one thigh. There were ghosts in Kate's Cottage, too many for her to feel comfortable, especially with only Linc for company. Their pasts were too inextricably bound together.

Linc, getting out of the Bronco, looked up when he heard the soft squeak of the screen door as she closed it behind her. She could see him frown, trying to make her out. Feeling exposed after her reaction to the kiss that morning, she'd purposely left the porch light off, unwilling to risk any more humiliation. His features, outlined in the truck's interior light, were harsh and unsmiling. The creases around his mouth seemed carved deeper than they had been that morning. Without looking away, he closed the door and started toward her.

"What's wrong?" he asked sharply. "Is Nikki okay?"

Always Nikki. She sighed and crossed the porch, descending the steps before he reached them. "Nikki's fine. I fed her and gave her a bath at my house. When it got so late, I thought it would be better to put her in her own bed, so here we are. She's sleeping now."

"Thanks," he said, absently rubbing at the muscles in his neck.

"You're welcome." When she reached him, she didn't pause, but sidestepped a little to get around him. He stopped her with a hand on her arm. She took a step back, dislodging him. He didn't appear to notice.

"Wait here," he told her, taking the porch steps two at a time. "I'll check on Nikki and then walk you home," he called over his shoulder as he disappeared into the cottage.

Ignoring him, she picked her way past new lawn furniture and odds and ends of Nikki's things strewn in the yard. She'd meant to have Nikki put them away properly, but she'd forgotten once they started fixing omelets. Then they'd dawdled over her bath, both of them soaked when Nikki finally climbed out, all rosy and sweet-smelling.

"Why didn't you wait?"

She gave a little squeak and stumbled as Linc caught her by the arm. How had he managed to come up behind her without making a sound?

"I don't need an escort to find my way across land I've lived on all my life," she said in a tight voice, shaking off his hand.

"It's not a question of knowing the way, Camille. It's dark as sin out here. Things happen."

"I've managed all these years," she snapped. "You can go back to Nikki now."

"I plan to walk you home and keep an eye on the cottage at the same time," he told her.

That tone probably had Pearce's employees—correction, Camille reminded herself, Linc's employees—jumping to do his will. She shrugged. "Suit yourself."

"What is it, Camille?"

"I'm just not used to this."

"What? Using a little common sense?"

"No. This." She gestured vaguely. "Having a... bodyguard." When he just grunted, she said, "I've been taking care of myself a long time, Linc."

He stopped, and for some reason Camille did, too. "You've only been a widow a month, Camille."

But I've been alone far longer than that.

She almost said it aloud, but what would be the point? How could Linc understand the kind of loneliness and isolation that drove a woman to take risks, to stretch beyond the world of home and husband? For her, the other option had been to crawl into the bottle with Pearce and eventually become as sick as he was.

Frowning, Linc shook his head and said, "I can't believe Pearce let you traipse around at night alone. That's risky even in the rarefied atmosphere of a plantation."

Camille wondered how much he knew about her relationship with Pearce. Had Pearce confided in him? Had he discussed her shortcomings with Linc? Did Linc know how totally she'd failed as a wife? Just then, the moon emerged through a bank of clouds. The willow pond lay a few yards in front of them, the water still and silent, the surface silver in the moonlight. Between the trees that ringed the edge, drooping limbs created a small, isolated space. Seeing it, she suddenly remembered another night. Linc had been beside her then, too. But they hadn't been standing and they hadn't been arguing. She turned and found him watching her. Her breath caught in her throat, and her pulse raced wildly. Although his features were in shadow and his body as still as the pond, she knew he was remembering, too.

"Let's sit a minute." He caught her hand, and she let him pull her over to the old willow. Reaching up, he parted the leafy switches and, ducking, they both stepped through. Instantly, as before, they seemed alone, cocooned in the small, dark space. He released her hand and, after a moment, she dropped to the ground, drawing up her knees and wrapping her arms around them. Other than the nocturnal chorus of nature and the soft whisper of the water, nothing seemed real. In the silence, she was suddenly, intensely aware of him. The memory of what had once happened in this place was too close. Her heart began to beat raggedly.

Urgently, she searched for a safe topic. "How was your trip?"

"Successful."

"They had the parts you needed?"

"Yeah, fortunately. They'll ship within the week."

"That's good."

With a restless move, he sat down beside her, propped on one elbow and stretching his legs toward the water's edge. Feeling his eyes on her did nothing to ease Camille's discomfort. Between their unsettling encounter that morning and Christine's bizarre behavior that afternoon, she'd had a very trying day. The only bright spot had been the time spent in Nikki's beguiling presence.

"I've been thinking about something Jack said this morning before you appeared," she said.

He reached for a small twig on the ground and began idly snapping it in his fingers.

"He said you wanted to see the books for the past five years."

"That's right." He glanced at her. "Do you have a problem with that?"

She shook her head. "No, I..." She shrugged. "No."

He laughed, an almost silent, humorless sound. "Good, because I mean to see them."

"That's not what's bothering me, Linc. Jack's concerned about his campaign. You know how people are about the least little thing in a candidate's background.

I don't want to do anything to discredit him in the eyes of voters.''

Linc picked up a small stone and sent it sailing over the surface of the pond. It fell into the water with a soft plunk. ''*You* can't discredit him, Camille. Only Jack can do that.''

She looked directly at him then. ''I won't be a party to anything that will hurt Jack's campaign,'' she said quietly. ''No matter what he did in the past.''

''Nobody's asking you to.''

She turned the words over in her mind. ''I had the craziest visit from Christine today. Actually, I'm a little worried about her.''

''What is it, campaign fatigue? This is probably the longest, most consistent stretch of real work she's ever done.''

She looked at him, resting a cheek on her knees. ''You don't like Christine or Jack, do you?''

He laughed shortly. ''Let's be honest, Cami. Just between you and me and the bullfrogs, wouldn't you say that those two people are pretty difficult to like?''

''He's my brother, Linc.''

Linc reached over and gave her shoulder a little squeeze. ''I'm sorry, honey. I know that, although sometimes it's hard to believe.''

''Chris knows you hate Jack, and she's convinced you're going to destroy him before the election.''

There was a small silence. ''How does she think I could do that?''

''She says he has secrets, things that he's done to get where he is that wouldn't go down well with the voters.''

''Not an uncommon predicament among politicians.''

''I told her you wouldn't do such a thing.''

''And did she believe you?''

"I'm not sure."

He turned then, studying her face profiled in the moonlight. "What do you think, Cami?"

She looked at him. "Why would you destroy him? For spite? Revenge? For old time's sake? And then what? Sit back and enjoy watching a man try to pick up the pieces of his shattered life?" She shook her head. "I don't think so. You're not that kind of person. You've had too many personal setbacks in your own life to deliberately inflict pain on anyone, even a man you despise."

He sat up so abruptly that she was startled. "Linc?"

He was shaking his head. "Camille, you're incredible."

"I am?"

"Yeah, you are."

Camille met his look with bewilderment. She sensed the turmoil in him but didn't have a clue as to what had caused it. Was he angry with her? Irritated?

"Do you go around expressing that kind of blind faith in everyone you meet?"

"You know I don't, Linc."

He passed a hand over his face. "Didn't you learn anything from Jack's treachery?"

"Just that even the people you love can hurt you."

Linc drew in a deep breath, letting his gaze roam the purity of her features, the grace and feminine allure of her throat. When he spoke, his tone was low and intense, like a caress, although he didn't touch her. "I'll never hurt you again, Camille, not if I can help it."

"Does that mean you aren't planning something to discredit Jack?"

He was silent for so long that she started to rise. "Wait—" He stopped her with his hand and, after a

second or two, she settled back. "I haven't thanked you
for taking care of Nikki today."

"I thought we went through all that this morning,"
she said with a trace of exasperation.

"Yeah, but what happened to Maybelle? She's supposed to stay until I get home in the evenings, no matter
how late I am."

"She got a call from her son. I could tell she was
concerned, so I offered to stay with Nikki." With his
eyes on her like that, Camille's whole body seemed too
warm. She shifted uncomfortably. "It was fun...for both
of us."

"Was it?" His tone dropped. "What did you do?"

Camille shrugged. "We made omelets, and then she
had a bath. I read her a story, and she went right to
sleep."

"Omelets?" he repeated.

She looked at him. In the moonlight, his half smile
was a white Cheshire grin, impossible to resist. "Yes,
omelets. What's so funny about that?"

"She's never had anything but scrambled eggs. What
did this gourmet delight have in it?"

Camille leaned back with her hands locked around
one knee, rocking slightly. "You won't believe it."

"I won't?"

"Uh-uh. I let her choose."

He groaned. "Then I can rule out onions, green pep-
pers, mushrooms, cheese, pepperoni, olives—"

She smiled. "You're getting close."

He stared. "Olives?"

"Grapes."

"A grape omelet?"

"With raisins."

"Oh, yeah. A grape and raisin omelet. Sure. That
makes all the difference."

She gave him a quick, sideways glance. Their eyes met. A second or two passed and then, simultaneously, they both laughed. The sound rang out over the water, uplifting and free.

After a minute, Linc lay back flat on the grass, his hands behind his head. "God, that felt good."

"What? A good laugh?"

"Yeah."

Still smiling, she lifted one shoulder. "To me, too. I've had a terrible day."

His smile disappeared. "I hope Nikki—"

"No, Nikki was the only good thing."

Around them, the sounds of night seemed to close in, inviting intimacy. Camille plucked a leaf from a drooping willow switch. She gave him a soft smile. "I don't think I've told you this before," she said, idly tapping her mouth with the leaf. "Nikki is a wonderful child, bright and beautiful. You're very lucky."

He was silent. Again she sensed the turbulence within him. When he did speak, his voice was low. "Thank you." He snapped another twig between his fingers. "I don't feel as though I deserve her. Her mother—"

Camille tossed the leaf aside and wrapped her arms around her knees. She didn't want to hear about the woman who'd given birth to Linc's child. She turned from him, fixing her eyes on the white fence line that separated the Twin Willows.

"Joanna wanted a divorce."

His words fell into the silent night with the same effect as the stone Linc had tossed into the pond. Whatever her thoughts about the perfection of his marriage to Joanna, his statement destroyed them.

"It was all my fault," he said, his gaze vague, as if fixed on another time and place. "She wanted a home and family and so did I. At the time, I thought it was enough. She was a nice person, attractive, kind, intelligent. But those are the traits you look for in a friend, not the woman you marry.'' He looked at Camille. ''There has to be something else, call it chemistry, that special something, I don't know. Whatever it was, it just wasn't there between us. And Joanna sensed it. She felt...we both felt that having a child might make a difference. It didn't.''

He shifted a little closer to Camille. ''I knew that the moment I held Nikki in the hospital. I felt almost overwhelmed with love for that tiny baby girl. It was as though a door in my heart that had been closed was suddenly thrown open. I'd never been able to open that door to Joanna. She needed a man who could give her that, who could love her as she deserved to be loved.''

His gaze fell to his hands, and Camille had a chance to study him. With his dark head bent and his voice speaking of failure, he appeared vulnerable, weighed down with guilt and defeat. She pushed the thought aside. Linc, vulnerable? It must be the moonlight playing tricks.

He glanced up, meeting her eyes. ''Then she died suddenly, violently. Can you understand how I felt?''

Camille stared beyond him to the elegant outlines of Willow Wind. Did she understand failure? Guilt? The ceaseless searching of the heart in the midnight hours? Yes, oh, yes. She understood perfectly.

''If she loved you,'' Camille said softly, wanting to offer him some small comfort, ''she would want you to put it behind you and go on with your life. She wouldn't want her memory to be a burden.''

With her own words came a sudden flash of insight. Pearce wouldn't want his memory to bring her pain, either. With all their problems, he had understood her, loved her. He wouldn't want her crippled with guilt. He would want her to be happy.

Linc was still for a long time. She felt his eyes on her. Heat rose in instant response, and her heartbeat accelerated into a quick, uneven tempo. She lifted her chin. It was time to leave. Past time. But her limbs didn't seem willing. It was the night and the moonlight and the echoes of things they'd shared back when they were both different people. Altogether, they wove a spell that defied good sense.

"Camille?"

She heard him move, felt the heat of him, sensed him crowding her. She closed her eyes for a timeless second and then opened them. He was close, so close, but still she didn't turn. She felt the caress of his breath on her cheek. Suddenly, the memory of their kiss that morning was vivid in her mind.

His hand went to her jaw as he leaned forward and touched his mouth to her temple. "Is this wrong, Camille?"

Her whole body began to tremble, yielding to him. "I don't know." She frowned, pushing away thoughts of Pearce and Joanna. Her mind was cloudy with desire, as though she'd taken a heady drug, one that made her body liquid and pliant, ready for loving. Dear heaven, how long had it been since she'd felt this way?

His hand slipped into her hair and then grasped a silky handful, holding her head tight against him. "If this is wrong," he said in a ragged voice, his lips at her mouth, "then I'm damned forever. I want you and I'm tired of fighting it, Camille."

"Yes," she said, turning and putting her arms around his neck. Pulling her close, he covered her mouth with his and she was lost.

Nothing had prepared her for the fierce rush of emotion that welled up to consume her as they fell back onto the thick, lush grass. Her senses exploded in an orgy of discovery, as she reveled in the feel of him, the taste and the smell and sheer male strength of him. From somewhere deep inside herself, she sensed his hunger, and it touched the part of her that had gone untapped and waiting for so long. Whatever caution she'd felt only moments before fell away before the intensity of the emotions that coursed wildly through her.

"I want you. I want this," he told her, covering her with quick, openmouthed kisses all over her face, her throat, her hair. His hands were everywhere, cradling her face, molding her shoulders, gliding over the soft contours of her breasts, lower to the line of her hips, cupping her round bottom tight against him.

He groaned, pushing his pelvis into the heated flesh between her thighs. "I've waited so long. Too long."

Hot, feverish needs clamored inside her, drove her hands to fumble at the buttons of his shirt, to pull at it until she had his shoulders bare. With a frustrated sound, he shrugged it away, helping her. At the first touch of his skin, damp and rough with a heavy growth of hair, her fingers curled greedily. He sucked in air harshly at the pure pleasure of her touch. A fire storm of pleasure. How did she know that? But she did. She *did*. It was instinctive, coming from some deep wellspring of feminine knowledge. For her, it was liberating knowledge. After living for years in a passionless marriage, it was glorious to know that she could trigger deep, elemental desire in a man. This man.

She leaned back to look at him, then brushed kisses over his collarbone and into the hollow at his throat while her fingers buried themselves in the dark hair on his chest. Blood and heat raced through her veins, urging her to do things she'd never done before. He was beautiful and he smelled good, felt good, tasted good. She blew softly on a flat nipple, smiling when it contracted, kissing it slowly, erotically, enjoying the rough sound of his breathing.

He caught her head and kissed her hard on the mouth. "My turn," he told her in a voice made husky by emotion and arousal. His hands went to the bottom of her T-shirt. "I want to see you, too."

She lifted herself slightly, helping him take it off, her gaze fixed on the taut, moonlit planes of his face as he unsnapped her bra and slipped the straps from her shoulders. Her breasts felt tight and heavy. When they sprang free, he paused. For a second, she thought about covering herself. But something about Linc, his stillness, stopped her.

"Camille..." He closed his eyes and drew in a deep, unsteady breath. Bending, cupping both breasts with his hands, he softly kissed one and then the other. With a smothered moan, he closed his mouth over one aroused tip and drew an answering sound from Camille, half pleasure, half pain. It was as though a sensual cord linked her breast to the deepest part of her womanhood. With every tug he made, desire quivered, intensified, ached.

Whispering her name and endearments, Linc ventured lower with his kisses, pulling at the elastic waist of her shorts and drawing her panties down at the same time. He found the soft core of her and she cried out, writhing and digging her fingers into soft, grassy earth. With a gruff inarticulate sound from deep in his throat, he began a sweet, rhythmic massage that drove her into a mindless, hot realm of sensation and then suddenly catapulted her into climax.

She fell back, gasping, her body thrumming. Linc caught her close against him, murmuring a mixture of

erotic words and gentle reassurance, letting her bury her
face in his chest. His skin was hot, and he was breathing
as though he'd run a marathon. Denied satisfaction, his
body was drawn as tight as steel wire. Against her thigh,
she could feel his aroused manhood as hard as the
ground they lay on. Beneath her fingers, his muscles
were bunched and quivering. He had been every bit as
aroused as she. Still, he was stroking her hair, bringing
her down with a sensitivity that made tears spring to her
eyes and thicken her throat.

"You didn't…I mean, we still haven't—"

He released a painful burst of laughter. "Tell me
about it," he said in a fervent tone.

"I'm sorry." She tried to push back to get a look at
his face, but he held her head against his chest with one
hand. "It can't have been very good for you," she said,
genuinely distressed. "I don't know what happened. I've
never—"

"Oh, yes, you have ever," he told her. "In this same
place, at about this same hour, about seventeen years
ago."

"We were just kids then!"

"You were a kid, Camille. I was old enough to know
better, and look what happened. I wasn't prepared then
and I wasn't prepared tonight." He laughed shortly. "Of
course, I didn't think of that until it was too late."

It was a good reason for stopping, she thought. The
best. And yet… Why did she have this feeling that there
was something else? That he had some other reason for
calling a halt? He had been as aroused as she. She hadn't
imagined that. She supposed she should be glad he was
the kind of man who remembered to take care even in
the throes of passion. Heaven knows, she certainly
hadn't. Suddenly chagrined, she caught up her T-shirt.
No one else had ever had that effect on her. Only Linc.

"What *were* you thinking?" she asked.

"Thinking?" Linc laughed again, softly this time, his thoughts focused on his aching, strung-out body. "How good you felt. How good you made me feel. How great it would be to take those feelings all the way."

"It's been a while for you?"

With a frown, he thought of Joanna and the night she'd demanded a divorce. It had been three months before she died, and they hadn't shared a bed since that night. He hadn't felt enough interest in any woman since then to want to go to bed with her. Until Camille. "Yeah, it's been a while."

"For me, too."

He was silent, debating the wisdom of asking what he wanted to know. But just as he'd been unable to keep his hands off Camille tonight, he was unable to keep himself from asking. "How long has it been, Camille?"

"Three years."

His silence now stemmed from shock. Had they been one of those couples who didn't need sex? No, that couldn't be. At least, not for Camille—she'd gone up like a firecracker. Had Pearce been impotent?

She sat up suddenly, fumbling with her T-shirt. "I suppose this was inevitable."

Linc propped his weight on one elbow, watching her shimmy into her clothes. He shifted to ease the steady throbbing in his groin. "What was inevitable, Cami?"

She paused and looked at him. "This." She waved a hand that took in the pond, the leafy glade, the two of them. "Us. Just tonight I was telling myself I was wiser and older, that I'd have enough sense to avoid a situation like this.

"The problem is…" She waved a hand helplessly, her face turned from him. "It's like you said, I'd forgotten those good feelings, the pleasure, the heat, the hunger...."

"Camille—"

"Forgotten how easy it is to get carried away." She laughed softly, ruefully. "Must be the full moon."

"It's not the moon."

Even in the dark, he sensed the intensity of the look she gave him. "Then what is it? I noticed you managed to stay in control."

He turned his face away. "I told you, I behaved like a fool once. I...care for you too much to take another chance like that again."

"Well..." She cleared her throat. "It makes me feel a little selfish." Her hand fluttered as she laughed again, the sound soft and husky. "But not so much so that I'd want to take it back."

"I'm glad." He chuckled, too, softly. "That means I'm the only fool out here tonight." When she made a faint, inarticulate noise, he reached over and caught her chin in his fingers. "I don't want you to have any regrets, Camille. I'm not denying I feel a little frustrated, but we're not kids any longer. I'll survive. Hell, it was wonderful. You're not the only one who tapped into some long-ago memories. When you climaxed, I felt about ten feet tall. A lot like that first time—" He stopped. That recollection was already a little too vivid tonight. "Anyway, I don't want you to be sorry. I can handle a little frustration."

At least he hoped he could. His expression impassive, he watched her resume dressing, her face still soft in the aftermath of passion. Just as well she didn't know that there was nothing he wanted more than to pick up right where they'd stopped. She had been so hot and soft and yielding. He ached to just reach out, the hell with scruples. The hell with condoms.

She looked up from fastening her shorts. "You know something?"

"What?"

"This was really good for me."

He stared.

She laughed. "No, no. Not in the sense you're thinking. What I meant was..." She stared beyond him as though gathering the courage to speak her mind. Her eyes came back to his. "I don't want to talk about my relationship with Pearce, because it's over. He's gone and he was my dearest friend in the world. But for such a long time, I haven't felt—" she glanced at him, then quickly away "—sexual. Since long before Pearce died. I'd even begun to wonder if I'd ever experience anything like that again." She shot him another shy look. "At least I can put that fear to rest."

"Camille..." His voice husky, he touched her cheek. "That's the craziest thing I ever heard."

"What? That I haven't had much of a sex life for a long time?"

"No, that you'd doubt your sexuality. You're a beautiful, sensual woman, but you're also loyal and constant. With Pearce as ill as he was, I don't see how things could have been much different. I think you probably suppressed all those feelings until now, but they're still there. Take it from me."

"Well—"

"You're still the sexiest woman I know." Looking down at her, all he could see were the dark crescents of her lashes on her cheeks. But she was smiling. He felt it.

"Well, it's nice to feel sexy." She lifted her eyes to his. "Thank you."

For a moment, he was trapped in her gaze. The words to reassure her had come easily to him. The idea that

Camille was less than womanly, sensual, wholly feminine was preposterous. She was everything a woman should be. Everything he'd looked for in a woman from the moment he'd left her all those years ago. Suddenly, his plan to destroy Jack seemed stupid and smallminded. What if Camille was somehow caught in the cross fire? He didn't want to cause her pain again, ever.

"I need to go now," she said softly. "It's late."

"I know. Thanks again for watching Nikki." He pulled his shirt over his head and caught her arm to help her over a tangle of roots. As they made their way out of the glade, he released her to reach up and part the willow branches. The sounds of the summer night surrounded them—crickets and cicadas, bullfrogs and mourning doves—sounds that usually comforted him, soothed him. Camille's thigh brushed his, renewing the ache of unsatisfied desire.

"Tomorrow we're defoliating," he told her, needing to break the silence. "I expect the pilot at dawn."

"I hadn't realized it was time for that."

"Yeah, it is. Probably take several days." He looked up at the sky. "Let's hope the weather holds."

They had reached the edge of the lane that led to Camille's front door. "I'll wait here," he told her. "Be sure to lock up."

"I will." She hesitated, not looking at him. In the moonlight, her dark hair had a silvery sheen. And her face…

She seemed vulnerable and more beautiful than ever, everything about her still soft and blurry on the edges, her eyes dark, dreamy. Renewed desire tore through him.

"Good night," he said. Even to his own ears, he sounded abrupt.

With a final quick look at him, she murmured a goodnight and slipped inside.

Still wrestling with emotion and his own torment, he stood without moving after the door closed behind her. For a minute back there in the grassy glade, at peace with the night and with Camille, soft and willing, in his arms, he'd felt almost whole again. And overlying all had been his sense of possessiveness, a wholly male sense of ownership. Camille was his.

But then his conscience rose sharply, taking the edge off his pleasure. Camille might well hate him when she found out what he planned for Jack. But, God help him, he'd come too far. It had to be this way. But could he engineer Jack's downfall and still have Camille, too?

He turned and started swiftly across the yard. Bourbon. That was what he needed. A good, stiff shot of bourbon. A double. He kicked at a green pecan that had fallen onto the path from a limb high above. The best thing to do was to keep away from Camille. Forget that he'd sensed in her the same deep needs that bedeviled him. Overhead, the full moon mocked him. As he watched, a distant star flared briefly in the western sky and then fell into oblivion.

Denying his deepest needs was nothing new.

CHAPTER TEN

DEFOLIATING THE CROPS was hot, dusty, nasty work. During the week set aside for it, Linc worked from early morning until darkness made it unsafe for the crop duster to fly. The long hours and hectic schedule provided a convenient excuse to avoid Camille, and he grabbed it. The truth was that after Camille had expressed such blind faith in his integrity, no matter how he attempted to justify himself, he felt lower than a weasel for what he planned to do to Jack Keating.

At night he fell into bed, slept hard for a couple of hours and then, tormented by erotic fantasies of Camille, tossed and turned until dawn broke and he could finally get up. By the end of the week, he was hollow-eyed and had dropped ten pounds. The irony of his situation would have been funny if he'd had any sense of humor left. His desire for Camille was once forbidden because of Jack's lies. Now she was forbidden to him by obstacles he'd made himself.

By Friday, his need to see her was so compelling that he finally collared his foreman, Rufus Johnson, a big black giant of a man, and instructed him to give the hands the rest of the day off. Then, leaving the keys to the heavy equipment with Rufus, he headed home to Kate's Cottage for a shower, the first one he'd taken before eleven p.m. in a week.

Maybelle gave him a surprised look when he told her

she needn't make the drive into town to get Nikki. He
was past making excuses to himself. He admitted flat
out that he was hungry just for the sight of Camille.
What he would say to her, he wasn't sure.

He was on his way out when Maybelle came out of
the kitchen to tell him that a package had arrived. His
eyes went to the distinctive red and white envelope lying
on the table near the front door. He knew what it was
instantly. Picking it up, he turned it over and studied the
return address. He held it a moment as though weighing
it mentally. Then, almost reluctantly, he slipped a thumb
under the flap and broke the seal. Tilting the envelope,
he pulled out a sheaf of papers and briefly scanned the
top page. It was exactly what he'd expected. With Maybelle watching curiously, he tucked everything back into
the envelope, reached for his hat on the rack beside the
door and stepped out into midafternoon sunshine.

Crossing the yard, unmindful of both the heat and
Maybelle's curiosity, he headed for the Bronco. Everything had seemed so simple a few years back when
Pearce had first approached him for financial help. Then
Pearce had died, and fate had practically handed him the
means to destroy Jack. It had been so simple, so easy
that he had focused only on the satisfaction it would give
him to see a man like Jack brought to his knees. Camille
was a complication he hadn't counted on. With her in
the picture, there was no satisfaction. Instead, he felt like
a man about to make a world-class mistake. He felt
guilty. As guilty as sin. He turned onto the highway and
shifted the truck into a passing gear. The last thing he
needed in his life was more guilt.

Sometimes he thought he had cornered the market on
guilt.

Easing off the gas, he ticked off the list in his mind—

his abject failure as a husband, his shortcomings as a father, his empty marriage. Together they were grounds for a lifetime of guilt. But when he added his desertion of Camille, pregnant and seventeen, all those years ago, it tipped the scales beyond the limits of decency. Would any of it have happened if Jack Keating hadn't lied? He rubbed a hand over his face, and with the sting of fatigue behind his eyes, he once again experienced the frustration and pain and bitter anger of that time. And with it, like a bad habit, rose a renewed lust for revenge. He had come back to Blossom to make Jack pay. And pay he would.

STANDING at her office window, Camille watched the children, marveling at their energy in the heat. She'd been so careful when selecting a site for Sunny Day. One of the main reasons she'd chosen this one was that two huge sycamores shaded the grounds in the summer. Now she wondered if kids ever noticed heat, even when it soared in the upper nineties.

Camille put a hand on her stomach. Maybe if she'd had a child of her own, she would have known things like that. Maybe—

Jess walked into her office, a letter in her hand.

"We heard from the wholesaler today about that playground equipment we ordered. It's going to be delayed another four weeks," Jess said, waving the letter at Camille's back.

"This is the third delay, Camille," Jess complained. "At this rate, we'll be halfway through the new semester before it's in place."

Camille's eyes strayed to the jelly jar on the windowsill that held a sweet potato in water. A few scraggly green leaves had come forth, and with a little luck, might possibly survive. With one finger, she touched a struggling shoot. It was Nikki's garden project. She knew she showed blatant partiality to Linc's child, but she didn't seem able to help herself.

"Camille?"

Just as she wasn't able to help the partiality she felt toward the man himself.

"They're upping the price," Jess drawled from behind her. "It's ten thousand dollars."

From the window, Camille watched Nikki shyly and silently refuse as Tracey tried to pull her into a boisterous game with half a dozen other little girls. Although she liked Tracey and seemed to love Sunny Day, Nikki had yet to say a word to her classmates. She would only speak to Camille when they were alone. That was the reason she spent so much time with Nikki, Camille told herself. Nikki needed her, needed the one-on-one attention. She'd considered the possibility that Nikki might be substituting her, Camille, for her mother, but even if that were true, she didn't see what she could do about it now. She refused to think about the time when Linc would move on, taking Nikki.

"You don't have a problem with that?"

"Hmm."

"Ten thousand dollars for a jungle gym?"

"Yes, all right."

At Jess's loud sigh, Camille turned. "What?"

Jess studied her for a moment. "Never mind. It'll keep." She crossed the threshold of the office and sat down in a chair across from Camille's desk. "What's wrong, Camille?"

"Wrong?" Did it show? Camille wondered. Since Linc had come back to town and Nikki had become a part of her life, she felt as though her world had been turned upside down. Could Jess see it?

"Something's been on your mind for several days," Jess told her. "You want to talk about it?"

Moving away from the window, Camille gave a helpless laugh. "I'm so mixed up that I wouldn't know where to begin, Jess," she said, sinking down in the chair behind her desk.

"It's Linc, of course. And Nikki."

She winced, her eyes sweeping the ceiling. It *was* obvious.

"You're in love with him."

Camille looked up sharply. "No! I—" She shook her head. "At least, I don't think…"

"Camille, Camille…" Jess's tone was soft with understanding. "Let's have a little honesty here, okay? You light up like a Roman candle when the man appears. If Maybelle Franklin picks Nikki up in the afternoons instead of Linc, you look so pitiful I want to offer you a lollipop to make you smile again. As for Nikki, you should be on my end watching the two of you together."

Camille dropped her head into her hands. "Oh, Lord."

"It's hard to hide love."

Love? Camille sprang up from the chair. She'd felt this way about Linc seventeen years ago, and the cost had been dear. Was she a fool to flirt with that kind of danger again?

"Anyway," Jess was saying, "why would you want to hide? It's not as though you don't know Linc. The two of you have a lot of history. If you still feel that way about the man—and the feeling's mutual—then why in the world would you even hesitate?"

"I'm not in love with him, Jess," Camille said firmly.

"Oh? What is it, then?"

Camille shook her head, lifting her shoulders helplessly. "It's...it's...I don't know. It's passion, sexual attraction."

Jess nodded with understanding. "I wondered if it had gone that far."

"It hasn't! I mean, we haven't..." As clearly as though it were flashing on a screen in front of her, Camille saw herself and Linc cocooned beneath dark, leafy willows at the pond. Linc's body was curved to hers, his hands seeking her most intimate places, doing the most intimate things. She glanced up to find Jess watching her.

"I'll just say one thing," Jess remarked, openly amused. "If I were having this discussion with one of my teenagers, I would be feeling distinctly uneasy. Blushing like that gives Jennifer away every time."

"I haven't been to bed with him, Jess."

A moment passed while they stared at each other. "You want my advice?" Jess asked, settling back in the chair.

"I can see I'm going to get it anyway."

"Do it."

Camille rubbed her temple with unsteady fingers. "It's not so simple."

"How so?"

"I don't think he wants to go to bed with me."

Jess snorted in disbelief.

"It's true." Camille turned back to stare out the window, thinking of the night at the pond. "We were together a few nights ago. He kissed me." She sent Jess a quick, embarrassed look. "It was...wonderful. I felt like Rip van Winkle waking up, Jess. I had forgotten how passion felt." Looking out the window, her expression became unfocused, dreamy. "How intense and wild and...and...just plain wonderful it felt."

"That's understandable. It's been a long time for you."

"No, you don't understand. I never felt that way with Pearce."

Jess was silent.

"He must think I'm some love-starved, middle-aged crazy person," Camille murmured, staring unseeingly out the window.

"You're a normal, healthy woman in her prime," Jess put in firmly. "I'd be more concerned if you didn't respond to a man like Linc, especially after years of coping in a dysfunctional marriage. Pearce was sick for a long time, Camille. You were a good, faithful wife. Give yourself permission to live again."

A good, faithful wife. The words sent a dart of pain through her heart. In all the years she'd been married to Pearce, she had never looked at another man. But suddenly she realized it wasn't because of her devotion to Pearce. It was because she'd never stopped loving Linc. If he had come back into her life while Pearce was still alive... In a flash of insight, the truth came to her. If Linc had come back to Blossom, she would probably have fallen back into his arms as fast and easily as she'd fallen this time. She closed her eyes and drew a deep breath. It wasn't something she felt good about. It just...was.

Behind her, Jess smiled softly. "But you don't love him."

Staring through the window, Camille's gaze fell on Nikki's dark curls, and pain and loss swept through her. "I can't love him, Jess. For some reason—I don't know what it is—I just get the impression that he doesn't want to get involved with me again.''

"Then why did he kiss you? Why doesn't he simply do the job he claims he came to do and avoid sticky personal situations with the woman he used to love?''

Mystified, Camille lifted her shoulders. "There is this…attraction between us, but he still always manages not to lose control. Unlike me.'' She gave a weak little laugh. "All he has to do is touch me and I'm lost, Jess. But not Linc.'' She frowned, searching for answers. "He goes to a certain point and then it's almost as though something, some internal alarm or something, goes off to bring him to his senses.''

"Maybe if you asked him, he'd explain.''

"He did, sort of. He talked a little about his marriage, his relationship with his wife. Joanna was unhappy, he told me. She'd asked for a divorce, but before she could file, she was killed. He feels guilty, I think.'' She paused. "But there's something else, too. I feel it, but I don't know what it is.''

"Sounds like both of you have some emotional baggage that needs to be dealt with before you can make any long-term commitments,'' Jess said. "But that doesn't mean you can't enjoy getting to know each other again.''

"Even if I wanted to, that might be a problem,'' she said. "Linc is avoiding me. I haven't seen him since that night when we talked. He's been working from dawn until long after dark. Haven't you noticed it's Maybelle who drives Nikki to school and picks her up? It's never Linc.''

Jess folded the invoices she held and stood up. "Well, as the old saying around here goes, maybe he's taking some cogitating time.''

Camille smiled, almost. Maybe. And maybe that was a good thing. There was no denying that she was still attracted to Linc, but she was not the inexperienced, idealistic teenager she'd been years ago. If it came to an affair with Linc, her eyes would be wide open. Linc's reluctance bothered her. She wanted some answers. Besides, she was human enough to want to feel that he found her irresistible.

She turned to gaze out the window again, wondering if, put to the test, she would be able to keep her head. When she was away from Linc, she had a firm grip on all the reasons she should keep him at arm's length. But when she saw him, or at night when she lay wide awake, her body restless and yearning, something more powerful seemed to take over. She—

A shrill scream scattered her thoughts. Startled, she exchanged a look with Jess, and then both women dashed for the door. Classes were over for the day, and some of the children had already been picked up. Those who were still waiting were crowded around the big, colorful plastic cube, where the screams were coming from.

As Camille and Jess hurried forward, the childish screams seemed to escalate. Spotting her mother, Tracey broke away from the group and ran toward them, her small face white with distress. "It's Nikki! It's Nikki! Hurry, she's hurt."

Camille's heart stopped and then lurched to life again in a painful, frantic rhythm. In a vivid flash, she pictured Nikki hurt and bleeding, imagined Linc crushed with another tragedy. This one, he wouldn't be able to bear.

Two aides, college girls Camille had hired for the summer, were crouched at the small entrance to the cube. One looked up, her face relieved as Camille approached. She moved aside.

"Oh, Ms. Wyatt, thank heavens. We didn't know what to do. She won't let us touch her."

"What happened?"

"We don't know. She just started screaming when Joey—''

Abruptly, Nikki quieted.

Camille, her hand at her heart, looked inside the cube. For a second, the world tilted, and little pinpoints of light flitted in and out on the edge of her vision. Nikki was curled in the far corner, her small dark head buried in her lap, her arms wrapped tightly around herself. There was blood everywhere, on the sides of the cube, on the toys that littered the floor, on the bedraggled blue bunny rabbit hanging half in, half out of the window. On Nikki. On her hands and clothes. On her small pink Reeboks.

"Oh, Lord, Nikki." Frantically, Camille reached for the small figure, but couldn't quite make contact. Where was the wound? *Oh, God. Please, please don't let it be serious.*

But all that blood!

Swallowing, Camille backed away and looked around wildly. "I can't reach her," she told Jess. "We'll have to pull off the top of the cube."

"I told Joey not to do that," Tracey said with an air of righteous indignation. "He's in trouble now, I bet."

Camille stood up and clawed at the plastic piece that formed the cube's top. With a desperate yank, she tore it from its groove and flung it aside. With the top piece off, the side came away easily. Camille dropped to her knees beside Nikki, unconsciously whispering reassurance and endearments. Without looking up, Nikki launched herself into Camille's arms, burrowing deeply and surely into the soft security of her embrace.

It was not the teacher in Camille that responded. Her feeling was wholly maternal, a desperate need to comfort and reassure, to do what was necessary to overcome whatever threatened. And overriding all, a fierce, instinctive fear for Nikki. Linc's child. Her—

She glanced down in surprise when she felt the sticky wetness on Nikki's skin.

"What is it? What's wrong?" Linc's voice suddenly cut through the shocked crowd like a gunshot.

Looking up, dazed, Camille met his eyes. "Linc, it's—"

She didn't get a chance to finish. Linc realized suddenly that it was Nikki in her arms, Nikki drenched with blood. He called his daughter's name hoarsely, putting out a hand to brace himself on the bright pink side of the cube that was still standing.

"Joey's gonna get in big trouble for this." Tracey's knowing whisper carried to every ear in the stark silence.

Her eyes locked with Linc's, Camille held out a red-smeared palm. "It's okay," she said unsteadily. "It's paint."

"What?" he croaked.

"Paint." She shook her head in pained disbelief. "It's red finger paint. It's not blood. Nikki's not hurt."

"God. Oh, God." She saw the shudder that ran through him, watched him take off his hat and push shaky fingers through his hair. And then, flinging his hat aside, he dropped to his haunches, his hand on Nikki's head, cradled on Camille's bosom. His eyes held a bright sheen as he looked at his hand, smeared with the obscene color of blood.

Around them, Jess began to muster order in the wide-eyed children. As she nudged her own daughter away, Tracey dodged the hand at her shoulder to get in a final word to her best friend. "I'm gonna talk to my mother and get Joey 'spelled for this, Nikki. Don't you worry. He won't ever get to play a trick on any—"

"Tracey!" In a tone she rarely used, Jess quelled Tracey's threat. With her free hand, she caught the mischievous Joey by the upper arm and marched both youngsters away from the scene.

"I don't know what happened," Camille whispered, looking into Linc's eyes. Fear had stolen the color from her face. Her mouth was unsteady. It didn't take a psychologist to interpret Nikki's reaction. With one hand, she stroked the small, dark head, wondering if Linc would take her out of Sunny Day.

"It was just a childish prank," Linc said.

Camille swallowed to ease the tightness in her throat. Looking down, she tried to lift Nikki's chin. "Nikki, it's okay, honey, it's okay."

Bending his head, Linc found his daughter's chin and lifted it a tiny bit. "Nikki, punkin, look at Daddy."

Nikki shook her head, her eyes squeezed tight "I don't want to see any red stuff."

Camille drew in a deep breath, hoping she was doing the right thing. "This isn't blood, Nikki," Camille told her gently. "This is paint. The same finger paint you used just this afternoon to paint that pretty picture of Firefly."

"Firefly's not red. She's brown."

"No, but Tracey used red for those flowers in her picture. Remember?"

"I don't like red."

"Lots of nice things are red."

"Blood is not nice."

"But we can't live without the blood that is inside us," Camille pointed out in a loving voice. "It makes us warm and soft. It makes our arms and legs work. It makes our hearts beat. Here, feel it." Moving gently, she placed Nikki's hand in the center of her small chest. "Now feel mine." She held the tiny hand over her own heart. "Now feel Daddy's."

For a long moment, Nikki let her hand rest on Linc's chest. Without lifting her head, she said, "I saw a lot of blood on my mommy."

Camille's heart turned over. "I know, sweetheart. That was a bad thing. I'm sorry such a bad thing happened."

Nikki clutched a fistful of Linc's shirt. "I don't want a bad thing to ever happen to my daddy."

Camille gave Linc one quick, intense look. "Your daddy knows that, Nikki, so he's always extra careful."

Nikki finally stirred and lifted her head. She looked at Camille. "I don't want a bad thing to happen to you either, Camille."

Her heart full, Camille smiled softly and touched Nikki's baby-soft cheek. "I'll be careful, too, sweetheart."

After a moment of solemn thought, Nikki nodded. "Can we go home now?"

"Yeah." Linc put his hands under Camille's elbows, helping her and his daughter to their feet. Camille bent to straighten Nikki's shirt and shorts, frowning with concern at the big, red blotches that desecrated the front of the child's outfit.

"Tell Maybelle to use cold water when she washes Nikki's things," she told Linc. Her frown deepened as she took in the damage to the pink Reeboks. "As for her shoes, I just hope—"

Nikki placed a hand on Camille's shoulder. "Can you come, too, Camille?"

Camille shot one quick look up at Linc and found him watching her with an intensity that made heat bloom inside her.

"Can you come, too, Camille?" he repeated.

"Oh, I…" She made a vague gesture to her car parked behind her. "My car…"

"I'll see to your car later."

"Can I talk now?" Tracey, her hands on her hips, stood peering at them intently.

"What is it, Tracey?" Camille asked.

"My mama told me I could help Nikki wash off," Tracey said. "We're gonna use the water hose."

"I can't," Nikki said, speaking directly to Tracey. "I'm going home with my daddy and Camille, and *they're* gonna wash me off with the hose." She turned to Linc. "Huh, Daddy? Isn't that so?"

Camille and Linc exchanged startled looks. For weeks, they'd waited for Nikki to begin talking naturally. She still hadn't spoken to anyone except Linc or Camille. She had mingled happily with the other children, especially Tracey and Joey, entering into almost every phase of play, but until this moment, she had not said a word.

"Aren't you gonna wash me with the hose, Daddy?" Nikki demanded impatiently.

Linc laughed, a little unsteadily at first. "Yeah, punkin," he told his small daughter. And then the sound grew stronger, richer. Heartfelt. "You bet."

"And Camille's gonna help, huh?"

He caught Camille's hand and squeezed it, hard, almost losing himself in the too-bright morning-glory blue of her eyes. "Yeah, Camille's gonna help."

CHAPTER ELEVEN

"SHE'S GOING TO BE okay now, isn't she?"

Camille heard the anxious note in Linc's voice and sympathized, wishing she were truly an expert. Wishing that she could tell him unequivocally that the hideous experience that had stolen Nikki's voice was fading into the mists of the little girl's memory and would never cause her another moment of distress.

"I don't know, Linc." Standing at the sink in his kitchen, she rinsed the glass that had held Nikki's milk and then placed it in the dishwasher. "I think the fact that she's beginning to talk is surely a good sign. However, I'm not an expert."

He moved closer. Without looking, she felt the heat and the masculine power that seemed so much a part of him, and her pulse quickened in response. "You're expert enough for me," he said, touching her hair. "And for Nikki, too."

"I don't know about that," she said, her voice husky. "If I'd been a true professional, I wouldn't have panicked when I found one of my students covered with red finger paint."

"You didn't panic. You were scared and it showed." He reached out and stroked the sensitive spot beneath her ear. "I'd rather have a warm and caring woman run to the aid of my child than a coolheaded professional."

Camille laughed, but it came out shakily. "Not if

she'd broken her arm, you wouldn't, or if that had been real blood.''

''But it wasn't, thank God.''

Clutching the sponge in one hand and the handle for the water in another, Camille warned herself to keep her head. She was so susceptible to anything Linc did that called up the feelings they'd once shared; she couldn't trust herself when he got that sound in his voice. And if she looked at him, she would find a look in his eyes that would turn her knees to jelly.

She fought an urge to tilt her head. There was a place between her shoulder and neck that only Linc knew. When he stroked it, kissed it, it felt so good. Everything he did to her felt good. As if reading her thoughts, he gently kneaded the tense muscles in her neck. She ground her teeth to keep from moaning.

What was she doing here still? she asked herself in disgust. Why had she stayed after cleaning Nikki up? Why had she allowed herself to be persuaded to join father and daughter in the kitchen to fix Nikki's favorite meal? Hot dogs gave her indigestion. Only a handful of potato chips made her gain a pound. Now here she was doing the dishes. As soon as Nikki got out of the bathroom, she was going straight home before she did something dumb.

Linc dropped his hand and leaned against the counter. Crossing his legs, he shoved both hands in his pockets. ''I've missed you,'' he said suddenly, staring at his feet. ''You probably haven't even noticed, but I've gone out of my way for days to avoid you.''

''I know.'' She wrung the water from the sponge.

''I thought if I didn't see you, I wouldn't think about you.'' He shook his head, his gaze still fixed on the floor. ''It didn't work. I dreamed about you instead.''

She pictured him in his bed, naked, the covers hot and wrinkled, his long limbs in a sensual sprawl, his skin burnished and satin-slick with sweat. Her mouth went dry.

Beside her, he shifted restlessly, uncrossing his legs. "I haven't had a decent night's sleep since I moved into this damn place."

Good. She was glad to know she wasn't the only one whose nights were hellish.

He turned his head then to see her. "Were your ears burning?"

Not her ears, no. But her body was as sensitized as though she'd entered into a hot, torrid affair. It was a state she'd been in since that renegade kiss under the willows.

"Camille?"

She turned to him then. "What do you want from me, Linc?" she demanded in a low, intense tone.

His eyes dropped to her mouth. "I don't know." He moved a shoulder restlessly. "Nothing. Everything. I really don't know, Camille."

"Is this some kind of game for you? Playing around with the passion between us?" Camille's gaze was steady, accusing. "If I've given you the idea that that's okay, then you'll have to think again. I came with you this afternoon because of Nikki. She asked, so I came. I want to see her well and happy again as much as you do, but that's as far as I'm willing to go. Two times now I've been stupid enough to get caught up in whatever it is you're doing, but I'm not buying into it tonight." She tossed the sponge onto the counter. "I'm going home."

"Wait, Camille—"

"Okay, I'm finished!" Nikki, her face innocently eager, appeared at the kitchen door. She gazed up at the two adults. "Can Camille come in my bedroom and see all my stuff, Daddy?"

"I saw all your stuff just a week ago, Nikki," Camille reminded her.

"Well, then, could you come tuck me in?"

Only the wicked witch could refuse the appeal in those big eyes. Without looking at Linc, Camille took Nikki's hand, and together they left the kitchen.

"It won't be long until I get a kitty," Nikki informed Camille as she crawled between sheets covered in cartoon characters and allowed herself to be tucked in. "Daddy promised."

"Have you got one all picked out?" Camille smoothed a dark, silky curl away from the downy softness of the little girl's cheek.

"No." Nikki frowned sleepily. "Do you know where we can look at lots of kitties? Maybe I should have two." She yawned and snuggled a cheek into Camille's hand. "Maybe a puppy, too."

Camille hid a smile, thinking of Linc saddled with the chore of house-training a puppy. Kittens were less trouble, as he'd doubtless known when caving in to Nikki's plea for a pet.

"Good night, sweetheart," she whispered, bending to drop a kiss on a delicate temple.

"Daddy always says—" another enormous yawn "—goodnight, punkin."

"Shall I call your daddy?"

But Nikki was gone. Clutched in the crook of her arm was her beloved bunny rabbit, still damp and tinted pink in a few places. It hadn't been possible to remove all the red paint, but they'd finally cleaned him up enough to suit Nikki.

Camille rose gently, letting her hand linger a moment

on the small arm flung above Nikki's head, and then, tiptoeing to the door, she turned off the light and left the room.

She stood still a moment in the hall, thinking that if there had been another door, she would simply walk out of Kate's Cottage and go home to Willow Wind. But there wasn't another door and she couldn't get away without at least letting Linc know. Besides, she was puzzled enough by his behavior to want some answers. While alone with Nikki admiring the child's possessions, a part of her had been turning over in her mind some of the things he'd said.

Why had he been avoiding her? He'd admitted being attracted to her, and she'd obviously been willing that night under the willows. With little or no effort, he could have had her. What reason could he have for denying himself? Was it simply that he hadn't been prepared? Or was it the fear of pregnancy that had stopped him? Something told her it wasn't that. She frowned. What else could it be?

And wasn't it for the best anyway? she asked herself, walking slowly down the hall. She wasn't the type of woman who would be satisfied with a lover. At least, not for long. She had her reputation to consider, even in this day and age. Sunny Day was a kindergarten. She catered to families. She influenced children. Whether she liked it or not, her personal life and how she conducted herself mattered.

Still, the attraction between her and Linc was a powerful thing. Just how powerful, she was only beginning to realize. Her sensuality had been awakened after too many years in a sterile marriage. If she hadn't met Linc again, if he hadn't stirred the ashes of desire, then walking away from him would be a lot easier.

At the living room door, she stopped. Bending her head, she rubbed at her temples, remembering something Jess had said. Was she throwing away something worthwhile for the wrong reasons? Even Abigail had cautioned her not to close her heart and her mind to Linc too soon. Should she wait a bit before deciding there was no room in her life for him? She stood still for a moment and then, with a deep, measured breath, went into the room where he waited.

He had turned out the overhead light, leaving on only a multihued Tiffany lamp that bathed the room in a soft, rosy glow. Camille looked around slowly. The furnishings were old-fashioned, mismatched for the most part. An old oak desk took up most of one wall. Kate used to sit there, Camille remembered suddenly, feeling a rush of nostalgia. Directly opposite it was a sofa, and Linc was stretched out on it, his head propped on the arm. He was very still. Moving closer, she realized that he had fallen asleep.

He had been working long hours and not sleeping well lately, disturbed by dreams of her, if he was telling the truth. Fascinated, she stood a moment watching the slow rise and fall of his chest. One arm was thrown over his head, his hand relaxed and curled slightly. The other rested at his belt buckle. The sofa was too short, so one leg was propped against the back, bent at the knee. The other had fallen into a relaxed, open position. His tight jeans accented his amply endowed physique. Camille felt an odd little quiver deep inside, and discovered that she enjoyed looking at him.

Realizing how it would seem if he woke and found her watching him, she looked around to locate her handbag. She spotted it on the floor beside the sofa and bent to pick it up. Just then, Linc made a soft, muffled sound.

He was still asleep, but she could tell that he was dreaming. Not a good dream, either. He moved his head restlessly and frowned. He shifted his legs. The cramped confines of the sofa seemed to add to his agitation.

She knew the hell of a nightmare. Unable to watch his distress, Camille put out a hand to wake him up. The instant she touched him, his hand closed on her wrist. She was bent in an awkward position, and when he pulled, she tumbled against his chest.

His arms went around her, capturing her as easily as though he'd planned everything. He hadn't, though. He wasn't yet awake. That was the only reason she wasn't more forceful in resisting him, she told herself. She turned her head, but he didn't seem to realize she wasn't cooperating. With a groan, he buried his face in her hair, nuzzling, searching. He began to kiss her, erotic, open-mouthed kisses on her temple, her cheek, her ear. Wherever his tongue touched, wherever his hot breath reached, delicious sensation erupted like unchecked electrical charges.

Suddenly he found her mouth. Opening his own over hers, his tongue plunged home, warm, wet, seductive. Camille moaned. His kiss was symbolic of the elemental joining that he'd denied them before. And he would this time, she knew with sinking certainty. Still not fully awake, he'd been in the throes of whatever hell his nightmare had taken him, and she'd stepped unknowingly into that hell with him.

She knew that, the instant he began to regain consciousness. He made a sound, a deep, guttural sound, and tore his mouth from hers. His voice, when he spoke, seemed ripped from his raw throat.

"Joanna…"

Until that moment, Camille's thoughts had been a disjointed jumble of anxiety and sensuality and need. Now pain eclipsed all. Hearing his dead wife's name sent a spear of such sharp anguish through her that she literally cried out.

"What—" Disoriented, Linc tried to push through the dark web of the nightmare. Joanna's cold white face was still etched in stark, macabre detail in his head. She'd been in a coffin. But when he'd reached out and touched her, she was warm. And she smelled like Camille. He'd needed that warmth, that sweet, seductive feeling that came over him when he held Camille. But then, just as he gathered her in his arms, he looked up and saw Jack Keating. Jack was going to take her away from him. The knowledge was heavy, like lead in his chest. Jack would never let him have Camille.

Jack began to laugh and point. Linc looked down at the woman in his arms. It wasn't Camille. It was Joanna. Cold and lifeless. Joanna, dead.

The strange weight on his chest intensified. In the purgatory between wakefulness and sleep, his senses registered everything in clouded confusion. Shaking his head, he realized suddenly that it was Camille, that he still held her. The kiss he'd stolen in his dream had come from Camille.

She struggled fiercely, making soft, vulnerable sounds that might have been sobs or, just as easily, curses. As though she were a flame burning him, he thrust her away, swearing softly. The instant he freed her, she was up and off him. Whipping around, she scooped up her purse, which lay on the floor beside the sofa, and raced for the door.

"Camille, wait!" He stood up.

She fumbled a little at the door, but before he reached her she had managed to jerk it open.

"Camille!" She whipped around as she felt him catch her arm. His hand fell at the fierce look in her eyes, but he blocked the doorway with his sheer size. "Let me—"

"What? Apologize, explain?"

He lifted his shoulders helplessly. "Both, I guess. I was asleep, Camille. I was dreaming. It was—"

She closed her eyes and turned from him. "Believe me, I know you were dreaming, Linc. Now, move, I want out of here."

"No! I mean, don't go yet. It isn't what you think." He looked down suddenly, shaking his head. "It isn't what you think," he repeated in a low tone. "It was a nightmare."

"I'm sorry," she said without sympathy. "Maybe you should try meditating."

"It was about Joanna."

"I caught that much," she said with a harsh laugh.

Her sarcasm was lost on him. He frowned, focusing on a point beyond her shoulder, seeing it all again. "She was dead. Cold and deathly white in a coffin. I touched her. I don't know why. Next thing I knew, she was warm and..." He stopped as his mind cleared, and he looked into Camille's eyes. "She became you, Camille. When I touched her, it was suddenly you."

Camille's anger faded, leaving her in a much more vulnerable state. She wrapped both arms around herself. "Please, just...don't say any more, Linc. It really doesn't matter."

"Suddenly I felt good." His laugh was strained, mystified. "So damn good. And happy. I kissed you. Just...wrapped my arms around you, tight as I could." His tone changed, hardened. "Then Jack appeared. And Joanna reappeared. The dream became a nightmare. That's when I woke up."

She turned from him, saying nothing.

"I know you're furious. I don't blame you. I'm sorry. It's just that—"

"I'm not mad at you, not really. I'm angry with myself. For letting this crazy thing between us turn me into an irrational…I don't know what. Today we were both off balance from Nikki's accident, I knew that. I had already decided to go home, to simply get away from you, when she called out." Her smile was more natural. "I can't resist her any better than I resist you."

"Camille—"

"No, let me say this and then I'm going." She gave a weary sigh. "After Nikki fell asleep, I sat for a minute thinking. Somebody cautioned me about throwing away a second chance for happiness with you. I thought about that. I'm only human, and I like the way you make me feel when we're together. It would be nice just to go with that, see where those feelings take us. Maybe it would be a little crazy, but I've lived so cautiously, so circumspectly for so long that a little craziness seems oddly appealing. I missed one chance at happiness seventeen years ago when I lost my baby. But I've paid my dues, Linc."

Looking beyond him at nothing in particular, she nodded her head slowly. "Yes, I've paid my dues." Her eyes met his again. "So, when I left Nikki's room a few minutes ago, I was halfway convinced, for once, to take a chance."

Linc stood as still as granite. His heart thudded, braced for the kicker. He felt as he used to when a crucial deal was going down and the odds were stacked heavily against him. The sense of impending loss was almost overwhelming. To save his soul, he didn't know why Camille still held that kind of power over him.

"But you know something, Linc? It's you who's holding on to the past. It's you who doesn't really want to take a chance on us. I don't pretend to know anything about interpreting dreams, but one thing about yours seems clear, at least to me. As long as your feelings about your marriage and Joanna go unresolved, you can never be free. Maybe you should ask yourself why."

He watched silently as she walked across the porch and down the steps. As she reached the last one, she turned back. "Let me know when you've worked it all out."

Tortured, he watched her walk across the yard. He wanted to call her back, but the words stuck in his throat. What could he say? Come back and we'll work it out? She didn't know how much there was to work out.

There was no moon. In seconds, she had been swallowed up in the dark. Somebody was out running a string of hounds, and their mournful baying had a lonely, desolate sound. It was a sound that matched Linc's mood. He stepped off the porch and started after her, intending to keep her in sight until she reached her door. He hadn't forgotten what a fuss she'd made that one time he'd insisted on walking her home. She certainly wouldn't want his protection tonight.

At the pond, he stopped. From that point, he was able to see the rest of the way to the lights of Willow Wind. Camille had been walking so fast she had almost reached her front door. It was obvious she wanted to get far from him as quickly as possible. Only her fierce pride had prevented her from running, he suspected. Watching her, knowing she ran from him, was almost more than he could stand.

How in hell had it happened? When she'd taken Nikki in to bed, he'd sat down to wait for her, aware that

having her in his house gave him pleasure. The last thing
he remembered was lying back on the sofa enjoying the
sound of his daughter talking to Camille. Nikki sounded
happy and carefree, the way a child should.

Next thing he knew, he was dreaming. About Joanna.
No, Camille. He groaned, thrusting a hand through his
hair as the full force of what he'd done came to him.
She'd never forgive him.

What on earth made him call Camille by his wife's
name?

"WE GOT A NICE NOTE from Joey's mother."

"Really?" Stretching on tiptoe, Camille pinned the
last colorful autumn leaf to the wall above the black-
board. She stepped back, tilting her head to one side.
"Does that look okay?"

"Fine," Jess said, giving the display a casual glance.
"She apologizes very nicely for Joey's finger-painting
caper and then in the next sentence asks us to try and
place four kittens that they just happen to have."

Camille turned around. "Kittens?"

"Yeah, kittens. Can you beat that? The woman has
some nerve. If another kid caused half the consternation
in class that Joey does, a normal mother would want to
keep a low profile."

"It was just a prank, Jess."

"Hmm."

"Joey's not bad. He's just…creative."

"Well, I hope she wore his creative tail out when he
got home that day."

Camille laughed. "I wouldn't count on it. But I don't
think he'll do it again. Nikki's reaction made more of
an impression on him than a spanking."

"He won't do that again, no," Jess agreed. "I just hope his next idea isn't something worse."

"Me, too. Now what's this about kittens?"

Jess waved the note. "Their mama cat had four kittens, and they're up for grabs. Are you thinking about getting a cat?"

"Not for myself," Camille murmured. Her eyes strayed to Nikki playing in the Sesame Street house with Tracey and—she looked closer—yes, Joey. Nikki would be thrilled to know about Joey's kittens. She wondered if she should—

Even before the thought formed, she dismissed it. She hadn't seen Linc in more than a week. He was apparently as intent on avoiding her as she was on avoiding him. Nikki was delivered and picked up every day by Maybelle Franklin. There were no more casual morning encounters when Camille rode Firefly, because she went in a direction opposite to wherever Linc was likely to be. Even his conscientious business reports on the plantation had ceased. Now, he reported everything in writing. A part of her felt relieved. Another part felt perversely disappointed.

"How old are the kittens?" she heard herself ask.

"Eight weeks," Jess said, eyeing her curiously.

Camille looked over at Nikki again. She drew in a deep breath. "I think I know someone."

CHAPTER TWELVE

LINC WAS STRUGGLING to fit the corner of a fresh sheet on Nikki's bed without disturbing her, when the telephone rang. He looked up, swearing.

"Don't leave me, Daddy." Nikki's voice was thin and weak. Her face was flushed and her eyes heavy with the unfocused look that fever induced.

"I'm not leaving, punkin." He dropped the sheet without finishing the job. "I'll just answer the phone and be right back. Don't try to get up, okay?"

"I think I have to throw up again."

Damn. He scrambled for the plastic trash can that had seen a lot of action since the onset of some kind of intestinal upset an hour before. He was too late. Nikki rolled over weakly and managed to get on her knees before more deep retching racked her small body. Linc held her, feeling helpless and concerned and increasingly worried. She was so tiny, her little frame so fragile beneath his hands. She was so sick. What should he do?

The phone had stopped, but after only a few minutes—which he spent mopping Nikki's face, stripping her again and settling her on a spot on the bed that wasn't soiled—it began again.

Cursing, he threw the washcloth in the direction of the clothes hamper and stalked into the kitchen where the nearest phone was on the wall. "Yeah, hello!"

"Linc?"

His heart jumped. "Camille?"

"Is something wrong, Linc?"

He slumped a little against the wall. "Camille, thank God. I—" He dropped his head, squeezing his eyes closed. "I need...I mean, it's Nikki. She—"

"Is she sick?"

"Yes, she—"

"I'll be right there."

He sent a grateful look heavenward, searching for a way to express what he felt. Before he managed it, he heard a click and then the blankness of an empty line.

"IT SEEMS TO BE a twenty-four-hour bug, and so far, at least half of the kids at Sunny Day have come down with it."

Camille sat in the old-fashioned rocking chair that Linc had dragged into Nikki's room for her. Across the bed, in a straight chair, Linc still bore the strain of having to stand by helplessly and watch his child battle against a vicious but invisible virus that had invaded her system.

"Is the worst over?" Linc asked, his eyes on Nikki.

"Probably."

"Thank God."

Nikki had been resting quietly for more than an hour. She was still pale, but she seemed more normal somehow. Linc wiped a hand over his face. But what did he know about kids, sick or well?

"Don't worry," Camille said softly. "Kids are tough."

He shook his head. "If you could have seen her... It was awful." He looked up suddenly. "Did I remember to thank you? I don't know what I would have done without you."

"I'm glad I was able to help, but you would have done just fine without me." She gave him a smile. "I just happened to call at a crucial moment."

"This is one of the times I feel overwhelmed being a father." His laugh was strained. "If I'd had more experience, maybe I would be better at this. I mean, if I'd spent more time doing the nitty-gritty stuff, like fixing meals, bathing her, choosing her clothes...." He sent her a rueful look. "Unfortunately for her, I didn't. One day I was wrapped up in the demands of my business, and the next thing I knew, I had the full-time responsibility of a four-year-old."

Camille rocked quietly, saying nothing. Suddenly, a thought seemed to strike him.

"That reminds me. You never mentioned why you called."

"Oh, it was just—" she gave an embarrassed shrug "—an impulse. I probably shouldn't have."

"I'm glad you did." His look, capturing hers, was so intimate, so intense that she had to look away. "I was so relieved, I wanted to—" He laughed. "But, you'd probably have slapped my face if I'd tried."

She caught her breath, too vulnerable at the moment to follow up on that. "I called about Nikki's birthday."

"Her birthday?"

"Yes, surely you haven't forgotten?"

He shook his head. "No, no, I haven't forgotten. But what about it?" She wasn't rocking anymore, he noticed. She leaned forward, her face as eager as Nikki's sometimes was. Watching her, he realized just how much he liked seeing her smile. When she was with him, she didn't smile nearly often enough. He'd have to work on that, he decided.

"You've promised her a kitten, haven't you?"

"Yeah, I promised her a kitten."

"I found one."

Catching the sparkle in her eyes, he leaned back. "Oh?"

"Now don't freak out when I tell you who—"

His brows went up. "So long as it's not your brother."

She rolled her eyes. "Hardly. Jack would never have a pet of any kind."

"Better not tell that to the voters."

She made an impatient gesture. "Forget Jack! These kittens—"

His chair legs came down on the floor with a soft thump. "Kittens!" he hissed, so as not to wake Nikki. "Who said anything about more than one?"

She struggled to stifle a laugh. "Okay, okay. But there are two in the litter that are just precious, Linc. Nikki would love them both." She shrugged with feigned disappointment. "But if you can only bring yourself to give a home to one of them, I guess somehow we'll have to choose between them."

"Damn right."

"The tiger-striped one is adorable, but he's male. They're not quite as affectionate or as gentle as females. Now, the little female is a tortoise with lovely markings. She'd be perfect."

"Maybe you should take one," he suggested slyly.

"Oh, I don't know. Abigail might not—"

"Abigail would love a cat, Camille."

She tilted her head as though considering it, her mouth pursed. Suddenly he wanted to kiss her so much that he could almost taste her.

"So..." He cleared his throat. "Getting back to the point—where are these little darlings?"

"They belong to Joey."

"Joey? Joey Thigpen?"

At his expression of disbelief, she hurried on. "I know, I know. Jess and I had the same reaction at first. But I don't see how he could influence kittens, Linc."

"Could we get that in writing?" he asked dryly.

She gave him a slow smile. "Nikki's going to be so thrilled."

Nikki's tiny night-light flickered suddenly. Then came a rumble of thunder, gentle and distant.

"Rain!" With a look of dismay, Camille got to her feet. "I'd better run while I can."

Linc stood up, too, his eyes clinging to hers. Suddenly, a gust of wind lashed against the window, spattering the panes with raindrops. "You'll get soaked. I would drive you, but I'm afraid to leave Nikki. You can take the Bronco." He dug in his pocket for the keys. "Let me—"

"Don't bother." Camille hurried out of the room, heading for the front door. "It doesn't matter. A little rain won't hurt me." At the door, she flinched as lightning flashed vividly, lighting up the whole room.

Behind her, Linc waited for the thunderous boom to dissipate before saying, "You can't go out in this, Cami."

"But I can't stay here," she said, unaware of the near-desperate tone of her voice. She wrenched the door open and dashed out onto the porch. Instantly the wind caught at her dark hair, whipping it wildly against her face. She reached up, raking it out of her eyes and mouth. The storm was approaching rapidly from the west, pushing a wall of rain across the fields, past the pond. On the porch, both Camille and Linc were unprotected from the brunt of it, and in seconds both were drenched.

"Come inside, damn it!" With a hand at the small of her back, Linc urged her through the door and slammed it against the lashing of the wind.

Neither of them said a word for a minute. Though she felt him watching her, Camille wouldn't look at Linc. She felt ridiculous and embarrassed. It had been stupid to run out in the rain, but the thought of being shut in with him in the intimacy of Kate's Cottage had been more than she could bear. It had been different while Nikki was sick, demanding their attention. But now...

"You don't have to run from me, Camille."

She looked at him then, her heart suddenly beginning to pound, not at his words, but at the low, intense tone. Before he could say another word, she pushed at the wet strands that clung to her cheeks. "Yes, I do."

"No." He shook his head, just one short vehement movement. "What do you think I am, damn it! You've spent half the night helping me with my daughter. Jesus, Camille, do you think I'd do anything to hurt you?"

She stared at him. Like her, he was wet to the skin, his hair molded to the shape of his head, his T-shirt soaked and plastered to his body. To Camille, he seemed even more blatantly male than usual. More dangerous. She turned again to the door.

"Don't go," he repeated, touching her arm hesitantly. "I need to talk to you. For days I've been trying to think of a way, but after...everything and knowing how you felt when you left the last time, I didn't expect you to welcome a call from me."

"What did you want to say?" she asked, not looking at him.

"First, you need to get out of those wet clothes." She allowed him to usher her along to the bathroom. "Hand your wet things out and I'll toss them in the dryer," he told her. "I've got some sweats you can put on."

She felt a little more in control by the time she'd stripped out of the soaked clothes and wrapped herself in a bath towel. She was using his blow dryer on her hair when he rapped on the door. Opening it, she took the soft, gray sweats.

"They'll be big, but what the heck." He grinned at her. "It's the style now, isn't it?"

"Thanks." She closed the door quickly, before he could suspect how susceptible she was to that grin. If she had any luck whatsoever, the storm would blow itself out soon and she could escape.

"Looks like we're in for it," Linc said as she slipped into the living room. He patted a place on the sofa beside him, and she sat down a little gingerly. Before leaning back, he handed her a cup of coffee. "I made it while I still had a chance. The way the wind's howling, I wouldn't be surprised if the electricity goes."

She looked anxiously at the window and cringed when another jagged bolt lit up the world.

"Are you afraid of storms?" he asked.

"Not really. I'm just a little…nervous. I should be at home. Abigail will be worried."

"Didn't you tell her where you were going when you left?"

"Well, yes…"

"Then she'll know you're with me and she won't expect you to drive home in a rainstorm."

Wrapping both hands around the warm cup, she settled back a little deeper in the corner of the sofa. "What did you want to talk about, Linc?"

He rested an arm across the back of the sofa. "You and me, Cami."

"There is no you and me."

Even before she had the words out, he was nodding in contradiction. "Yes, there is. No matter how we beat around the bush or try to deny it, even after all these years, there is definitely something between us."

She turned her head and looked out the window.

"Cami…" When she didn't move, he released a long breath. "I've spent a lot of time thinking since you walked out last week. I can't blame you. It must have sounded weird hearing me call Joanna's name like that."

"Not weird, just…unsettling."

He laughed dryly. "Yeah, I guess that's a good word." When she still wouldn't look at him, he reached out and touched her cheek, curling his fingers around the delicate bones of her jaw. "Please look at me, Cami."

She didn't want to, but when he spoke to her using that tone, her resolve melted. Her heart melted.

"I want you, Cami, not Joanna." She made a move to leave the sofa, but he put a hand on her shoulder. "No, wait, please. Just let me try to explain." He fell silent for a moment, seeking the right words. "You were right. Between my marriage and Joanna's death, I've been hauling around a load of guilt and regret. Without the accident, we would probably have ended up the way so many other couples do today. I'd be divorced and sharing custody of Nikki. But when you suggested that I might be hiding behind that for some cockamamy psychological reason, I spent the next two days telling myself you didn't know what you were talking about.

"When I finally cooled off, I realized it could be true. It took me a while to work it all out. I've been carrying a torch for you for seventeen years, Cami, and that's a long time. Especially since all that time I believed you were forbidden to me. One look at you at Pearce's funeral and I knew that what I felt for you was ten times more powerful than anything I had ever felt for my wife.'' He shook his head ruefully. ''My half sister, for God's sake. It shocked me that I felt that way.'' He lifted one shoulder helplessly. ''It terrified me, Cami. I needed to block it out, and I did.''

He leaned forward, resting his elbows on his knees, staring at his feet. ''Even when I found out Jack had lied, I hid behind my rage at him, because that was safer than the emotional risk I'd have to take if I let myself love you again.''

Camille's heart began to pound. She looked at his bent head, longing to slide her fingers through his dark, still-damp hair. To keep from doing it, she locked her hands together in her lap. She was trembling all over. With hope. With anticipation. With a wild need that threatened to burst its bounds if he didn't touch her soon.

He looked up suddenly, catching her eyes, holding her still with the sheer intensity of his look. ''I'm not running anymore, Cami. I want you.'' He reached for her, curling a hand around her neck, pulling her to him. ''I need you.''

She went willingly into his arms, her face lifted to meet his kiss.

Lightning flashed, a brilliant, dazzling blue-white spectacle, and the cottage was suddenly plunged into total darkness. In the ear-splitting boom that followed, mouths sealed, breath mingling, they fell back on the sofa.

Camille's pulse leaped in anticipation of what was to come as she gloried in their rising passion. She had been a girl all those years ago. Now she was a woman, her need as honest and urgent as his. All her senses burst into vivid life, and her heart soared in satisfaction. It had always been this way between her and Linc. She loved him. She had always loved him. She always would love him.

Camille wrapped her arms around him, taking his weight gladly, a heavy, sensual burden that stirred something primitive and deeply feminine in her. Without breaking their kiss, he touched her everywhere—on her face, her neck, her breasts—as though he couldn't explore her fast enough. Taking the time for prolonged foreplay seemed beyond him.

"Camille, Camille." He breathed into her ear, his mouth moist and erotic, his tongue wild and plunging. Then he pushed her slightly away, just far enough to get a hold on her shorts. He pulled them off and flung them to the floor, closely followed by her panties. Whispering soft, fervent love words, he caressed her stomach, her inner thighs, and then finding the silken nest of her femininity, he went still a moment.

"We've got to slow down," he groaned, his forehead resting between her breasts. But even as he said it, he was bending her leg to wedge himself tightly against her, his hips already moving in a sensual, measured rhythm that triggered the same instinctive response from her own hips. He was warm and hard, his need building urgently.

"This is too fast," he moaned, shaking his head. He withdrew his hand from her seductive softness, sought the fullness of her derriere instead and squeezed it gently. "If I don't slow—"

"No." She arched against his hardness. "No, don't wait."

Her plea sent him over the edge. He pulled her T-shirt over her head and tossed it aside. When he fumbled with her bra, she moved to help him, even though her own fingers were shaking and the familiar clasp baffled her for a second or two. He levered himself off the sofa, pulling his shirt over his head as he rose, tossing it aside. Quickly he shed his jeans and shoes and socks. Just before sinking back onto the sofa, he stopped.

"Not here. The bed."

Finding his bed meant a delay. With a protesting sound, she shook her head, reaching for him.

He bent and kissed her hard on the mouth. "Ah, sweetheart, I've waited too long for this," he told her. "Let's not waste it on this damn sofa. Come here." Then, scooping her up as though she weighed no more than Nikki, he carried her down the hall to his bedroom.

The electricity was still off, and the room was in total darkness. As Linc laid Camille down on the bed, he ran both hands over every inch of her, as though touching her could somehow satisfy his need to see her. "You're beautiful and sweet," he murmured against the soft lushness of her breasts. She shivered when his moist breath feathered over her skin. With it came a rush of desire so intense she felt almost faint.

"I wish I could see you," he whispered, his fingers splayed wide on the skin of her abdomen. "You're so soft and silky, like satin." He bent and kissed the tip of one breast and then bit it gently. She shivered and her vision went hazy.

"You like that?" With his tongue, he traced the sensitive areola.

"Yes, yes." Blindly she caught his head between her hands, moaning at the warmth of his mouth, writhing when he sucked hard and deep. He sensed that she was at the edge, and his own passion quickened. His hand swept lower. Her breath caught, and a dull roaring filled her ears as he found her wet and ready. With his thumb, he touched the tiny, pulsating nub of her desire.

Sensation after sensation spiraled through her. Her body was no longer her own. Pleasure, deep and dark, robbed her of her will, ruled her. Still, it wasn't enough. Even while glorying in the feeling, she wanted more. She wanted—

She moaned as his hands and mouth drove her higher. She sobbed even as instinct had her reaching, reaching. Clawing at the sheets, her head tossing fitfully as she tried to hold off the inevitable. She did not want it this way again.

She opened her eyes. In the stormy light, she could see his face, harsh and strained with passion. His mouth moved with words she couldn't hear as he found a cellophane packet in the bedside table. Feverishly, she reached for him, dragging his mouth to hers.

"Please," she whispered, her breath catching on a sob.

"Together," he grated softly, kissing her. "This time, we go together, Cami love."

"Yes. Yes." It was what she wanted.

The room flared with fierce, prolonged lightning. Rain and wind slammed against roof and walls, lashing windows and shaking rafters. Outside in the rainswept field that separated the Twin Willows, a tree split suddenly and then burst into flame.

Inside, Camille and Linc rode a whirlwind of passion. He rose above her, quickly finding his place between her thighs. With a groan and a thrust of his hips, he was inside her. For a moment, both were breathless with the sheer joy of it. Then instinct and need overwhelmed them, and they surrendered to the storm within.

"WHAT ARE YOU THINKING?"

Linc pulled his gaze from the rain-washed window and brushed a kiss against Camille's temple. "You don't want to know, love."

Camille waited a minute before replying, thankful that the electricity was still out. Uncertainly, she asked, "Were you disappointed?"

It took a minute for that to sink in. "Disappointed?"

"Yes. I know I'm not very…" Her voice trailed off; she was unable to say it.

Astonished, he pressed back into the pillow so that he could see her face. "Are you serious?"

She gave a tiny shrug.

With a husky chuckle, he tightened his arms around her in a bear hug. "Sweetheart, if it had been any better, you'd probably have to haul me down from the ceiling."

"Really?"

"Yeah, really." He lifted her chin and lowered his face to hers. Rubbing her nose with his, he gave her a loving kiss. "It was fantastic. You're fantastic." He rained tiny kisses all over her face. "And beautiful. And special. And oh, so sexy."

She smiled against his mouth. "Okay."

He propped up on one elbow and gazed at her. "But if you want to get into a critique—"

"I don't!" Laughing, she pushed at him, but he didn't budge.

"Then I have to say it went too fast."

"And whose fault was that?"

He traced the shape of her mouth with his finger. "Yours."

Because his voice had dropped, her own came out husky. "Mine?"

"Yeah. If you weren't so beautiful and special and sexy, I'd have been able to last a lot longer."

She kissed his fingertip and then cradled his palm against her cheek. "I don't see how it could have been any better." After a minute, she said, "I really thought that kind of…ecstasy—that's the only word to truly describe it—was something I would never feel again. That summer…" Her eyes narrowed as if trying to fix the memory. "Whenever I remembered how it was with you, I convinced myself it hadn't been that good, that incredible. I told myself it was the silly fantasies of a seventeen-year-old. Because with Pearce—"

She stopped quickly. The shortcomings of her relationship with Pearce were in the past, and the past had no place here.

He lay back, tucking her head beneath his chin. Then he said in a low voice, "We've missed so much, Cami."

"Maybe it just wasn't meant to be."

"I can't believe that."

She hesitated, knowing he was thinking of Jack. "What's done is done, Linc."

"But not forgotten. I won't ever forget."

She brushed a hand over his chest, enjoying the feel of him. Jack had cheated her, too, but snuggled close to Linc, warm and replete from their loving, there was no room in her heart for resentment, not tonight. Tonight she had reclaimed something precious, something she'd never expected to know again. She was happy, full of wonder and delight. It made her feel generous. "We have to let it go, Linc."

"I can't just let it go, Camille. He took everything. And it wasn't just me—he shortchanged us both. He doesn't deserve forgiveness. I'm not letting him off scot-free."

She closed her eyes and burrowed her face into the pocket of his shoulder, not wanting to tempt fate with talk of revenge. Discussing Jack's perfidy seemed to taint what they'd just shared.

Turning to him, she linked her arms around his neck. He groaned and sought the warmth of her flesh. She smiled when she felt his instantaneous response. She was filled with a sense of her own power. *Let me love you,* she coaxed him with her touch. *Let me make you forget.*

Suddenly he shifted so that she was beneath him. Covering her mouth with hot, crushing kisses, he pressed into her soft, welcoming warmth. *Yes, oh, yes,* she thought. *Let me burn your lust for revenge to ashes.*

It was the last thing she thought before passion claimed them both.

"I THINK THEY'RE SLEEPING together."

"So what?" Jack took the glass Christine handed him and gulped down half the contents in one swallow.

"So you'd better do something about it, that's what!" Christine took a quick, tense puff from her cigarette. She'd been pacing the room for the past twenty minutes, oblivious of the storm. "Who does he think he is?" she muttered. "He's nobody! I don't care how much money he's made. His mother was a servant, and he existed on the judge's charity. Nothing will ever change that."

Jack glowered at her before dropping down in a deep-cushioned chair. "Don't let anyone else hear you talking like that, you hear? The minute you open your mouth, your prejudices show. I've told you a thousand times, Christine. And put out that damn cigarette. It looks bad."

Christine took one last greedy drag and ground the butt into a crystal ashtray. "It won't be me jeopardizing the campaign, Jack. I'm telling you, your precious sister and that...that glorified hired hand are going to do you in."

"She's over twenty-one, Christine. She can sleep with whoever the hell she wants."

"What if the press gets wind of it?"

"What if they do?"

"Jack—" She gave him an exasperated look before fumbling again with her cigarettes. Lighting another she went over to stand in front of him. "You've got to do something to get rid of him."

"Like what? Have him strung up on a dark night? Ride him out of the state on a rail? Be reasonable, Christine."

She made an impatient sound. "I can't believe you have to sit here like a pigeon waiting to be broadsided." She shot him a challenging look. "Am I going to have to take care of this?"

It worried him when she talked like that. There was a dark streak in Christine that matched Jack's own. It was one of the things that bound them together. But lately, he'd begun to wonder if she was losing her grip. He realized how disastrous it would be if his constituents ever caught a glimpse of that side of Christine. So far, she was not a liability. Not yet, anyway. Besides, she knew too damn much.

"We don't even know for sure that he has anything on me," Jack argued in an attempt to placate her. "And even if he does, he'll think twice about using it, because it'll jeopardize what he's got going with Camille. She's family, Chris. She won't just sit by and let him wreck my campaign."

Or so he hoped. Jack went to the window and stared out at the fury of the storm. Christine had hit a nerve.

But what the hell could he do? He'd asked himself that question a thousand times lately. Cantrell was like a wily fox. He had to show his hand before Jack could play his own cards. Until then, all he could do was walk a tightrope and pray Cantrell didn't have anything so damaging that he couldn't successfully explain it away.

Jack grunted as a particularly fierce bolt of lightning rent the sky. Timing. That was everything in a campaign. Potentially explosive material could blow him right out of the water if it was timed just right. He drew in a deep breath. Christine was right. It would be best to get rid of him. Camille could send him packing. When he put it to her, she'd come around. She always had.

Christine, distracted, took a sip of her drink, rattling ice cubes as she placed it back on the bar. "I want to live in the governor's mansion, Jack. You promised."

Jack hunched his shoulders defensively, still facing the window. "You're going to, Christine, you're going to."

"I can't live here all year long," she complained, her tone changing. "You know that, Jack. You've always known that. We agreed it's good for your image to own the Twin Willows, but we just can't live here. It's like being buried alive." Her voice rose with distress. "I need good shopping and good entertainment. I need the right clothes. We need to be seen in the right places. We need the company of the right people. You see that, don't you, Jack?"

Jack tossed back a hefty swallow of bourbon to quell his uneasiness. Lately Christine's moods seesawed so, he never knew what to expect. One day up, one day down, nagging, nitpicking. It was enough to unnerve him, too. Right now he needed Christine. Her family was powerful; her connections reached all the way to Washington. This was not a good time for her to fall apart on him.

Christine drew fitfully on her cigarette. She turned and faced him through a cloud of smoke. "I promise you this, Jack—if you lose this election, I'm divorcing you."

Jack's hand clenched on his glass. The years rolled back and he was a scared boy again, listening to his mother threaten to leave Willow Wood. Echoes of the judge's futile arguments to persuade her to stay rang in his ears.

Katherine, you can't mean that!

I mean it, Joseph. As soon as this hateful pregnancy's over, I'm leaving this godforsaken place.

You don't mean that, Katherine. You're my wife. Your place is here. Of course you're going to stay.

No! I hate it, the heat, the dust, the boredom.

And me, Katherine? Do you hate me? And our son? Do you hate Jack?

Yes! Yes! Everything. I hate everything!

Crouched behind the big armoire in his parents' bedroom, he'd wrapped his arms around his knobby knees and prayed the baby would never come. But the baby had come. And as soon as Camille was born, his mother had left.

He tossed back the rest of his drink in one gulp. Land. Land and power. Those were the only important things.

CHAPTER THIRTEEN

IT SEEMED INCREDIBLE to Camille that for the second time in her life, she found herself helplessly in love with Linc. She had come full circle from the passionate innocent who had given her heart and body without a thought to consequences. The sum total of her life experiences had taught her caution and doubt, but it made her value joy and…feelings. What she felt now was more complicated, more intense, deeper by far than the youthful sexual enthrallment that had been the essence of her love then. This time, she loved as a woman. It was wonderful, it was heady. It was scary.

As August gave way to September, blistering heat matured the cotton. Linc was spread thin as summer's lazy pace accelerated to the frantic activity necessary to bring in the crop. Even so, they found time for each other, seizing every available moment to be together. Sometimes it was early morning, before dawn, when Linc would steal into Camille's bedroom at Willow Wind and wake her with slow, languorous loving. Sometimes it was tumultuous midnight trysts, moments stolen at Kate's Cottage after Nikki slept. With a whisper and a touch, he was hers. And she was his. Always it ended with soft murmurs of satisfaction savored in moments of close intimacy and a sense of the rightness of being together again.

It also felt right having Linc running Willow Wind.

Camille's misgivings had vanished along with her guilt at having him in Pearce's house, sitting at Pearce's desk, making decisions with a skill and confidence Pearce had never displayed. Willow Wind flourished under his supervision.

"Heavens! Is this right?"

Linc looked up from the desk as she came toward him, her eyes on a long printout. "What, the quarterly report?" He took the paper from Camille, tipping his head slightly to focus through his glasses. Giving the figures a quick look, he tossed the printout aside. "What's the problem?"

Perched on the edge of the desk, as close to him as she could get, Camille shook her head. "Nothing, if those figures don't lie."

He leaned back, smiling at her. "They don't lie, lady. A month ago, we locked in one hell of a price on our cotton. It'll take Willow Wind out of the red this year. Next year, barring a major natural disaster, the plantation will be a paying proposition again."

"Thanks to you." She glanced around the room that had once been Pearce's study, but she could no longer picture him there. There had never been a computer at Pearce's elbow. He'd never bothered with plans for future expansion. No paperwork ever cluttered Pearce's desk after midnight. The stamp of Linc's personality was everywhere.

"Just doin' my job, ma'am," he drawled. Leaning even farther back, he rested his hands on his flat stomach, eyeing her over the tops of his glasses.

"You look cute in glasses," she teased.

He made a choked sound. "Cute?"

"Uh-huh." He wore reading glasses when he did paperwork, she'd discovered. It was one more little fact about Linc, a tiny nugget to be added to her store of knowledge. Her curiosity about him amazed her. She was insatiable. Now that they were lovers, it was as if a dam had broken, releasing her hunger to know everything. She wanted to learn his secrets, his favorite things, what pleased him, what made him grouchy, whether he was neat or messy, whether he was moody in the morning, whether he liked broccoli or golf or fishing. She longed to fill in all the blanks, to bridge the gap that their seventeen-year separation had forced upon them.

She watched him, knowing her heart was in her eyes. Linc studied her slowly in return. The brief, strapless jumpsuit showed off her long legs and bare shoulders. She'd worn it deliberately, knowing he was here working in the room that had once been Pearce's private domain. When his gaze lingered at her breasts, she felt them tighten and pulse with heat. Meeting his eyes, she knew he'd discovered that she wasn't wearing a bra.

"Cute, huh?" With a throaty growl, he wrapped an arm about her waist and hauled her into his lap. She tumbled onto him with a little squeal. "Let me see what I can do to change my image," he said, heedlessly tossing his glasses on the desk. He caught hold of her waist with both hands while tugging her elastic top down with his teeth. As he'd intended, her breasts promptly spilled out. Under his scrutiny, a flush tinted her skin.

Suddenly, her playful mood subsided as he bent and softly kissed first one rosy tip, then the other. She made a soft sound, closing her eyes as her head fell back. He moved to kiss the hollow of her throat, then nipped at her earlobe. Using one hand, he kneaded her breasts, then cupped them in his palms. "You're beautiful here, did you know that?" he murmured. "I love touching you."

"Linc." Vaguely, she remembered the unlocked door. "We can't—"

"It's okay, sweetheart. We're just playing."

This wasn't play. This was serious business. Her need was strong. As was Linc's. She knew the signs well after all they'd shared in the past weeks. She sighed when his hand slipped into the loose leg of the jumpsuit and worked under the sleek satin of her panties.

"Doesn't that feel good?"

"Yes, yes." She was hot and creamy, ready for him. She should be embarrassed, she thought from some distant pleasure-drunk corner of her mind. Instead, she simply craved more. She wanted to take everything he knew how to give and then to turn the tables and give him a taste of his own medicine.

"This is crazy," she protested weakly, breathlessly.

"I love making you crazy," he murmured against her ear. His breath sent thrills coursing through her. She moved restlessly. With his fingers, he drove her a little higher.

"We can't, Linc. Abigail might—"

"We'll stop," he promised in a ragged voice. While his hand worked magic, he kissed her hotly and deeply, tearing his mouth away to explore her ear. "We will...we will...soon...."

Trembling, she wedged her hand between them and encountered the hard bulge of his arousal, pressing it urgently. Needing no further encouragement, he shifted, breathing hard and fumbling with his zipper. He held her hand there as he worked around his briefs. Then she felt his hot, velvety length. She closed her fingers around him and he groaned, shuddering powerfully.

All thought of stopping disappeared. She gave him an openmouthed kiss as her hands touched him, caressing him voluptuously. In moments, she sensed he was beyond control, his body clamoring for release. It sent her own desire to the edge.

With a frustrated sound, he put her aside just long enough to adjust the jumpsuit and her panties and then, before he pulled her back onto his lap, their eyes met. She sent a fleeting look to the door.

"We can't quit now," he told her and kissed her hard.

Shaken, they both laughed—strained, this-is-crazy laughs. Without a second thought, he positioned her in his lap and then with a groan and a matching whimper from Camille, in one swift thrust he was inside her.

She gasped at the power of it. He was long and straight and hot and hard. She rocked once, experimentally. Shifting, groaning with gratification, he helped her accommodate his erection. Then, like perfectly choreographed dancers, they set a slow and steady rhythm on their sensuous climb to the top. Climax, when it came, was deep and mindless and powerful. When it was over, they lay panting against each other, foreheads touching, the light of laughter in their eyes.

"I'm not paying attention to your promises anymore," she told him, shivering in the aftermath of orgasm.

He chuckled softly.

"What were we talking about before this started?"

Smiling against her temple, he said, "The plantation. Your profit projection this year."

She shook her head. "I can't believe those figures. I know you're a far better farmer and manager than Pearce ever was, but the difference is staggering. What's your secret?"

"Pearce hasn't been farming Willow Wind for more than three years, Camille. Jack has."

She didn't want to talk about Jack. Whenever they did, they always wound up in an argument. Linc would never be able to see any good in Jack, and although it bothered her to admit it, she'd felt the sting of Jack's insensitivity so many times that she couldn't really put up much of a defense for him.

She bent for a lingering kiss.

"What was that for?" he asked when he could catch his breath.

Smiling, she rested her forehead against his. "Because I felt like it." With a mock growl, she rubbed against the evidence of his arousal.

"What about Abigail?" he managed, pressing her hard against him while nuzzling her bared breasts.

"Too late," Camille teased with a soft laugh. "Even as we speak…uh, act, she's probably seeing everything in her teacup."

His head snapped up as though it had been yanked with a cord. She almost fell off his lap in his mad scramble to put himself and her to rights.

"I thought you were a skeptic," she said, laughing.

"I am…I was.…" He swore, stuffing his shirt back into his jeans. "But she comes up with some strange stuff occasionally, just enough to make me doubt."

"Like what?"

He sat on the edge of the desk and pulled her down beside him. "Like telling me months ago that it was meant for us to be together."

She touched his face gently, her eyes soft. "Did you need to hear that from a psychic?"

He captured her hand and kissed her palm. "No, but it scared the hell out of me. I still thought you were my sister."

She snuggled close. "Thank goodness I'm not."

Hugged to his side, she almost felt that nothing bad could ever touch her again. It was so *good* loving Linc. Life was full of surprises, she decided. After Pearce died, she had sincerely believed there was little left for her to look forward to. She had her home, she had Sunny Day, and she had a nice circle of friends. That apparently was meant to be her fair share of happiness. No dizzying heights, no abysmal lows. Just an unexceptional, safe, even sort of existence.

Until Linc. And Nikki.

The joy she felt now was so keen, so breathlessly beautiful that it scared her. One part of her focused intensely on the here and now, relishing happiness while it was offered. Another part, that flawed, uncertain part that had been conditioned by years of neglect—by her father and family, by Linc's abandonment and her miscarriage, by years of stoic acceptance in a dysfunctional marriage—that part braced for the moment when the joy might end.

So much lay unresolved between her and Linc. It bothered her that he seemed obsessed with making Jack pay for what he'd done all those years ago. Why couldn't he see that that kind of thinking was destructive and futile? It bothered her, too, that they never talked about the future. She lay awake nights wondering whether a man who'd lived Linc's sophisticated lifestyle could ever be satisfied to stay forever in a place like Blossom, Mississippi.

"DON'T WORRY, Linc's where he wants to be," Jess told her one day as they tidied up the premises at Sunny Day for the upcoming weekend. It was Friday and the kids were gone. She bent over to scrape up a blob of modeling clay that was stuck on the floor. "Nobody forced him to come back to Mississippi, and he's too much his own man to tolerate a situation that doesn't suit him."

Camille went about the room collecting workbooks. "Yes, but how long will he be content in a place like this?"

Jess straightened, looking at her. "He loves you, Camille. His roots are here. And Nikki loves you, too. Why would he leave?"

"Do you think so?"

"That he loves you?" Jess inquired with a disbelieving look. "Of course he does. It's written all over him when he's around you, Camille. Don't tell me you doubt it?"

Camille shook her head and attempted a laugh. "It's silly, I guess. It's just that I love him so much, Jess. And Nikki, too. I'm happier than I've been in a long, long time. It's a little scary. I worry that it could be snatched away from me somehow."

Absently, Jess rubbed the small of her back. "That's not so hard to understand. Happiness has been snatched from you before. But that doesn't mean it'll happen again. Believe in yourself, Camille. Believe in Linc and what the two of you have together now."

Camille paused, the workbooks held close to her chest. "I'm not sure what we have. I'm not sure where we're headed. Linc hasn't said anything about the future." She frowned suddenly. "The reason is, he's no more certain about the future than I am, I think."

When Jess looked confused, she said, "It's his obsession with Jack that worries me. Until they cease hostilities, I don't think there's a chance for us. Linc knows something that can ruin Jack, I'm sure of it. If he decides to use it, I'm afraid it will destroy what we have together."

"Does Linc know how you feel?"

"We've discussed it, but he's...obsessed. That's the only word, Jess. He wants Jack to pay for what he did."

"Even if it means losing you?"

"I don't know." Moving slowly, Camille opened the cupboard and stacked the workbooks inside. It was possible.

"I just can't believe that," Jess said, shaking her head. "I can accept that he might be human enough to fantasize about something like that, even that he might go so far as to plan it. But things have turned out differently from what he expected when he first came back. Look at Nikki. She's attached to you. You've taken the place of her mother. I can't see Linc doing anything—anything, Camille—to jeopardize that."

Camille stood with her hand on the cupboard door. "I hope you're right." Both she and Linc had had more than their share of losses and regrets. What good would it do to open fresh wounds, to cause more pain?

Jess dusted off her hands and looked around for her purse. "The party's still on for Sunday afternoon, I suppose?"

"Hmm?" Camille stared blankly a moment before replying. "Oh, yes. Nikki's birthday. Two o'clock."

"At Kate's Cottage?"

"Uh-huh."

Jess picked up her purse. "Do you think Linc will manage to break away for a couple of hours?"

"I hope so." Camille closed and latched the cupboard before picking up her own purse and settling the strap on her shoulder. "Barring an emergency, that is. He promised Nikki. I expect he'll have to go back to the fields once it's over. He's been keeping horrendous hours, but thankfully picking will be finished in a few more days, he tells me. A week at most.''

After locking the main door, they went down the steps together. "I never knew Pearce or Jack to keep such long hours," Jess commented. "Is it really necessary?"

"Pearce delegated a lot of the responsibility, and so does Jack," Camille said, searching for her car keys. "Linc prefers to be in the thick of things. He knows every section and acre of Willow Wind, its peculiarities and exactly how much cotton we can expect from it." She smiled softly. "I think if he thought it would make a difference, he'd sleep out there with the pickers and balers."

"He sounds like a born farmer."

Camille smiled gently. "He always loved the land. That's all he ever talked about when we were kids. He had such plans and dreams."

"It must have been doubly painful for him when he was driven away all those years ago," Jess observed thoughtfully. "It's hardly any wonder he wants to punish Jack for taking everything away."

Camille's doubts resurfaced as she drove home. Punishing Jack would not fix anything. It wouldn't turn back the clock or erase the mistakes. And once done, it would be a burden Linc would carry forever whether he realized it or not. With her thoughts in a muddle, she took Keating's Corner a little faster than usual. Then the graceful lines of both Twin Willows materialized through the glaze of September sunshine.

Her eyes stung as she gazed at them, both so beautiful, but both harboring such painful secrets. How sad that so much beauty housed such unhappiness. She sighed. Maybe Willow Wood was cursed forever, but at Willow Wind, she knew there was a chance for something good and enduring, for a new beginning. For joy and warmth. For love.

Surely Linc would count the cost before deliberately destroying that chance.

"HAPPY BIRTHDAY to Nik-keee, happy birthday to-oo youooo!" A flurry of clapping and childish shouts accompanied the end of the birthday song. Flushed and laughing, Nikki scrunched up her small shoulders and blew with gusto, managing to extinguish three of the five candles before Joey Thigpen leaned forward and quickly finished the job.

"Joey!" Tracey yelled indignantly. "Are you trying to get 'spelled from Nikki's party like you was almost 'spelled from school?"

"I was not!"

"You was, too!"

Linc leaned close to Camille who was cutting the cake. "Are they going to fight?"

"It's possible." To distract them, she handed each of the antagonists a piece of cake. "Tracey takes a very protective attitude toward Nikki, and Joey delights in challenging her."

Shaking his head, Linc surveyed the dozen or so small fry who were clustered around the picnic table busily consuming cake and red punch. "They only slow down to eat or sleep, it seems. How do you manage thirty of them all day?"

"I have help. Lots of help. The secret is to keep them occupied." The cake and punch were fast disappearing, she discovered. Joey and Tracey especially were getting restless.

"Looks like the lull is over," Linc observed as Joey got down first, and then Tracey, stuffing the remains of her cake in her mouth, scrambled down, too. "I think I'd rather manage the plantation," Linc murmured.

Nikki abandoned cake and punch and ran over to join her two cohorts at the small side table heaped with her gifts.

"Can we start opening, huh, Miss Camille?" Joey yelled.

"Not us," Tracey reminded him in a bossy tone. "Nikki's the birthday girl. She's the only one who can open, huh, Miss Camille?"

Camille started toward them. "That's right, Tracey. But everyone gets a party favor."

Her remark was greeted with a chorus of "Yaaaay!" and much jumping up and down. Linc smiled, watching Nikki tear into the gifts with as much uninhibited enthusiasm as the other children displayed. When everything was opened and oohed and aahed over, Nikki looked up, searching for her daddy.

Linc went over and squatted beside her. "What is it, sweetheart?"

Nikki gave him a bewildered look from wide blue eyes. "You forgot to get me something, Daddy."

Linc smacked his forehead in exaggerated surprise. "Gosh, I'm glad you reminded me." He looked up at Camille. "Camille, isn't there something somewhere…" He frowned as though trying to recall.

Joey, hopping from one foot to another, couldn't stand it. "Over there! Over there!" he shouted, pointing to the front porch of the cottage.

"Jo-o-e-y," Tracey warned with a fierce look. "You hush!"

Wide-eyed, Nikki gazed where Joey pointed.

Camille laughed, knowing Joey couldn't contain himself much longer. He had a proprietary interest in Nikki's special surprise and had been sorely tested by Camille's insistence that he keep quiet until the other presents were opened. At the porch she picked up the basket, carried it over to Nikki, who stood encircled in Linc's arms, and set it down. It was a picnic basket with a hinged wooden top. Over Nikki's small, dark head, Linc and Camille exchanged a brief look.

"Open it, punkin," Linc coaxed his daughter, his eyes filled with warmth.

Laughing, Camille managed to hold a dozen four- and five-year-olds at bay while Nikki bent down and opened the basket. Up popped a mottled kitten, mewing plaintively. Nikki gasped softly, a look of wonderment on her small face.

"Daddy! Daddy! It's a kitty!"

Linc chuckled softly. "Well, whaddaya know! So it is."

Nikki dropped on all fours and picked it up, snuggling it against her chest. Then, looking at Linc with shining eyes, she said, "I knew you wouldn't forget, Daddy."

He ruffled her hair affectionately. "How'd you know that, punkin?"

"'Cause you're the best daddy in the whole, wide world!"

As CAMILLE HAD PREDICTED, Linc went back to the work site after the party. Then, for several days afterward, he worked almost around the clock. As the end of picking approached, the frantic pace increased. Mechanization was a great boon, but weather was always an uncertain factor.

Friday afternoon, as he watched a bank of dark clouds, he thought with a smile that the original farmers who'd cultivated delta cotton two hundred years before him must have felt the same way when they looked at the changeable sky. Today, with luck, the clouds would dissipate before causing rain.

Movement on the dirt road caught his eye as three minivans pulled to a stop. He'd promised Camille and Jess that the kids from Sunny Day could come and watch for a few minutes. Doors opened and, like colorful jelly beans, four- and five-year-olds spilled out everywhere. Glancing quickly at the huge mechanical pickers, he found three of the giant machines already in place as he'd directed for the next day's work. Another was positioned to make a final swath down the rows. With some relief he noted that besides Camille and Jess, there were three additional women to keep the kids in order. He remembered all too well the high-spirited rowdiness of Nikki's birthday party.

Nikki's party. A smile played at his mouth. To his surprise, he'd enjoyed it so much he'd been reluctant to leave. Instead of returning to work, he'd wanted to stay and rehash everything with Camille, to wring the last ounce of fun from the occasion. He'd wanted to chuckle again with her over Joey Thigpen's antics, to share in Nikki's delight—for the fifth or sixth time—over every gift. Remembering Nikki's face and his own pleasure shared with Camille, he felt a sense of peace, a quiet satisfaction that he could not recall ever experiencing before. It made him want to shut out the world around them and for the rest of the evening simply…enjoy.

As the kids noisily grouped together on the cotton field, he signaled a driver to get ready to give them a demonstration of the cumbersome cotton picker in action. Once picked, the cotton was dumped into the mechanical compactors alongside the road, then compressed and baled and placed at the roadside to be hoisted onto long flatbeds. Later, it would be hauled to the gin. When he was satisfied that the site was relatively childproof, he turned and gave Camille a thumbs-up. Incredibly, she had the children all gathered around her in a colorful knot while she explained what was going on. Nikki, he noticed, kept as close to Camille as possible.

Staying in the background, he watched Camille gesture and talk while the kids looked on in fascination. He was fascinated himself. She was a marvelous, gifted teacher, stopping to answer questions, listening patiently, gently chiding when necessary. Smiling, he saw her hand settle on Nikki's small, dark head. It was the natural, unconscious touch of…a mother to her child, he realized, feeling a sweet pain in his chest.

Nikki's expression as she leaned against the security of Camille's thigh was one of complete trust and belonging. There was something about Camille and Nikki, even in the chattering throng of kindergartners, that set them apart. They might have been alone on the dusty road, they were so right together.

After a few minutes, the children were ordered back to the minivans. All except Nikki and Tracey and Joey. Linc watched Nikki tug at Camille's arm, and with a quick smile in Linc's direction, Camille nodded and followed as the three imps dashed toward him.

"Daddy! Daddy! We saw the pickers! We know how to make jeans now," called Nikki as she ran.

Linc caught her as she bumped into his thighs. "Whoa, lady. How about a hug?" Squatting with his daughter between his legs, he grinned at Joey and Tracey. "Hi, kids."

"We're supposed to say thank you," Tracey chirped.

"Yeah, thanks, Mr. Linc!" Joey said. "This is neat!"

Over all their heads, Linc sent Camille a special smile,

taking pleasure in the soft color that bloomed in her skin. "Now," he said to Nikki. "What's this about jeans?"

"I'll tell," Tracey said, assuming her favorite role as spokesperson. "Blue jeans are made out of cotton, Mr. Linc. And it all starts here." She swept a small arm to encompass the nearly shorn fields.

"I like the machines," Joey stated with unerring male instinct. "I bet that big dumpster would be fun to play in." He eyed the huge rectangular container bulging with loose cotton.

"It looks soft and mushy," Tracey said with a gleam in her eye.

"It's so white," Nikki said. "Just like snow."

"We don't have snow here," Tracey informed her.

"We do so!" Joey disputed instantly with a glare. "It snowed last year, because I put some in a plastic cup."

"That doesn't count for real snow," Tracey said with a sniff. "Nikki means like on Christmas cards and stuff."

Joey stuck out his tongue. "You think you know everything, Tracey Perkins!"

Camille clapped her hands. "Okay, kids, back to the vans."

"Aw, Miss Camille." The three spoke in unison.

"The vans," Camille repeated firmly, pointing to the waiting vehicles. As they trudged off disconsolately, she gave Linc a smile. "Thanks for having us. The kids enjoyed it."

He grinned. "No problem. Tracey and Joey are always good for a break in the monotony."

She shook her head. "Aren't they a mess?"

He gave an emphatic nod.

Laughing, she rolled her eyes.

"Thanks, Mr. Linc," she said with a teasing smile

and a wave as she started off toward the van. Not caring if his crew and all of Sunny Day saw him, he caught her around the waist, growling a little as she squealed, muffling and finally quieting her with the heat and hunger of his kiss.

"Now you can go, Miss Camille."

Her cheeks bright pink, Camille ran.

A FEW HOURS LATER, tired and hot and dusty, Linc surveyed the acres that remained to be picked. The weather had held, enabling his men to put in a long day. The equipment was shut down for the night but already positioned for an early start-up the next morning. If all went as well as it had today, they'd definitely finish up tomorrow. As the pickup carrying the last of his crew pulled away, he stood for a minute savoring the peace of the silent work site with a sense of satisfaction.

Turning slowly, he surveyed the vast, flat expanse of land that surrounded him. Willow Wind. Beautiful, bountiful Willow Wind. Moonlight shed a ghostly sheen over the fields. Alongside the precise rows sat the mechanical compactors. As far as the eye could see, the huge baled rectangles rested on the roadside, ready to go, the evidence of Willow Wind's munificence. The crop this year had exceeded his expectations. Next year, he would—

He raked a hand through his hair. He couldn't plan on being at Willow Wind next year. For more than a week he had been holding an envelope containing everything he needed to destroy Jack Keating. There was little doubt that once the facts were revealed, Jack would have to drop out of the race for governor. Then, barring a miracle, he'd be lucky not to find himself indicted by a grand jury. Whether or not he got out of the criminal charges Linc had documented, his credibility and his image in the state would be destroyed. He would be lucky just to hold on to Willow Wood.

Linc climbed into the Bronco and pulled out, refusing to explore why the thought of Jack's downfall didn't fill him with glee. In moments he was at the Twin Willows. He could never look at them side by side without remembering his failed dreams, the judge's betrayal, the double losses of his mother and his love, Camille. At the drive that led to Jack's big house, he stopped the truck. His fingers clenched on the wheel, he forced himself to look.

At that moment, Jack stepped out onto the porch. He stood with his legs slightly splayed, his attitude one of power and possession as he surveyed Willow Wood's rich acreage. Then he turned and spotted Linc. For a long time, the two men stared at each other. Jack's hostility and arrogance were almost tangible. Even from two hundred yards away, Linc felt their impact, as he knew Jack meant him to. Something inside him snapped, and his decision was made. With one explicit curse, he threw the Bronco in gear and swung it onto the curved driveway, his lust for revenge mirrored in his eyes.

AFTER HIS CONFRONTATION with Jack, Linc went straight to Camille. He had a key to her house, but after what he'd just done, he knew he no longer had a right to use it. Standing before the beautiful leaded-glass front door, he took a deep breath and leaned forward to ring the old-fashioned bell.

Upstairs, Camille came out of her bathroom wrapped in a deep purple bath towel. She didn't often take long, scented tub baths, but tonight, anticipating a visit from Linc, she'd indulged herself. After drying off, she dropped the towel, released her hair from its loose top-knot and shook it out, enjoying the feel of it on her naked shoulders. Sitting down in front of her dressing table, she reached for a bottle of ridiculously expensive body emollient. Feeling sensual and supremely feminine, she began leisurely applying it. Tilting her head, she stroked it over her throat and breasts, on her arms, down her abdomen, onto her thighs and calves and feet.

Catching her reflection in the mirror, she smiled slowly, feeling sexy. There was something almost pagan in her enjoyment of her body now. It was because of Linc, of course. Loving him had released a latent streak of sensuality she'd never known she possessed. It was amazing. How had she managed to subdue so vital a part of herself for so long?

At the sudden peal of the doorbell, she frowned. Linc had a key and she wasn't expecting anyone else. Hesitating, she waited to see if Abigail would answer, but after a few moments she decided her aunt must have gone to bed. Slipping into a satin robe, she secured the sash as she hurried down the stairs.

"Linc!" She pulled the front door open with a surprised smile. "I was just thinking of you."

For a moment, before he stepped inside, he simply looked at her. Then he swept her into his arms and held her close. Camille went willingly, delighting in the feel of him, warm and hard-muscled, strong, so right. She buried her nose in his shirtfront, loving the musky, masculine smell of him, the smell that was Linc and no one else.

"Did you forget your key?" she asked softly, looking up after a few moments.

"No." His mouth was against her temple. She felt him draw in a deep breath, as though filling his lungs with the smell of her. He held her for another moment and then let her go.

"I thought you might be here tonight," she said huskily, touching him just because she wanted to, needed to. "I took a long, delicious bath."

He glanced at the ivory satin robe and then away. "I know. You felt warm and soft and—" he made a move with his shoulder that seemed curiously distracted to Camille "—damp."

Damp? Not exactly a romantic comeback. She laughed, a little puzzled. Usually, when she gave Linc anything approaching a suggestive remark, he was all over her. She watched as he took a step toward the living room. It was almost as if he were deliberately putting distance between them. Then she saw the envelope in his hand.

"Did you wrap things up at the work site?"

"Yeah. We'll be ready first thing tomorrow morning. Another day or so and it's all over."

She wrapped her arms around herself. "That sounds…pretty good." But it didn't. It sounded ominous.

"You look beautiful."

"I do?" she said.

"Yes." He moved closer and put out a hand to touch her hair. Damp from the recent bath, it curled around his fingers. "Beautiful," he murmured.

She stared at him. "What is it? Why are you saying it like that, Linc?"

"Because I may not ever get to tell you so again."

She closed a hand around his wrist. "What's wrong, Linc? What is it?"

He pulled away from her and went to stand by the window. Across the way, the lights of Willow Wood blazed as usual. He stared at Jack's house for a long moment before turning to face her. "I've got to tell you something, Camille."

She tried to laugh. "Is it so serious?"

"Yeah, it is. It's about Jack. I just left him."

Jack again. At something in his tone, she put a hand on the back of a chair. "What about Jack, Linc?"

"Judgment day," he said, savoring the words.

"Judgment—" She shook her head. "You aren't making any sense."

"Jack's been running a nice little scam with Pearce's land, Camille."

"Scam?"

He watched her a moment. "Yeah, scam."

She turned, rubbing her forehead. "What exactly did he do?"

"Lied, cheated, stole. All those things Jack does so well."

"Linc—"

He looked away for a moment. "The hell of it is, Pearce made it so easy. For the past few years, he allowed Jack to negotiate his cotton on the commodities market along with Willow Wood's. The lock-in price that Jack actually negotiated for Twin Willows' cotton was always more than the price he told Pearce."

Camille's expression was filled with disbelief. "Pearce wasn't that stupid, Linc. What about contracts? Paperwork?"

"Contracts can be forged, Camille. Paperwork can be altered."

She put a hand to her heart. "How can you be sure?"

"I suspected it for years. I knew for certain when I demanded a copy of the current contract as a condition of a loan. I talked to Tom Pettigrew, then to my contacts

in New York. I knew the actual price that was paid for
Willow Wind cotton. The price paid to Jack, that is.''
He held up the envelope he'd brought with him. ''It's
all right here, everything.''

She looked at the envelope in horror. ''Linc!'' she
said in a shocked whisper. ''What have you done?''

CHAPTER FOURTEEN

SHE DIDN'T NEED an answer to that question. It was written all over him, in the bitter tilt of his mouth, the cutting look in his eyes. The ammunition to destroy Jack was in that envelope. The more important question was: what did Linc plan to do with it?

"You say you've known this for some time," she managed. "Why didn't you say something before? Why wait until now?"

"I didn't have proof until now. Besides, I was a silent partner until Pearce died. It wasn't up to me to tell him how to run his business."

"But you apparently subsidized him when he came up short," she reminded him, thinking of the mortgage he held.

"Did you want me to refuse him and let Willow Wind go into foreclosure?"

"It wouldn't have gone into foreclosure and you know it. Jack would have come to the rescue."

He made a sound of disgust. "Jack would have stolen it outright, you mean. He's always wanted both plantations, Camille. You know that. It was a sweet setup for Jack. From his point of view, Pearce's alcoholism was an advantage because it left him in a fog most of the time. With Pearce dependent on him and married to his sister, he could afford to wait as long as it took. And if something had happened, you would have turned to your brother, right?

She was shaking her head, resisting the ugly picture that was emerging. "You make him sound so...so calculating."

"He *is* calculating. And manipulative. And dishonest." Linc faced the window again. "Pearce was sick and sinking deeper with every passing day. Jack saw it and realized how it could work to his advantage." Linc paused, then added bitterly, "Pearce had something Jack wanted, so he set the wheels in motion to take it."

And who would know that better than Linc, an unseen player in the background? What a perfect way to turn the tables on Jack. Camille recoiled to think of the secret satisfaction Linc must have felt, knowing he could beat Jack at his own game. He'd waited until he had Jack trapped, his political life and his reputation on the line, just at the moment when he thought he had it made. She realized now that Linc had simply been biding his time. Swallowing against a feeling of nausea, she said in an unsteady tone, "How...how did Pearce manage to hold things together for so long?"

His back to her, Linc focused on something in the distance. "He always came to me to make up the shortfall."

"But...but...for years?"

"Yeah. Years."

"Why did you keep pouring money down the drain like that?" But she knew. He wouldn't take Willow Wood away from Jack, but he could acquire Willow Wind, and that would gall Jack almost as much.

"I knew what Jack was up to. If Pearce hadn't come to me or some other outsider, he would have had to go to Jack, who would have been delighted to take a mortgage on Willow Wind. Which is what he planned all along, naturally.''

''Instead, Pearce handed it over to you.''

He turned from the window and faced her. ''He trusted me, Camille.''

''What about me! Didn't he care that I was left dependent on you, too?''

''What is this, Camille! Would you rather he had gone to Jack? Jack treated you like a poor relation all your life. He manipulated you, he cheated your husband blind, and if I hadn't stepped in, he would have grabbed your house and land right out from under you. Are you crazy? Or blind? Or both?''

She looked into his eyes and then away. ''Please, could we stop this?''

''And then what? Hope it'll all go away? He'll be the next governor, Camille. He shouldn't be in such a powerful position.''

After a moment, she faced him again, her heart beating with fear. ''You aren't going to let it go, are you?''

''I can't.'' He turned, his hand pressed to the back of his neck. ''Damn it, Camille. I just can't.''

Suddenly, she heard her name being shouted at the front door, accompanied by a repeated ringing of the doorbell.

She stared at Linc. ''It's Jack.''

He lifted one eyebrow. ''The big man himself.''

She gave him an exasperated look.

''To get you to bring me into line, no doubt,'' Linc said, cramming his hands deep in his pockets.

''We know you're there, Camille. Let us in.''

Christine, too. Sighing, Camille went to the door and pulled it open.

For a moment, the sight of her ... es made her so

tired, so heartily disgusted that her first inclination was to slam the door in their faces, to send them away before they could cause any more damage to her life. But why she should blame her sense of impending doom on them, she couldn't say. It was Linc who held the key to everything, Linc who planned to destroy everything for the sake of this stupid, futile obsession with paying Jack back for his injustices.

She saw Jack's gaze move beyond her to Linc, who was standing nonchalantly in the wide archway to her living room.

"Has he told you what he's done?" Jack demanded.

"You've got to reason with him, Camille," Christine said. She, too, darted a look around Camille as though checking out the location of a rabid animal. Her eyes were blinking rapidly with a wild, unfocused look. If Camille hadn't felt so raw and vulnerable herself, she would have made an effort to reassure her. As it was, she had nothing left to give. She stepped back wearily, holding the door open.

"Come in, Jack. Christine."

Jack hustled Christine in front of him and shut the door herself. "Well, did he tell you?"

"If you're referring to whatever's in the envelope, we've been talking about that, Jack. I'm not quite sure what—"

"He's crazy, Camille. I told you that when he first showed up after seventeen goddamn years, but you wouldn't listen." Jack shot Linc a malevolent glare. "Now I guess you see I was right."

"Jack, please calm down," she began. "I'm sure we can—"

"Calm down! He's manufactured a pack of lies in that

envelope, and if he uses it, it can destroy everything I've worked for, Camille. You don't realize—''

"Pack of lies?" Linc repeated softly, pulling his hands from his pockets and coming away from the archway to join them.

"Damn right, it's lies!" Jack blustered, turning to Camille. "You don't believe that stuff, do you, Camille? You know me better than that, don't you, honey? You're family. Pearce was family. I wouldn't have cheated my own brother-in-law, would I?"

"You'd cheat your own grandmother if you had half a chance," Linc said contemptuously.

Christine grabbed Camille's sleeve. "You've got to stop him, Camille. You don't understand what could happen here. The press will have a field day. Dirt like this can ruin Jack. Please, Camille."

Camille put her hands over her ears. "Everybody, hush! Just…hush. I haven't even seen what's in that damned envelope! Linc and I were just talking about it. It's…I…I'm still trying to take in the fact that you cheated Pearce, Jack. He was sick and you took advantage of him."

"Sick? He was a damn drunk, Camille! If I hadn't done it, someone else would have. And then where would you have been?"

"I thought he was 'family,'" Linc sneered. "Is this the way you Keatings treat one another?"

"It wasn't like that!" Jack shouted. "It wasn't wrong to step in to keep Willow Wind off the auction block, damn you!"

"There was never a remote chance of that," Linc said softly.

Jack glared at him. "No, because you were busy behind the scenes with your own sleazy scheme."

"What scheme?" Christine demanded.

"Buying up Pearce's bad debts to get a foot in the door at Willow Wind," Jack answered without looking at his wife. "Right, Cantrell?"

Linc shrugged. "You seem to have all the answers, Keating. You don't need me to fill in the blanks."

"Then if he croaked, you were more than happy to step in and console the widow." Jack's tone was snide. "At the same time, of course, you'd shoulder all the other responsibilities that came with the poor bastard's estate."

"But why would Pearce do that?" Christine asked with a confused frown. "He should have looked to you to take care of Camille, Jack."

"Yeah, Jack," Linc put in silkily. "Why did Pearce do that?"

"Because he was a stupid jerk."

Linc folded his arms on his chest. "I don't think so, Jack. I think he saw through you. He looked around for someone he could trust to do the right thing by Camille."

"The right thing! You're crazy, Cantrell!"

"Yeah, the right thing. He trusted me to take care of Camille, to put her interests before my own. And you know why, Jack."

Camille and Christine looked on, both completely bewildered.

Jack made a dismissive gesture. "The booze had him addled as a loon those last few years. He didn't know what he was doing."

Linc laughed shortly. "A circumstance you must have thanked your lucky stars for."

"Why did he do it, Linc?" Camille asked quietly, her eyes searching his face.

Linc glanced at her before looking away. "He knew I'd treat you better than Jack."

"Why? Jack is my brother."

After a second, he met her eyes again. "Pearce thought I was your brother, too."

She stared at him. "What?"

Jack said something in disgust that they both ignored.

"When I left years ago, Pearce came after me," Linc said. "He demanded to know why I'd deserted you. I told him everything—" he shot Jack a hostile look "—the way Jack had told it to me."

Camille put a hand to her throat as a dark foreboding settled in her chest. There had always been something about that time in her life. She'd sensed it, but in her pain and inexperience, she hadn't really wanted to know any more. She'd lost Linc and that had been all that really mattered. Now that the veil was torn aside, she wasn't sure she was ready to hear it, even after all these years.

Linc saw her confusion. He put out a hand as though urging her to listen. "Pearce agreed with me that no good would come from telling you, Camille. He knew we'd been intimate, but I don't believe he knew about your pregnancy. Or the miscarriage. If he had, he would have told me and I would have come back." Linc's eyes held hers, willing her to believe him. "In spite of everything, I would have been here for you if I'd known."

Would he? She stood staring at him, numb with the shock of everything. The greed, the manipulation, the duplicity of the people she loved. Was nothing as it appeared? Was everything she'd shared with Linc these past weeks a sham, too? Did he want her for herself, or was this the culmination of years of planned revenge?

Would the takeover of Willow Wind, her own seduction and Jack's downfall be the ultimate revenge?

"All these years…" She looked at Linc, her expression tortured.

"This is all a lot of crap," Jack scoffed, suddenly running out of patience. "Pearce wasn't half as big-hearted as you're painting him, Cantrell. Hell, I told him the truth when he came to me asking about it, and it was way before he married Camille. He had plenty of time to let you two in on the secret if he'd been so inclined."

Both Camille and Linc turned to look at him incredulously.

"It's true," Jack insisted, shrugging as though the web of deceit he'd spun hadn't altered the lives of three people.

Linc pinned Jack in a narrow-eyed stare. "He married Camille knowing she was not my sister?"

"I just said so, didn't I?" Jack returned sourly.

Camille frowned. "He knew all along the reason Linc left me," she said, speaking the words carefully, as though picking her way through a dark and dangerous path, "and he went ahead anyway? Without telling me anything? Without telling Linc?"

"Well, if he didn't say anything," Jack replied, "then I guess so."

Stricken, Camille looked at Linc, who seemed just as shaken.

"It's water under the bridge now, Camille," Jack said. "It hasn't got a damn thing to do with what's happening here tonight. Now, what I want to know is—"

"Just a minute, Keating."

Linc's tone was enough to stop Jack abruptly.

"You may think it hasn't got a damn thing to do with anything that's happening here, but I think it does. If

Pearce knew about Camille and me and went ahead and married her, you're right about one thing. It's water under the bridge. Nothing can change it now. Maybe he loved her too much to let a chance to have her as his wife slip through his fingers." He gave Camille a look that made her breath catch in her throat. "Hell, I can even understand it. For myself, I know nothing short of the lie you told me could have kept me away from Camille seventeen years ago. So, if Pearce did know, it's interesting to speculate why he came to me when he was in trouble. The way he set up his estate is also interesting—making Camille almost completely dependent on me, not you, Jack—when he died. What could have been Pearce's motive?"

Camille's heart was beating frantically. Her head whirled with unanswered questions. Had Pearce set it up so that she and Linc would be thrown together? Her marriage to Pearce had been so troubled. Had he been trying to make amends in case something happened to him? Linc was free and he knew it. Joanna's accident had happened months before. Another thought, dark and disturbing, struck her. Pearce's death had been ruled an accident. He'd hit a bridge abutment. His blood alcohol level had been high, but not over the limit. *Surely* it had been an accident.

Oh, Pearce.

Jack caught her arm, his tone urgent. "Camille, can't you see this is more of his bullshit? Don't get sucked in again. You know how unstable Pearce was. He wasn't even capable of thinking up a complicated scheme like this." He threw Linc a hard look. "More than likely, it was Cantrell pumping him full of lies about you and our family that influenced him to do what he did." He gave her arm a little shake. "It was crazy for Pearce to put it all in Cantrell's control, Camille. But he did, and we've got to live with it, I guess. We don't have any choice there.''

She pulled her arm from his grasp. "Please, Jack—"

"But this other thing, Camille…" Still insistent, Jack bent, trying to get her to look at him. "This isn't something you can just blow away. I want you to tell him if he uses the stuff in that envelope, you won't see him again. It's the only chance we've got, the only chance I've got, Camille. He has that little kid who's crazy about you, and he's still stuck on you himself. I don't care what he says—he'll do whatever you ask."

Camille raised her eyes and found Linc looking at her with an inscrutable expression. In her ear, Jack's low, cajoling voice droned on and on. Would Linc do as he'd threatened? So far, only Jack had seen whatever was in the envelope. He obviously believed that when and if it got to the media, it would be the death of his political ambitions. If she didn't do what she could to stop Linc, it would destroy her relationship with Jack forever. He was the only family she had in the world. She could tell Linc was waiting to see if she would cave in to Jack's demands, if she would once again allow herself to be manipulated by him. But what was the difference between being manipulated by Jack and being held hostage by her love for Linc?

"I want you to go now, Jack," she said suddenly.

"What?" Jack looked startled.

Linc moved swiftly to the door and opened it. "You heard the lady. She wants some privacy."

"Now look here—"

"No, you look, Keating." Suddenly, Linc dropped all pretense of civility. He was hard and purposeful and utterly believable when he said to Jack, "Your sister wants you to leave, and that's the way it's going to be." He pushed the door wide and stepped aside, his gaze encompassing both Jack and Christine. He couldn't resist one last zinger.

"Do keep in touch," he said.

After they left, there was only silence in the room. The heat of the summer night did nothing to dispel the empty chill that penetrated all the way to Camille's bones. Briskly, she rubbed both arms above her elbows, her jaw tense and clenched. Behind her, Linc waited.

"Are you going to give it to the media?" she finally asked.

"Are you going to ask me not to?"

"What's in it besides the…crimes he perpetrated against Pearce?"

"And you, Camille. Don't forget you lost right along with Pearce." When she didn't answer, he moved away. At a table, he toyed with a heavy paperweight that had once belonged to the judge. "For starters, he's involved with some shady investments at a savings and loan in Jackson. He's been buying up farms that have been foreclosed on by that same S and L—in another name, of course."

Oh, Jack! Closing her eyes against tears, she imagined Jack's horror when he discovered the extent of his exposure at Linc's hand. And Christine. Camille wasn't sure that Christine would be able to bear it.

She sighed. "Have you thought what's at stake here, Linc?"

He made a disgusted sound. "What? Jack's career? Jack's reputation? Jack's sick ambitions? Jack's wife's chance to be the first lady of the state of Mississippi? I don't give a damn what's at stake for Jack, Camille."

"I'm not talking about Jack. I'm talking about what's at stake for you."

"I get what I've wanted for seventeen years," he said in a voice vibrating with the hatred he'd lived with for so long. "I get to see him taste what it's like to lose everything. Everything."

"At the expense of your own soul, Linc!"

He gave her a fierce look. "I've thought of that. Don't you think I've thought of that! I knew you would hate me when I did it."

Pain rent her heart in two. If she'd needed proof that he was willing to sacrifice everything on the altar of his lust for revenge, here it was. For a moment she wanted to scream, to tear her hair, to do something violent for the price she was forced to pay, too.

"Camille—"

"You see the irony here, Linc?" She dredged up an unsteady smile from somewhere. "If you do this, you punish Jack for his behavior seventeen years ago. He stole your future, he besmirched your mother's name, he robbed you and me of the chance we had to be together." The look she gave him let him know she understood the magnitude of his loss at her brother's hands. "Okay, you can avenge all of that. But hear me on this, Linc. If you destroy Jack, you'll destroy yourself. It's the price you'll pay to have your revenge."

He stared at her a moment, then said quietly, "It has to be this way. I don't expect you to accept it, or even to understand it. It just has to be, Camille."

For a man making a decision of his own free will, he looked far from happy. Instead, there was stark desolation in his eyes. She did understand, Camille thought, suddenly wanting to touch him so much that her hands quivered. She wanted to draw his head down to her

breast and stroke away his pain, to give him the peace
and acceptance that would help him turn away from this
terrible thing before it destroyed him, too. But he didn't
need any of that from her. She must be mad to think he
needed anything she had to give.

Keeping her distance, she made a helpless gesture.
"And then what, Linc? After you see Jack on his knees,
will it give you satisfaction and peace of mind? After
it's done, what will you have?"

HE HADN'T BEEN ABLE to give her an answer to that. He
didn't *have* an answer to that. All the way back to the
cottage, Linc thought about it. Before he came back to
Blossom, he'd had it all figured out, but he hadn't reck-
oned on the way things had turned out, hadn't dreamed
that he and Camille would have a second chance. He
hadn't counted on Nikki blooming as she had, making
a bunch of little friends, finding a second mother in Camille. Somehow, without his realizing it, time had
passed and the rest of his world had changed, slowly
and surely, like the colored glass chips in a kaleidoscope.
But stubbornly, blindly he'd still focused on that one
destructive goal.

Maybe he was crazy, he thought, dragging the screen
door open and entering the dark cottage. He'd almost
accomplished what he'd set out to do. Everything was
in place to pull the great Jack Keating down in the mud
with all the other unscrupulous, dishonorable types
whose evil deeds eventually found them out. He pulled
off his hat and tossed it toward the brass hook on the
door. Where was the triumph? Where was the satisfaction? As for peace, he honestly didn't think he would
ever find peace. Not in this world.

Moving softly so he wouldn't wake Nikki, he removed his belt and began pulling his shirttails from his jeans. He could hear the faint sounds of late-night television coming from Maybelle's room. She'd finally straightened out her family life enough so that she could live in, at least most of the time. With the long hours he worked now, it had proved a godsend. Passing her door, he gave it a soft tap to let her know he was in and kept on going. Nikki would be sleeping, but he always checked anyway, just to make sure. Just to look at her. At her door, he stared a heart-stopping second at her empty bed before recalling that she was staying over with Tracey. Then, easing down to sit on her bed, he gazed slowly around the room.

Her childish femininity was apparent everywhere. There was a collection of dolls painstakingly arranged in a bookcase. In the window were several miniature crystal animals, each suspended from a line of thin filament to catch the morning sunshine. On the floor at his feet lay tiny pink ballerina shoes, which she'd assured him were necessary for the simple reason that Tracey had a pair. Idly reaching for a dainty ruffled pillow, he turned it over and over in his hands. With all the good things in his life, why couldn't he put aside this obsession to bring Jack down? Camille was probably right about one thing. Being the instrument of Jack's destruction—of any man's destruction—might well destroy him, too.

And what about Camille?

He loved her. He loved her so much that sometimes, after they'd been together, it was all he could do not to say the words. Shaking his head, he wondered why he'd stupidly thought that if he just refused to say it, it wouldn't *be*. Fat chance. What he felt now for Camille was as different from that immature, impassioned emo-

tion of his youth as night from day. What he felt now
was the stuff lifetimes were made of, families were built
on, futures were based on. He breathed in as the full
impact of what was at stake washed over him.

Tossing the pillow aside, he got up, heading for the
front door. On the porch, he propped both hands on the
railing, his head down. In a sweat, his heart thudding,
he played everything over in his mind. Camille's words
came back. What if he destroyed Jack? What next for
him, for Nikki? For Camille? It came to him then. Jack
Keating had destroyed his first chance at happiness, but
he himself was getting ready to destroy his second
chance.

Only if he was the world's biggest fool.

Staring across at Willow Wood's stately, well-lit
grounds, he felt the truth settle in his soul. He didn't
give a damn about Jack Keating one way or another. He
didn't need to engineer any man's destruction. He
needed Camille. He needed to build a life with her.
He needed her to mother his daughter and be the mother
of more sons and daughters that they would conceive
and rear in the love they shared. A love that had mirac-
ulously survived incredible odds.

Suddenly, he plunged down the steps, heading across
the ground toward Camille's house, tucking in his shirttails as he went. He was clear of his yard and over the
fence that separated the Twin Willows when he realized
something. He felt as if a load had been jettisoned from
his soul. Giving up his vendetta against Jack had its
advantages. As he approached the pond at a dead run, a
startled bullfrog jumped into the water. Throwing back
his head, Linc laughed out loud.

In her room, Camille was reaching for another tissue
to stem the flow of her tears when she heard someone

on the stairs. For a second or two, she didn't care enough
to be alarmed. If an intruder wanted to burglarize Willow
Wind, let him. What would he find but dead hopes and
shattered dreams?

"Camille?"

"Linc!" Sniffing, hurriedly dabbing at her eyes, she
rose to her feet just as he appeared. "What is it? How
did you get in?"

He shrugged, his expression strangely intent. "I used
my key."

She looked at the key in his hand. "I thought you lost
it."

"I never said I lost it, just that I didn't have the right
to use it anymore."

She shook her head in confusion and weariness.
"Don't, Linc. I'm just not up to this tonight. Say whatever you came to say and then please leave. I've had
about all I can stand."

"I love you, Cami."

"What?"

He smiled crookedly but didn't move. "That's what
I came to say. I love you and I'd like us to get married.
That is, if you think you can stand living with a man
who doesn't always know what the hell he wants even
when it's right under his nose."

She sank down on her bed abruptly. "What are you
talking about?"

He walked across the room and crouched on the floor
in front of her. "It took me about thirty minutes of soul-
searching and thirty seconds of thinking about never
making love to you again to forget about Jack Keating
and that damned envelope."

Chuckling softly when she didn't reply, he glanced
down, shaking his head. "It's no wonder you don't fall

into my arms and promise undying love in return. I've given you a hard time, sweetheart. I know it and I'm sorry.''

She watched him through narrowed eyes. ''What about Jack?''

''I told you. If I had that envelope with me, I'd burn it in front of you. I'm not interested in exposing Jack anymore. It's just not important.''

''What about Willow Wind?''

He looked a little puzzled. ''What about it? The crop is better than expected. Enough to make a substantial reduction in the indebtedness.'' He gave a dismissive shake of his head. ''But it doesn't matter anyway. If we're married, I assume your debts, honey. Tell you what—'' he winked at her ''—I'll write this one off. It'll be my pleasure.''

''That's very generous of you.''

His smile faded. He sat back a little, giving her a more searching look. ''What is it, Cami?''

She freed her hands from his and stood. ''I've been doing some thinking myself. The things I learned to-night...'' She gestured vaguely. ''I don't know. It's as though the people closest to me were suddenly strangers. The secrets, the duplicity, the greed. How could I have been so blind, so naive all these years?'' Turning, she said, ''It makes me question everything, my own judg-ment most of all.''

Linc rose, too. ''I'm sorry. I know how it must seem, but...'' He shook his head. ''Pearce never meant any of this to hurt you, Camille. You must know that.''

''It's not only Pearce I wonder about.''

He gave her a quick look.

''What about you, Linc? I've been turning everything

over and over in my mind. Do you want me for myself or do you want Willow Wind?''

"What do you mean?"

"It would be perfect. A clean sweep—Jack, the campaign, me, Nikki.'' She looked away.

Suddenly, Linc's heart was thudding with fear. He had never really worried about losing Camille, he realized. Faced with the prospect now, he couldn't believe his own arrogance. As he searched—no, prayed—for the right words to tell her how wrong she was, she spoke again.

"Was Nikki part of your plan, too, Linc? In case I proved a little too difficult? Did you think I couldn't resist a child since I don't have one of my own?''

Never had he wanted to take her in his arms as much as he did at that moment. But as long as she even halfway believed the things she'd just said, he knew she wouldn't tolerate it. Without touching her, he put out a hand of entreaty. "Is that why you were sitting here crying, sweetheart?''

She looked at him through eyes that swam with tears. "Isn't that something to cry about?''

"And you really believe that I could use you that way?''

"I don't know."

"I came here with the idea of taking your brother down, Camille. I've never denied that. But I never planned to use you to make it happen. And certainly not Nikki. What happened between us was meant to be. Maybe it's seventeen years late, but it was meant to be. Maybe I had to come back here and go through all this…torment to get to that." Tentatively, he touched her cheek, cupping her jaw. "You've got to believe me,

Camille. Without you, none of the craziness makes any sense.''

"Oh, Linc…'' She sniffed, closing her eyes with a sigh. "I want to believe you, so much.''

He pulled her close, his heart pounding. "Camille, if you don't believe me, I don't think I can take it.''

Tears welled up again. "I kept telling myself you had more integrity than to sink to Jack's level, but you'd suffered so because of him. Who could blame you really? I was afraid you'd hold on to that damned envelope just to watch him squirm, and all the while it would be eating at you like acid.''

He smiled a little unsteadily. "Well, the thought did occur to me.'' He looked at her sheepishly. "I'm only human after all, and he's such a rat. But I decided he wasn't worth sacrificing everything good and beautiful in my life for.''

Gently he pushed her down on the edge of the bed and sat beside her, keeping her close. Smiling a watery smile, she leaned her head against his shoulder. "I love you, too.''

The phone rang just as he tipped her mouth up for the kiss that would seal their new understanding. With a groan, he stopped. "Whoever that is, remind them what time it is. Only a dire emergency is going to keep me from getting you in that bed within the next thirty seconds.''

Eluding the hand edging up her thigh beneath her nightgown, she leaned over to the nightstand and lifted the receiver.

Linc realized the moment she looked at him that it was an emergency. With the color drained from her face, she listened.

Shifting the receiver, she said to him, "Is Nikki at home in her bed?"

"No." He stood up. "Why?"

"This is Maybelle. Jess called her. Nikki and Tracey aren't there."

"Then where the hell are they!"

"Jess sent them to bed, then watched a video movie. When she checked on them a while ago, there was no one in Tracey's bedroom."

He looked at her in stunned disbelief. "They have to be there! Where else could they be?"

Camille spoke a few more words into the receiver, then said to Linc, "They've combed the yard and their nearest neighbors', too. No one has seen them."

"Tell her to call the sheriff's office," Linc said over his shoulder as he headed for her bedroom door.

Her face pale, Camille stood, still holding the receiver. "What are you going to do?"

"Drive around and see if I can spot them."

"I want to come with you, Linc."

He clamped an unsteady hand on the back of his neck. "Okay. Hurry up and get dressed. We can check the road to the cottage to see if that's where they headed, but somehow I doubt it. It's a couple of miles from Tracey's house."

"It's so dark," Camille murmured, meeting his gaze across the room. In her eyes was the same unspeakable fear that Linc felt. She searched his face as though he might be able to work a miracle. "Linc, they're so little."

"I know." His jaw clenched with the effort to stay calm. "But don't worry, we'll find them."

CHAPTER FIFTEEN

FOREVER AFTER, Camille had only to think of that night to feel the helplessness and horror all over again. At first she and Linc had searched the area near Tracey's house. They'd reasoned that the two could hardly have ranged much farther than the neighborhood where the Perkinses lived. When they drew an absolute blank, they increased the area to include the road that led to Kate's Cottage.

Most of the law-enforcement people in the county turned out to help. It wasn't often a child was in jeopardy there, and with the vast expanse of land to be searched, every available person was needed. As the night wore on, Camille soon realized someone should be at home just in case Nikki should, by some miracle, find her way to Willow Wind. Maybelle was stationed at Kate's Cottage.

It was so dark. Searching in the shadows, Camille cursed the clouds that obscured the moon. The half-moon wouldn't have helped much, but at least it would have afforded some light. All the tragedies in her life, it seemed, happened in the dark of night.

Linc wasted no energy on omens and wishful thinking. With single-minded intensity, he searched for his daughter. It took only a short while to scour the town of Blossom. Next, he combed the rural roads, beginning with those closest to the Perkinses' house and then fanning out. Soon he was on Twin Willows land. First, Jack Keating's, then Camille's.

No one spoke their worst fears out loud, but neither could they discount the possibility that someone had picked up the girls.

Like a woman in a nightmare, Camille stared out the window, her heart mired in dread, her face ravaged with fear. In the distance over the eastern section of Willow Wind, she could see a faint, pink lightening of the sky.

"Come sit, awhile, dear. If Linc should pop in, you won't want to show him such a woebegone face." Abigail lifted a squealing kettle from the stove and poured scalding water into a teapot. She stood for a moment contemplating the swirling tea leaves and then firmly placed the lid over the steaming crock.

At her aunt's gentle urging, Camille sank into the chair, but she didn't take the cup Abigail pushed toward her. What would be the point? She couldn't swallow anything, not even tea. Lifting her gaze, she looked into her aunt's eyes. "Where could they be, Abigail?"

"They're not far, dear." Abigail filled her own cup, her rheumy gaze on the leaves. "They're safe."

"But where? *Where?*"

"I wish I could tell you that, Cami love."

"How do you know that? How can you tell?" This once, Camille longed to believe in her aunt's gifts. She'd already prayed and prayed, but she still felt numb. And scared. So scared.

Abigail peered into her own cup, looking perplexed. "There they go again," she murmured with a shake of her white head. "It's so confusing. You'd think without cream…"

"What?"

Abigail looked at Camille's cup. "Perhaps if you

would drink your tea, dear, I would be able to see more clearly.''

"Please, Abigail.'' Camille put her fingers to her temples and began a weary, circular massage. "I know you mean well....''

"Yes, yes.'' With a vague wave of her hand, Abigail dismissed Camille's skepticism. "I don't know what it is, but when Lincoln is involved—''

Camille looked up. "Linc?''

"Those other forces,'' Abigail murmured in distraction. "Just the way it was the last time.''

"Other forces?''

Abigail blinked and looked up. "What was that, dear?''

"What other forces, Abigail?''

"I can't read them, Cami. It's just the way it was that terrible summer all those years ago. Except then there was Kate, and the judge, of course. I always thought that was the reason. Violent death and sickness, you know. Powerful, powerful influences, naturally. But when Lincoln came home and revealed that nonsense that Jack concocted...'' She shook her head, clucking with disapproval. "Jack is just too, too wicked, Camille. He really should be ashamed.''

"Is he too wicked to become the governor of the state?'' Camille asked dryly, finding it impossible not to respond to Abigail, no matter how outlandish she got.

Abigail's delicate brows rose above her spectacles. "Oh, we don't have to worry about that, my dear. He'll never be at the state capital. No, indeed, not Jack.''

"Christine's going to be disappointed to hear that,'' Camille commented.

"Oh, we won't tell her,'' Abigail said sweetly as the doorbell rang. "But I believe she's here.''

With another penetrating look at her aunt, Camille jumped up, then promptly forgot everything except the rush of anxiety that filled her. Hurrying to the front door with her heart in her throat, she told herself it could as easily be good news as bad. To her amazement, it really was Christine standing there as she opened the door.

"I guess you don't know where they are yet," Christine said, stepping inside.

"No, we—"

"Now I suppose you can see what you've done, Camille."

"I don't know what you mean, Christine. Are you talking about the children? About Nikki and Tracey?"

"No! Don't give me that tearful, my-babies-are-missing act, Camille. I'm not in the mood." Lifting her cigarette for a brief, jerky drag, she pointed it at Camille. "I'm here about this rotten situation that Linc has engineered and is holding over Jack's head. You're the only person who can do anything about it, and we—Jack and I—expect you to do it. Right away, Camille."

"Christine, do you know what time it is?"

"It's time to quit meddling in business that doesn't concern you! That's what time it is."

"It's barely past four o'clock in the morning. What are you doing here?"

"Trying to talk some sense into you!" Christine began pacing the foyer. "What do you think I'm doing?"

That Christine was worried over Jack's dilemma came as no surprise to Camille. But it was more than worry causing that look in her sister-in-law's eyes. There was a peculiar, unfocused look that sent a shiver through Camille. Was it drugs? she wondered blankly. Christine had been running in some pretty sophisticated circles lately. But surely with the campaign, she would avoid anything that might reflect badly on her. Nevertheless, it was decidedly odd that she was at Camille's door at 4:00 a.m. babbling about Jack's situation and how Camille could fix it.

Using the tone of voice that almost always calmed her pupils, Camille asked, "What was it you wanted to say to me, Christine?"

"First of all, you've got to tell him to go back to wherever it is he came from."

"Who, Linc?"

Christine rolled her eyes. "Yes, Linc! Who else?"

"Why?"

"So he can't cause any more trouble and everything can go back to the way it was."

"Linc is here to stay, Christine," Camille said gently. "Whether it makes you and Jack happy or not."

A crafty look appeared in Christine's eyes. "Not if you go along with my plan. He's not the only one who can come up with a plan. He thinks he can plot and scheme and make us all jump when he pulls the strings, but every man has his weaknesses."

Camille eyed her narrowly. "And what is Linc's weakness?"

"You, oddly enough," Christine said. "And the kid, of course."

"He does love us both," Camille agreed, thankful all the way to her toes that it was true. "But how is that a weakness?"

"A man's weaknesses can be used against him."

Camille was still, considering the implications of that. She drew a deep breath, trying to resist the thought that sprang into her mind. "Christine, you don't know anything about Nikki's disappearance, do you?"

Christine gave her a defiant look. "I'm not saying

anything until I have your word that you'll break off
with him and make him go back where he came from!''

"Then you do know something!''

Christine crushed out her cigarette and reached for
another. She lit it with unsteady fingers before resuming
the conversation, as though they were discussing nothing
more crucial than the latest trend in fashion. "None of
this would have happened if you'd only done what Jack
told you to do."

"If you know where they are, please tell me, Christine," Camille begged. "You know how worried everyone is. It's not only Linc," she added, realizing her sister-in-law could hardly be touched by Linc's suffering.
"Tracey's parents are beside themselves, too. The whole
town is worried."

"Will you break it off with Lincoln Cantrell?"

Trying to reason with her was going to be useless,
Camille realized. There must be some way.... "Christine, if you're involved in the disappearance of these
children, think what it will do to Jack's campaign."

For a split second, she looked uncertain. "I...I need
to use your bathroom," she said suddenly. "I'll be back
in a second."

She turned and hurried down the hall to the powder
room at the bottom of the staircase. Frowning, Camille
started after her, but just then, the telephone rang.

It was Linc.

"Have you found them?" Camille cried, her heart
beating with hope and fear.

"No. I was hoping you'd heard something," he said,
sounding tired. "Or thought of something."

"No, nothing." She hesitated. "Did you uncover anyone who'd seen them? Is there any trace of
their...their...anything?"

"No, Cami. Nothing."

That was good, Camille thought. In a way.

"It's almost dawn, sweetheart. We were set to start the last day of picking, but most of the hands have been out with me all night. I'll get a skeleton crew started on that last section, but everyone else at Willow Wind will be involved in the search."

"What can I do, Linc?"

"Just wait for me, Cami. She may turn up, now that it's daylight. She'd come to you before anyone else."

"All right." The word was barely a whisper. Tears sprang to her eyes. "Aunt Abby says she's okay, Linc."

For a moment, Linc was silent. "Well, I hope she's right."

"She says she's close."

"Close? Anything else?"

"No…" At a sound, Camille glanced down the hall to the door of the powder room. "Christine's here, Linc."

"Christine?" he repeated blankly. "Oh, the campaign. I forgot for a minute. Even for the sake of appearances, I can't see Christine as the supportive type."

"Linc, she's acting…strange. Strung out." Her eyes troubled, Camille watched the powder room door. "I think—"

"Sweetheart, I can't stop to chat about Christine. I just hoped…I just thought maybe Nikki—" Camille heard the heavy intake of his breath. "I'll check with you a little later."

"Okay. I love you."

"I love you, too, sweetheart. Bye."

After hanging up, Camille stood where she was, wondering at the bittersweetness of knowing Linc loved her and that they would have a future together, but it could be without Nikki. If something had happened to Nikki—

"That was Linc, wasn't it?"

Camille turned as Christine reentered the room. "Yes. No news yet," she said, assessing her sister-in-law surreptitiously. Christine had been very agitated before going into the bathroom, pacing the floor, smoking one cigarette after another, her sentences disjointed. Now she seemed almost calm.

"It's all up to you, Camille. I've told you."

As her words registered, Camille's suspicions crystallized. "What did you take in there, Christine?"

"What difference does it make? I'm not here for counseling, damn it! I'm here to straighten out this mess you've made."

"Is it marijuana?" *Dear God,* Camille thought, *I don't know anything about dealing with this.*

"No, Ms. Goody Two-shoes, it isn't marijuana." Then, with a return of her usual sophistication, she went to the sofa and sat down. "Now he's worried, isn't he?"

"Cocaine," Camille murmured.

"Oh, for God's sake! Do you have to be a saint all your life? Come into the real world for once. I've fixed it so we can bring him down, Camille, but you've got to cooperate."

"What are you talking about, Christine?"

She lit a cigarette and blew the smoke impatiently to the side. "I'll show him where the damn kids are if he'll just leave us alone."

Camille sank onto the edge of the sofa. "You know where Nikki is? My God, is she safe? And Tracey? She's with her?"

"They're both perfectly safe. What do you think I am?"

Camille shot to her feet in a murderous rage. "I think

you're cruel and heartless and I'd like to tear you to pieces!'' she cried. ''Where are they? You tell me where they are this minute, Christine, or I swear I won't be responsible for what I do.''

Christine looked as though a pet kitten had suddenly turned into a wildcat. ''They're at the picking site, playing in the loose cotton in the compactor.''

''At five o'clock in the morning?'' Camille demanded, her tone incredulous.

''They wanted to play in the cotton, I took them there. It's as simple as that.''

Camille simply stared, beyond speech.

Christine shrugged sullenly. ''It's not my fault. What were they doing heading down the road at night in the first place? I just gave them a lift. Anyone could have picked them up if I hadn't.''

But Camille barely heard her. She was scrambling for her purse with the keys to her car. There was no way to phone the work site, and the radio was in Linc's Bronco. The cotton in the compactor. Why hadn't she thought of it herself? They'd been fascinated with it yesterday. Joey had mentioned what fun it would be to jump in it.

The compactor!

Oh, God, oh, God. The men were going to be at the site very early. What if they decided to compress and bale that load in the compactor while Tracey and Nikki were in it?

Her fingers closed on her keys and she snatched them out of her purse. She would deal with Christine later. The woman was sick. Sick. Without looking back, she ran.

CAMILLE NEVER QUITE remembered the drive from the big house to the work site. All she could see in her mind was the compactor full of cotton and the two children asleep in it. Soft, like snow, Nikki had said. Fun to jump in, Joey had said. Tracey's expression, Camille recalled, had been one of definite interest. The two little girls, with their lively curiosity and Tracey's intrepid nature, had probably decided to check it out. The trek from the Perkinses' house to the work site was about two miles. Both knew the route well. Neither would have hesitated to get in the car with Christine.

Please, please, don't let them be in the compactor.

But it was the logical place. The field trip had been a great success. The children had been fascinated. It was only a miracle that Joey Thigpen wasn't in on the return visit. Why hadn't they thought of the equipment when they were searching for the girls? *Why didn't I think of it?* Camille mentally flayed herself.

As she turned onto the dirt road that led to the work site, she met Rufus Johnson, Linc's top hand, driving the pickup with Willow Wind's logo on the side. Flagging him down, she told him what she suspected and asked him to radio Linc in the Bronco and then to turn around and follow her back to the work site.

Even with only a skeleton crew, the work site was a beehive of activity. One of the machines had already made several passes through the field, stripping the cotton from the plants, and was heading for the compactor to dump it. Several of the hands looked up curiously as she tore past them, driving as fast as she dared, stopping closer to the compactor than she normally would, a blatant breach of safety. Linc would never allow anyone so close to the machines. She was hoping the driver would notice and stop his own machine out of simple curiosity, if nothing else.

It was a futile hope. Engine roaring, the machine was

already positioned at the compactor, hoisting its load high over the cotton. In another ten seconds, more would be dumped.

"Stop! Stop!" Pushing her door open, Camille tumbled out of her car, rushing forward, waving her arms. She saw the operator give her a startled glance just as he began to dump his load. A flash of blue amidst the white caught her eye. Tiny jeans? And then yellow. A T-shirt? But the cotton was already spilling into the compactor. The noise was deafening, but not loud enough to keep her from hearing high-pitched childish screams.

"Nikki! Tracey! I'm coming!" Sobbing, she ran toward the huge metal rectangle, frantically searching for a way to climb the steep sides. There were no handholds to be seen and nowhere to put her feet. If the cotton had landed on top of them, how long would they be able to breathe?

Panicked, she looked at her car, wondering whether she could stand on it and climb over, when she felt firm hands at her waist, pulling her back.

"No, no! Nikki's in there. Tracey—"

"I'll get them, Cami." It was Linc's voice at her ear. "Wait here."

Her hands clenched at her sides, she watched him signal the driver to cut his engine. Then he leaped onto the huge machine, climbing up and over the cab. On the roof, he looked down into the sea of cotton.

"I see them!"

"Are they okay?" Camille asked, holding her breath. "They're okay."

With a faint sound, Camille leaned against the side of her car in relief.

Venturing out to the edge of the equipment, Linc found a foothold on the side of the compactor and lithely

balanced there, keeping one foot on the picker. He put
out a hand and Camille saw a much smaller hand reach
out to be caught up and pulled into the haven of her
daddy's arms. From her place on the ground, the scene
blurred as Camille burst into tears.

HOURS LATER, Camille found Linc under the willow at
the pond. It was dusk. A serene stillness lay over the
fields of both Twin Willows. The clear skies and sunshine had held, and the men had finished the cotton picking for the season. Nikki was tucked in her bed at Kate's
Cottage, sleeping the sleep of the innocent after her hair-
raising escapade, while Maybelle hovered protectively.

Camille stood at the edge of the pond a moment,
watching Linc before slipping under the leafy canopy
and sitting beside him. "I missed you," she said softly.

Shifting, he made a place for her between his legs,
settling her against him with an arm at her waist. "I was
just doing a little thinking."

"Hmm. Sounds serious."

"Do you realize," he said, studying the diamond-
bright surface of the pond, "that I almost lost everything
today?"

With her fingers, she stroked his arm, knowing he
didn't expect an answer.

"I don't think I've ever been so scared in my life.
Every time I came up empty after searching a particular
place, I panicked a little more. By the time I got that
call on the radio, I was a desperate man, Cami."

"I know. I was terrified, too."

For a few minutes, they were still, both thinking how
lucky they'd been. Then Linc rested his chin on the top
of her head. "I still haven't quite come to grips with
what she did," he murmured.

"You mean Christine?" When he nodded, she said, "She's not rational, Linc. It's sad really."

"I never thought I'd feel sympathy for Jack Keating," he said in a quiet tone. "But you could see the shock on his face when Christine admitted everything. I went over there ready to kill them both, but..." He shook his head. "It would have been like kicking an animal who was already down."

Camille murmured in agreement. There was little she could say in defense of her brother or his wife. Once the two children were pulled safely from the compactor, they'd been eager to tell how they came to be there. They'd cooked up the scheme in Tracey's bedroom, sneaked out the window and started off down the road to see if all that cotton was as much fun to jump in as it looked. Christine Keating just happened to be driving home and picked them up. She'd been at a women's political gathering where she'd had a little too much to drink. She'd still been keyed up with the strain of being "on" as the candidate's wife for several hours. A little cocaine always relaxed her, she'd admitted to her stunned audience. It had taken only a few questions before they realized how seriously dependent on the drug she was.

"To give her the benefit of the doubt," Camille said softly, "I don't think she realized the danger to the kids. She knows next to nothing about cotton farming, let alone the operation of the equipment."

"I know." After a moment, Linc said, "Jack didn't react as I expected him to."

"I was surprised, too. But when he realized just how close to the edge Christine was, I think it scared him more than anything." She gazed for a moment at the pale orange horizon. "Do you think he'll be washed up after this gets out?"

"Probably," Linc replied quietly. "The voters won't want a woman with Christine's problems as the first lady of the state. And whether it's fair or not, Jack's image is tarnished by his wife's behavior."

The surface of the pond rippled when a martin made a low pass at an insect. "All their plans destroyed by that one impulsive action," Camille said in a low tone. "It really is sad."

"Yeah." He rubbed his cheek against her hair absently.

"What is it?" she asked, sensing something more.

"I didn't come out of this looking very good myself," he told her after a moment. "If something had happened to Nikki, it would have been my fault."

Guessing the direction of his thoughts, she waited.

"I mean, when you get right down to it, that's the truth. I was so bent on making Jack pay that I lost sight of everything else. That's what I came over to tell you when we got the call that Nikki was missing. Jack was responsible for stealing everything I cared about years ago, but I only had myself to blame for almost throwing away my second chance, Cami. It amazes me that I nearly did that."

She laced her fingers through his and squeezed tightly. "There's a big difference between almost doing something and actually going through with it. The important thing is that you didn't."

"I wish I could dismiss it as easily as that. I don't think I can forget that my obsession almost caused the death of my daughter."

"Don't be too hard on yourself, Linc. There were a lot of lives off track around here for a very long time,

if you really think about it.'' For a second, she rested
her cheek against their interwoven fingers. ''First, there's
Pearce, unfocused, unhappy—drinking himself to death.
Then Jack, poisoned by jealousy as a boy and by his
greed and ambition as a man. And Christine, unbalanced
and unfulfilled, then broken and pitiful in the end.''

A chill skittering down her spine made her snuggle
gratefully into his warmth. ''Even me, Linc. I let myself
be cheated out of so much when you left. Then when
you came back, instead of following my heart, I was
resentful and fearful, filled with doubt. Life is simply
too precious to squander on those emotions.'' She
squeezed his hand again. ''So don't be so quick to shoulder a load of guilt on Christine's behalf.''

''That sounds good, but if I hadn't been so bent on
making Jack squirm with what I had on him, Christine
wouldn't have been pushed beyond her limit.''

''Did you force Christine to start experimenting with
cocaine?''

''No, but you don't—''

''Oh, yes, Lincoln Cantrell.'' She turned in his arms
so she could look him straight in the eye. ''You were
going to tell me that if you hadn't dug up that stuff about
Jack, then threatened them with it, Christine wouldn't
have been driven to do the crazy thing she did.''

''Well, isn't that the way it happened?''

''Do I need to repeat the question?''

''What, about the cocaine? Hell, no, I didn't force her
to do that.''

''So, would she have gone off the deep end if she
hadn't been using it?''

''Well...''

''You know she wouldn't, Linc. And if Jack hadn't
behaved reprehensibly in the first place, neither of them

would have had anything to worry about.'' She leaned back a little to get a better look at him. ''It's like what you told me that night we discussed the baby when I was wallowing in guilt over the miscarriage. What happened is no one's fault. It happened. It was a bad thing, but it didn't end as tragically as it could have. Jack won't be governor, but you and I know he wouldn't have been good for our state anyway. Christine will get treatment, which is a good thing.''

Camille smiled softly and put a finger against her lips, then transferred the tiny kiss to his. ''And you and I can put the past behind us and finally get on with whatever's meant to be.''

He looked as if he might have something else to say, but at the imperious lift of her eyebrows, he changed his mind.

''Good.'' She snuggled against him again, wiggling a little more than was absolutely necessary to get comfortable.

He chuckled softly in her ear. ''Keep that up and the frogs and fish are going to get an eyeful.''

She smiled. It was going to be all right. It really was. ''You remember what we were doing when we got that phone call last night?''

He slipped a hand beneath her shirt and began stroking her skin. ''Uh-uh. Refresh my memory.''

''P-proposing.'' She sighed as he found a bare nipple. ''You were proposing.''

He kissed her ear and sent a wave of erotic sensation washing over her. ''Proposing what?''

It was difficult, but Camille managed somehow to drag herself away from the mesmerizing pleasure of his mouth and turn around to face him. There was still enough light left to make out the devilish grin on his face. She didn't say anything. She didn't have to. As she gazed at him with all her love shining in her eyes, his smile slowly faded. He reached out and cupped her face in his hands.

"Seventeen years ago," he said softly, his eyes adoring, "we made love for the first time in this very place. We made promises that are as sweet and meaningful in my heart today as they were then. I love you, sweetheart. I always have and I always will."

"Oh, Linc."

"So…" He bent and kissed her. "Will you marry me, Cami Keating?"

EPILOGUE

THE WHOLE TOWN of Blossom turned out for the wedding. And a major event it was, thanks to Linc. Word had it he'd told Tom Pettigrew that he'd waited seventeen years for Camille Keating and when they took their vows, he meant it to be in the sight of God and everyone else in the county. As they stood together that sunny October afternoon within sight of the pond between the Twin Willows, Linc's judgment couldn't be faulted. Camille was certainly a beautiful woman. And that little girl… Well, she looked so much like Camille, she could easily have been theirs in the first place.

Poor Jack. He was there, all right, but looking like a shadow of the man he used to be. Of course he smiled and shook hands as always, but as he wasn't in the race anymore, it didn't mean much. Surprising thing was that he was there at all. Everyone knew he'd planned to have Willow Wind someday, planned to join the Twin Willows just as they used to be back when the original Keating brothers had built them. Now, with Jack's wife sick like that… Well, as he and Christine didn't have chick or child, Camille—or Linc and Camille's children—would probably inherit Willow Wood, too. Funny how things work out.

Yes sirree, the marriage of Lincoln Cantrell and Camille Keating Wyatt was something else. Sam Byrd closed his barbershop for the whole afternoon. And the icecream parlor didn't open that day at all; its owners catered the reception, according to Maybelle Franklin, whose daughter-in-law was in the business now that she was reunited with Freddy.

The Magnolia Café had originally planned to stay open, but as the hour for the wedding approached and there wasn't a customer to be seen, the shades were drawn and the doors locked. Much to Mavis Potts's delight. She would have hated missing Linc and Camille "plighting their troth." Of course, she'd known it all along, she told Sue and Tatum Hollis. Right from that day at the Magnolia when they'd bumped into each other. According to Mavis, romance was alive and well, at least at the Magnolia Café.

Over his fourth glass of champagne Sam commented to Wiley Dawson that he was reminded of that day back in early summer when Linc reappeared in Blossom. Hadn't he told Wiley that Linc could be a godsend to Camille, knowing the land the way he did? Hadn't he pointed out that Camille couldn't run a plantation by herself? A marriage between those two was only logical. At which point Wiley stomped off, insulted. If Sam was suggesting it was anything but true love between Linc and Camille, he could just think again.

Watching the bride and groom toasting each other with champagne, it surely was easy to believe in true love. Linc was relaxed and smiling, Camille was flushed and laughing, her eyes a vivid blue, as blue as…as…as those morning glories that climbed up the porch rail at Kate's Cottage. And as for little Nicole—well, it just warmed the hearts of everyone when she threw her arms around her daddy and Camille that way.

Yes, indeed, it made a person believe in happy endings.

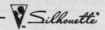
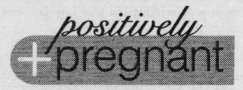

Romantic
SUSPENSE

Sparked by Danger,
Fueled by Passion.

This month and every month look for
four new heart-racing romances
set against a backdrop of suspense!

LIKE MOTHER, LIKE DAUGHTER (But In a Good Way)

with stories by
Jennifer Greene,
Nancy Robards Thompson
and Peggy Webb

Don't miss these three unforgettable stories about the unbreakable—and sometimes infuriating—bonds between mothers and daughters and the men who get caught in the madness (when they're not causing it!).

HARLEQUIN®
Next™

Available May 2007
TheNextNovel.com

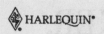